Historical Fiction: A Rancher's Dream -
Victorian American Western
by E. Ayers

Historical Fiction:
A Rancher's Dream -
Victorian American Western
A novel by E. Ayers
Published by Indie Artist Press
Eagle Mountain, Utah
www.indieartistpress.com
First Print Edition
copyright © 2015
All rights reserved.
ISBN-10: 1-62522-041-3
ISBN-13: 978-1-62522-041-7
June 2015

To George, who believed in me.

Acknowledgements

I'd like to thank the people who have made this book possible. Many thank yous to my editors and to so many wonderful people in from Texas to Wyoming who have taken the time to answer questions and provide me historical information. And a very special thank you to Indie Artist Press.

Part One

Ingrid Svensen wiped the tears from her eyes as two men held the ropes and lowered her father's coffin into the grave at Bluff Fall's only cemetery. If she wanted to survive, she couldn't spend another day crying. She needed to make plans and act quickly.

That evening she sat at the kitchen table in the house she had once shared with her father and brother. It hadn't been a solid week since her father had sat at his desk writing to the same people to inform them of Lennart's death. Deep inside she knew the deaths of her father and brother were related, but she didn't know why. What did you do Lennart? Am I next? No matter how hard she tried, she couldn't stop the tears as she wrote the letters.

After the most restless night of her life, where every creak and moan of the house had her holding her breath while she listened for more, she dragged herself from her bed. There was no time to figure out why her father had been killed, at least not now, not while her life hung in the balance. Stay calm.

An hour later, wearing the black gabardine dress she'd worn for her father's burial, she pulled the door closed on the house, locked it with the big key, and dropped the key into her pocket. She'd lived in this house for the last ten years. It was home.

On her way to the general store, she handed over her letters at the post office. One was to her mother's sister. It only told of her father's death, and she promised the woman that she would be safe. With luck, I will be safe. She forced a slight smile to the postmaster. "I am going to my aunt's in Delaware. I cannot stay here in Texas alone."

"Traveling alone isn't proper for a young woman." His immaculately waxed and curved mustache moved with every word.

"I know, but I have no choice. I am hoping my family will meet me half way."

The postmaster smiled at her and bid her well.

After walking another few doors down the street, she knocked on Mr. Mason's door and opened it. Mr. Mason, the town's only solicitor, a spectacled man, sat behind a cluttered desk. She forced a smile and said, "Good day, sir. I must leave town, but I wanted to do two things before I go. My father's records - I want to bring them to you for safe keeping. I'm sure the town will be hiring another doctor and the medical records of my father's patients will be needed."

"There will be a storage charge."

"I understand. Will you send a man this afternoon to collect the records?"

"Yes. I'll send Andy. How many do you have?"

She thought quickly. "Maybe four hundred." She was certain there were more. "And I wish to sell the house with the furniture. I will need the money."

"It's a fine house. If you aren't too firm on the price, I'm sure it will sell quickly."

"That is good news indeed. I shall leave on Friday. Maybe the town's next doctor will want it." She passed him a slip of paper that contained her aunt's name and address. "Please be certain any outstanding accounts my father might have in town are paid and send the check, payable to my aunt, for whatever is left." Except there won't be any check. "And please take whatever is reasonable for the storage of the records, and for the sale of the house."

She didn't want him asking too many questions. She bid him a goodbye and continued down the street. Walking to the general store barely gave her time to think. Supplies for extended traveling were almost too obvious. But fear kept her moving forward. As she stepped inside the general store, several people looked in her direction and then politely turned away. Ingrid cleared her throat and stepped up to the counter. "Good day, Mrs. Brook."

"I must say, I'm surprised you are out and about so soon after your father's death."

"Necessity. I cannot stay here. I will go home to my family in Delaware. I am no longer a child, but it is not proper for me to live here alone."

"That is true."

"I will need a few things."

She bought a few supplies at the general store, mentally reviewed her plans, and then went to the bakery. Again, townsfolk stared momentarily before looking away, as she entered the tiny shop.

The scent of bakery items filled her nostrils. As far back as she could remember, her father would often give her a few pennies so she could choose a sweet treat for her family. She looked at the pretty rolls studded with raisins and pointed to them. "A half-dozen rolls, please."

Whatever else she would need, she'd have to pick up on her way. But she had succeeded in giving everyone the impression that she was leaving for Delaware on Friday.

She hurried home and fixed a hearty meal for herself. This would probably be the last meal she would eat for a while, and she needed her strength. During the day, her movements inside the house would be almost invisible to the town, unless they put their noses to the windows, but at night, her every move would show.

In the carriage house, her father kept a small buckboard that he used for visiting patients and the carriage that they used for travel and Sunday church services. If she were going to travel, the coach would be the most likely vehicle to use. She pulled it close to the back door of the house. Must keep up appearances for the town.

She returned to the house and began to sift through the records in her father's desk drawer. That's where she found the letters her brother had sent him. She picked up one and read a few lines. Lennart's tone and what he said didn't resemble the letters that he sent her. He always stayed upbeat and joked as he wrote letters to her, but there was a graveness and a feeling of foreboding in the letters to their dad. Grabbing the wooden box that contained all the letters and running upstairs, she emptied the contents of the box onto her bed and stuffed the letters from her brother under her pillow. Then she took the box downstairs and replaced the letters with copies of bills to his patients. Almost everyone in town owed her father money, including Mr. Mason, and he never attempted to collect any of it.

The shelves in his office contained the medical records of almost everyone in the area; she only had to pack them up for when Andy came. She collected several medical supplies and instruments and took them out to the carriage house. They might be useful one day.

She tossed dress clothes and other useless things into the carriage. Important things, such as guns and ammunition, she placed in the buckboard along with anything that she would actually need. She also bundled the letters from her brother with her underclothes and put them in the buckboard. She'd read them when she had time.

A knock on her door caused her innards to do somersaults. Peering through the lace curtains assured her it was safe to open her door when she saw it was the boy Mr. Mason promised to send over for the medical records.

"Come in." It only took a few minutes to pass him the records. "Thank you, Andy." She handed the boy a few pennies. "I appreciate your help."

Her plans were coming together. She had the most important things out of the house. Her father's pocket watch said it was almost six o'clock. She was tired and exhausted, but she couldn't stop, not yet.

She walked from room to room checking on what was left and what she might still need. Satisfied that she had everything that she wanted or thought she might need from the house, she returned to the kitchen, spread some butter on a sweet raisin roll, and ate it. Her insides had jiggled so much, she wasn't certain that the light meal would remain in her stomach.

As she straightened up the kitchen, she spotted her father's whiskey bottle. Flammable! She didn't want a small fire; she wanted the place to go to the ground. She loosened the cork and carried it to her father's desk and placed it in the drawer with the box filled with bills.

Darkness was beginning to descend and the time had come. All the pertinent information that she needed was wrapped with her brother's letters. She went back to the kitchen. With a bucket of water nearby, she slipped her skirt off and used several matches to burn holes in her skirt. Then she burned a good portion of the hem. This needs to look real! Satisfied, she put her skirt back on, put the charred matches in a jar by the stove where they kept them, and returned to her father's office.

Her skin crawled. She had a feeling someone was watching her, and at this point, that was a good thing. There was no question in her mind that her father was killed because of Lennart. Her father didn't have enemies.

At first, she thought Lennart's death was a simple case of him trying to stop a train robbery. But when her father was killed for no apparent reason, she tied the two deaths together. Lennart must have had information concerning the recent robberies, and someone thought her father had it, too, probably in Lennart's letters. Destroy the evidence? If only I knew what it was.

She looked at the half-filled kerosene lamp and smiled. She lit the lamp on her father's desk and then blew it out. In a cabinet was a jug of kerosene and she filled the lamp, making certain to spill some across his desk and onto the floor. Using an old cloth, she made a show of mopping it up, while spreading the kerosene further. With a match, she lit the lamp. Then she filled another lamp and another, lighting each one as she finished filling them. Each time she managed to spill a few drops that required her to wipe off the excess. Then she left the kerosene jug by the desk.

In the well-lit room, she sat in her father's large desk chair and made a great show of making piles of paper, as if carefully sorting things. Her nerves were frazzled. This was it. Her plans were in place. She reviewed her mental checklist once more. Certain she'd not forgotten a single detail, she inhaled a deep breath and said a small prayer for her safety.

As the tall clock in the hall struck the half hour, she opened the drawer that contained the box of bills, and withdrew her father's bottle of whiskey. Her heart pounded in her chest as she placed the bottle on the desk. Then she lifted the box from the deep drawer. Placing the box on the desk, she deliberately knocked over the bottle, sending the alcohol pouring over the edge of the desk and onto the carpet below. She watched it for a moment, jumped up, and purposely knocked the desk lamp onto the floor, which broke the glass chimney and the oil font. Flames danced between the spilled fluids, and then in a deafening whoosh, flames leapt higher than she expected. She screamed and ran out the front door. "Fire! Fire! Fire! Help me! Fire!"

She turned and watched the curtains in her father's office catch fire. A moment later, the curtains in the front parlor danced with flames, and before more than a few men had arrived, the entire house was engulfed in flames. She screamed at the eerie groan as the flames curled back the metal roof. "Everything is in there. All my father's papers, everything is gone. Help me, please!"

She was terrified, but for a different reason. This had to work. Whoever might have been watching had to believe that any incriminating evidence that would link her to whatever knowledge her brother and father may have shared would be gone. She said a silent prayer for allowing her to escape unharmed. That initial burst of flames and its terrifying sound would certainly stay with her forever. Her body shuddered at the burning image before her.

The town's new fire wagon drew to a halt in front

of her house. Several men attached a hose to the town's water tower while another man uncoiled a hose from the big black belly on the horse-drawn red cart. Several men began to attempt to extinguish the flames as water spurted at high speed from the big brass nozzle on the end of the long hose.

The horses! My cart! She ran behind the house and discovered the carriage had already caught fire. In the carriage house, she hitched one of the horses to the buckboard and led both horses from the carriage house, taking them further down the street to safety. So far her plan was working, maybe a little too well, she thought, as she watched the roof of the carriage house catch fire.

Now she could once again have the luxury of crying. She stood with the townswomen and cried on Mrs. Brook's shoulder. The woman wrapped Ingrid in a comforting embrace. But it didn't stop the fear that Ingrid harbored.

Hot embers had damaged several buildings, but each flicker of flame had been extinguished before it could do severe damage. She hadn't meant to cause harm to anyone's building. Her intent was to only burn her own.

"Oh, our little Ingrid, come home with me. As if you haven't been through enough this past week," Mrs. Brook offered.

Several of the women in the town expressed the

same.

Ingrid dried her tears. "You are all so kind. But if I leave tonight, maybe I could catch the morning train." She patted her pocket. "But I only have a few coins on me. Everything was in there. I do not know what I'm going to do."

"Your father took care of me when I had my baby. Here." One of the women placed some money in her hand.

Soon all the townsfolk were doing the same. She wasn't certain how much she had been given, but it still didn't come near what most of them actually owed her father. The man believed in taking care of people. He could have made plenty of money in the city, but thought these people needed him more.

"Ingrid, I insist that you come home with me, wash up, and have a bit of supper before you do anything," Mrs. Brook said.

Ingrid nodded. "That is kind of you, most kind. But really I should be on my way. I shall sleep on the train."

The woman made tsking noises with her tongue. "First, you eat."

Ingrid washed her face and hands while Mrs. Brook brought Ingrid a clean skirt and some other clothes for traveling.

"You can't travel in a burned skirt. It's not proper for a woman such as you."

She gave Ingrid a bowl of stew and placed more of it in a jar for her to take with her.

Ingrid didn't think she'd be able to eat anything, but the tasty bowl of beef and barley was too good to ignore. "Oh, this is delicious. Thank you so much."

The woman handed her a slice of bread spread with jam. "There's a whole loaf in here and a jar of jam to go with it."

Ingrid accepted the flour sack filled with food. "Thank you so much. You are so gracious."

A half hour later, Ingrid headed east in her buckboard. The only things that remained of her house were the two chimneys standing like sentries; the rest was a pile of glowing debris. Not a single wall stood - even the carriage house had been leveled. She would never return to Bluff Falls, Texas. The only home she remembered was gone, along with her dad and brother. From now onward, she was on her own. It was up to her to survive.

Traveling alone at night in the dark was more than dangerous, and she knew she'd made a mistake when she heard a coyote howl. She stopped once, long enough to find the pistol she'd hidden under the seat and transfer it to her pocket. She stayed on the lonely road and pushed forward.

As morning light created a lighter blue sky above the horizon, she breathed a sigh of relief. The next town came into view and she blew out a few deep breaths. In the distance, she could hear the train's whistle. It's just as well. There's no need for me to go east.

The horses had stopped and she realized she'd fallen asleep. But she had no idea for how long. Shaking the reins, she got the horses moving again and they trod towards the town, which was larger than where she had lived, but she'd been here enough with her father to know her way around. With money for a hotel room, she pulled in front of the big granite building and called to a young Mexican boy standing nearby. "You'll watch my things?"

"Si, Señorita. I am very good."

She paid him a penny, passed him the sack with the stew and bread, then grabbed for the other sack with her things, and went into the hotel. The place was a beauty with marble and gold trim, but she was too bleary eyed to even care. She procured a room and then returned to the young boy outside. Handing him a few more coins, she instructed him to care for her horses and stay with them.

She returned inside and walked up the big staircase to her room. With blurring vision, it was all she could do to climb the steps. Sheer willpower kept her from sleeping on her feet. She unlocked her hotel room door and locked it behind her.

Waking once, she realized it was dark, and then

woke again to the sounds of a busy day. Uncertain as to what day it was, she pulled herself from her bed and washed up. The cool water felt good on her face, but did nothing to relieve her aching muscles. She changed into riding pants and a shirt before making her way downstairs. As much as she would have preferred to wait a week, she knew she needed to get as far away from Texas as she could.

She entered the dining room and looked across the tables. Each one shone in the bright light from the windows. She chose one in the corner near a window where she could see what was going on outside. The ability to watch without being watched was important to her.

A waiter brought her a menu. "We are no longer serving breakfast. You are welcome to wait a half hour for dinner."

"That's fine. May I order coffee?"

The man brought her a cup.

"I know what I want if you'd like to take my order now."

He nodded and she rattled off her choices. Over the next thirty minutes, several of the hotel's patrons wandered into the dining room. Trying not to stare, she attempted to evaluate each person who entered the spacious room to determine if they were a threat. She ate her meal, paid for it, and left a tip for the kind waiter.

After her midday meal, she collected her things from her room and asked the hotel desk where she might find her horse and buckboard. The livery was two blocks away. She passed a bakery, retraced her steps, and went inside. The delicious aroma of sweet treats and bread filled her lungs. She chose two pastries and had the bakery wrap them separately. Little Mexican boys would never be allowed in such a place, and the boy probably smelled the delightful aroma every day.

She stopped in the mercantile and bought a plain carpetbag for her things so that she didn't look like a beggar with a sack. She reached the livery, only to discover that her horses and buckboard were not there and never had been. Her heart fell someplace into her belly.

"You gave them to José?"

"I do not know the boy's name."

"He's this tall and skinny?"

"Yes."

The old man laughed. "Oh, I'm sure he has them. Getting them back might be a problem."

"And how do I do that?"

The old man at the livery sent her to a house about four blocks over. For a few cents, another man would take her to the ranch where the boy lived.

The old man gave her a ride from town to the gates of the compound where José lived and dropped her off. The old man refused to take her as far as the house. "I ain't goin' in there with those people."

She walked the last leg of the trip somewhat grateful she didn't have to ride. She hadn't realized how sore she was until she sat on the wooden bench of the old man's cart and was bounced some more. But the old man's refusal to take her to the actual house where the boy lived surprised her. What is so terrible about being Mexican?

The adobe house with a red tile roof and wrought iron trim was lovely. She knew such haciendas existed, but she had never actually seen one. Mentally she crossed her fingers that the occupants spoke English. Her knowledge of Spanish was limited to only a few words. As Ingrid approached the door, it opened.

"Welcome, señorita."

Her father said all people were the same on the inside and should be treated as the same. But that thought wasn't stopping the quaking inside of her. She squared her shoulders and looked at the strong-featured, gray-haired man before her. "I gave a boy named José some money, asked him to care for my horses, and to stay with my things. He promised he would keep them safe. Now I'm told he lives here."

"Yes. Please come in. You must be exhausted."

E. Ayers

She stepped over the threshold, and the man clapped his hands.

"Bring our visitor some refreshments."

She was ushered into a parlor that looked ten times more beautiful than anything she had ever seen. The tiled floor reflected light and the furniture was covered in brightly woven fabric. Big shutters kept the most of the daylight out, making the room cooler than the outside. It was elegant yet casual. The woman returned with a pitcher of cold orange juice that contained a hint of mint and a tray of tiny rolled tortillas filled with spicy meat.

She smiled at the man as she took her seat. "Your hospitality is most gracious. Allow me to introduce myself. I am Ingrid."

"I am Señor Colima. Welcome to my ranch. Does our young lady have a last name?"

She made an instant decision to hide her last name. "Smith. Ingrid Smith."

"And what is a young woman doing traveling alone?"

She picked at a spot on her skirt. Her father would have thrashed her for lying. "My family…" She looked at the man in the seat across from her. "I am the lone survivor. We were traveling to Laramie where we intended to live."

The man cocked his head. "Wyoming?"

She remembered seeing advertisements for land.

"Yes. My father was hoping to buy some land there. I believe the railroad is selling it."

"You cannot travel there alone. It is not safe."

"I don't see where I have any choice. I am strong."

The man shook his head. "Señorita, it is not safe. You may stay here as my guest until I can figure out how to get you to your destination. And that cart of yours will not survive such a trip."

He clapped his hands and in Spanish said, "Maria, show Ingrid to a room and draw her a bath. Bring her anything that she might need."

Ingrid followed the woman up a large staircase and to a room with a comfortable bed. Ingrid's attempts to chat with the woman fell flat. Figuring Maria probably didn't speak English, Ingrid gave up any attempt to converse. In an adjoining room, Ingrid watched through an open door as the woman drew a bath and scented it. Even the soap was scented with herbs. Maria motioned for Ingrid to get into the tub and then promptly took her clothes away. Uncertain what to do next, Ingrid sank into the tepid water, washed her hair and let her sore muscles relax.

When Maria returned, she virtually pulled Ingrid from the tub and proceeded to buff her dry with soft towels. Having never experienced servants, it all seemed very awkward. The woman towel dried Ingrid's hair and then took her back to the room with the bed.

"Siesta."

Ingrid knew that meant afternoon nap and crawled between the cool sheets of the bed as the woman closed the shutters, blocking the light from the room. Ingrid sniffed the sweetly scented sheets. Everything in the house smelled good. She looked around the room. Mosaic tiles created a tranquil landscape on the wall and outrageously painted ceramic lizards seemed to race up one of the other walls. Certain she was not tired, she assumed she'd lie there awake for an undetermined length of time. Instead she awakened to Maria bustling around the room.

The woman laid out the clothing that Ingrid had been wearing. Now everything was clean and ironed. The white shirt was as white as the day she had purchased it.

She dressed quickly and Maria helped to braid her hair and pin it up. Ingrid had never had a mother's touch, and Maria acted like a mother. When they were done, the woman took Ingrid downstairs, and the family introduced themselves. The best Ingrid could figure out was that there was the mother, father, three grown sons, and a teenager named José. The two oldest sons were married with children.

The youngest son was named Tiago, and the way he smiled at her made her blush. She tried not to stare at him, but he was handsome. and she could feel his constant attention on her.

Dinner was noisy with everyone chatting, and the food was spicy, but delicious. She had thought she wouldn't eat for days and yet so far, she was eating well.

The family switched between English and Spanish, sometimes in the same sentence, which Ingrid found confusing. For dessert everyone was served a bowl of shaved ice flavored with fruit juice. She had never had such a thing and it was delightfully scrumptious.

After dinner, everyone retired to a tiled patio that was lit with torches. That was when Señor Colima began to discuss Ingrid's journey.

"You want to go to Wyoming?" the father asked.

"Yes."

"And this land is in Laramie?"

"Um, no. It is… I believe it is north of Laramie. I would have to look at the advertisement and a map." She wasn't good at lying and her insides trembled with her compounding lies.

"How much land?"

She desperately tried to remember what she had seen. "Farm land."

"Farm? As in grassland?"

"I do not know." She added another lie. "My father was handling it."

"Tiago, what do you think?" the father asked.

The youngest of the three bothers nodded. "It would be worth checking. I have seen such advertisements for excess land. The U.S. government gave land to the railroads. Not all of if it was used and the railroads are selling the excess. But I'd rather go prepared to stay."

The older man nodded. "Yes, it is a long way." Then he turned his attention back to her. "Do you read and write?"

"Oh, yes. I have completed my studies. And I've continued to study on my own."

"Good. I want to hear you read." He left the patio and returned with a King James Bible. He opened it and pressed his fingers to a passage. "Read."

She cleared her throat, stood, and began reading. She read the entire passage and looked at the family. The father motioned for her to keep reading, so she did. She read the story until it was completed. She assumed he was satisfied when he took the Bible away, and she returned to her seat. Sitting motionless, she waited for him to come back with another batch of instructions, and she didn't have long to wait. But the conversation around her was in Spanish, and there seemed to be a great debate. The father brought her paper and pen, asked her to write several things, and then do some simple math problems. Finally the father held up his hand and quieted the family. "Ingrid, will you accept the position as governess to Alma in exchange for passage to Wyoming?"

She looked at the little girl who was curled in her grandmother's lap. "Yes, sir. It will be my pleasure to teach your granddaughter."

"Providence has smiled upon this family. Tiago has been looking for land to start his own ranch, but to make such a trip alone with his daughter would be fraught with problems." The man stood behind the chair where his wife sat and paced for a moment. "We have been blessed with a lovely young woman who can travel with Tiago and watch over his daughter. A woman who is educated and can teach Alma and José." He stared at Ingrid. "Yes, God has smiled upon this family and brought us a fair-haired angel named Ingrid."

In two days time, she would leave with Tiago, his young daughter, and José would go with them. They would be driving cattle northward for the summer.

"Do you cook?" Señor Colima asked.

"Oh, yes. When there is something to cook."

Tiago smiled and asked, "Can you do it over an open fire?"

"I don't see why not."

The father turned to his son. "Talk to our hands and choose wisely. Take only the men who wish to be part of such an adventure, and men who can be trusted around Alma and Ingrid."

That evening when Ingrid returned to her room, she sat near the open window and looked across the fields that surrounded the lovely hacienda of the Colima family. Their good fortune was indeed hers, a way to escape far from Texas and with the identity of governess to young Alma. She pondered that situation for a few minutes and slowly came back to the fact that she had no idea why she was running for her life.

She prayed there were answers in the letters her brother had sent. In her valise was the bundle that contained her money and the letters. She moved away from the window, retrieved the letters, and began to read them.

It soon became apparent that her brother, Lennart, had witnessed quite a few train robberies and a bank robbery. And he was certain that several men working for Red Hall Security were part of the ring of thieves. Ingrid's hands shook as she read the letters. Red Hall Security was the company where her brother worked. Against his father's advice, he had left the US Treasury department to work for Red Hall. He had been hired to protect the transport of federal government securities and U.S. mail, and those were the shipments that were being targeted for theft. Whoever these men were, they didn't want anyone to know about them, but Lennart had named them in his letters. His fear was clear, and he wasn't certain how high up the in the company the ring went.

The following day, her things were transferred to a coach and she would be traveling in that coach. The whole house seemed to bustle with activity. Tiago's mother would swing from barking orders at servants to wailing and clinging to her son. Ingrid thought the woman's behavior was strange, but having never had a mother, Ingrid had nothing for comparison. Her knowledge of Latin gave her a slight edge on the Spanish language, and she knew that Tiago's mother was certain that he would never survive the trip. His death would be hers for she could not bear the thought of losing her son.

***

It was late as Tiago read through the list of travel supplies and notes he had made as he walked the hallway leading to his father's private office. Certain he had taken care of everything he attempted to assure himself that his planning was solid. So absorbed in his list, he almost ran into Ingrid making her way to her bedroom. "Forgive me."

She stared up at him with pink cheeks and stammered, "Oh, I was the one not paying attention." She smiled. "I am looking forward to tomorrow."

He wasn't certain of her age, but he knew she had to be young, too young to travel alone. She was too well educated to have come from a poor family, but a woman with wealth would have been traveling by some other means and not in a rundown cart. "Yes, we all are. But it will be a long trip. Are you certain you are up to it?"

She blushed. "Oh, yes."

There was something about the way she looked at him, and he couldn't stop himself from smiling back. "That is good. We will start early."

She nodded and ducked into her room.

He stood for a moment and thought about her. She had willingly and without question accepted employment, in exchange for passage. Yet she was different from the other women he'd known, and very different from the women in his family. In a way, she intrigued him. Blonde and blue-eyed, he wondered if her heart was as icy as her coloring or was her coloring disguising a smolderingly sexy woman. It didn't matter, she was much too young for him and way below his class. Besides, his father had taught him not to dally with the hired help.

***

The day of departure, the sun was not up when Maria awakened Ingrid. The whole house was teeming with sounds, and there were even more sounds outside. When Ingrid looked out the window, she saw Tiago and José on horseback.

She could see the coach and a supply cart that was being loaded. The herd of cattle mooed, drowning the voices of the men except for a piercing whistle from one of the men. Behind her came the sounds of clapping and Ingrid knew Maria intended to hurry things along.

Maria brought a tray of strong tea and some sweet cakes made with cornmeal and topped with fruit. They were delicious. Ingrid devoured everything, made her toilet, and joined the men.

Ingrid didn't know that she would be driving the carriage until she was helped into the driver's seat. Alma scampered to sit next to Ingrid on the coach's bench. Alma looked adorable dressed in a short-sleeved white blouse with a pleated navy-blue skirt. She wore white silk socks and navy blue, kid-leather shoes with five small buttons. Her dark brown hair had been styled into several ringlets that fell to below her shoulder blades. She wasn't exactly dressed for such travel but maybe the child didn't own anything plainer. The little thing seemed to know almost no English, but she smiled brightly. Ingrid's instructions were to teach the child to speak, read, and write in English, and to educate her in other subjects, and to tutor José in English.

A Catholic priest appeared and everyone grew silent except for the bovines. From her perch on the coach, she barely heard a word of what the man said in Latin, but she knew he was praying for their safety. Then he sprinkled everyone with water, including her and Alma. Unsure of the significance of the water, she merely thanked the man.

The man looked at her and answered, "May God be with you."

A moment later, Tiago called and told her and José to start. José rode beside the carriage and chatted the entire time. Ingrid discovered José was barely twelve and actually a distant family member who had been entrusted to the Colimas at an early age. He had been well grounded in basic subjects, but apparently had only studied in Spanish. Although he spoke English, he admitted he could not read or write in it.

With José's help, Alma caught on quickly and was parroting songs, counting to ten, and reciting the alphabet.

Tiago pulled his horse next to the coach. She'd learned from José that Tiago had been married, but his young wife had died after giving birth to Alma.

Ingrid smiled at the man with dark hair and eyes the color of coal. His strong facial features were so different from the men in Bluff Falls. Tiago's features were more pronounced, and they matched his body, which was as solid. His hat had a large, flat brim. He wore a belt of ammunition across his shoulder, a pistol on each hip, and a rifle hung down his back. His clothing was plain, not adorned with the fancy stitching that he'd worn in the house, but still it was different from the other men. It was as though he had mixed American and Spanish styles together, but the quality of his clothing showed.

She never thought of her father as being a tall man, only average, and her brother had grown several inches taller than her father. But Tiago was probably the same height as her dad, yet Tiago's powerful body and the way he carried himself made him appear larger and more formidable.

He was solid-packed muscle with a broad chest and shoulders that tapered to a slim waist. Even his leg muscles showed through his pants as he sat on his horse. During the heat of the day, he'd roll up his long, white sleeves, exposing strong forearms.

The fanciful dreams of a young woman had never envisioned such a male specimen. She found herself blushing, because thinking about him sent little tingly feelings through her body.

Tiago sent José to join the men and then asked, "Are you doing well?"

"Yes. And I appreciate the padded seat."

He laughed. It was deep and throaty. For some reason, she found herself drawn to this strange, yet handsome man.

"It has been very difficult for me these last few years. My father wants me to have my own land and to start my own ranch. But alone, with a child, I could not do it. I also want her educated."

"So I am to be her teacher?"

"Yes. She cannot attend school. That is only for the children of white people. Seems we are not white enough."

Ingrid shook her head. "We are all the same. I do not understand why people think everyone is different or one is better than another. But for me to teach her, she must use more English."

"She will learn from listening to you. And you need to learn our language."

Ingrid looked at Tiago and nodded. "I am trying. I have studied Latin."

"I am educated - mostly in Spanish. She needs more English than what I had."

"I will do my best. She seems eager."

That evening, the men built a campfire and she fixed a hearty meal for everyone. She and Alma slept in the coach, but it wasn't exactly comfortable. Alma could stretch out on the seat, but Ingrid was too tall. A fly buzzed and the sticky air was still. She finally succeeded in killing the fly only to discover several more insects that feasted on her. She stood and pulled a sheet over Alma and then one over her.

Perspiration covered her body, but it was better than fighting off insects that seemed to want to drain her of all blood.

In the morning, she stirred the hot coals of the campfire and made cornbread to go with the eggs that she had tucked into the hot ashes. The eggs were far from perfect with slightly overdone whites and yolks that were still runny, but no one complained.

Moving a hundred head of cattle took time and each day seemed to drag. Alma was fine the first day, but became very wiggly on the second and third. By the end the week, Ingrid knew the child need to run and play.

"Tiago!" Ingrid called to the child's father.

He rode to her. "Yes. Is there a problem?"

"Alma needs to run off some excess energy. May we pull over there for awhile?"

He looked around. "No. Pull forward. I don't want you behind us."

"Thank you." She looked at the rope hanging from his saddle. "May we use your rope?"

He handed over the coil with a perplexed look on his face and she merely smiled at him.

She did as she was told and could see the herd behind her as she came to a stop. Teaching Alma to jump rope was fun for both of them. By tying one end of the rope to the side of the coach, allowed them both to jump. But as the sun bore down on them, she stripped Alma down to her underclothes and tucked her into the coach for a nap. She wished she could peel her clothes off, too, as she was drenched in perspiration. The men and the herd caught up to her and the decision was made to stop for a few hours.

Tiago's shirt, like the other men's, was soaked in sweat. And he had unbuttoned the top few buttons, showing off his muscular chest that was covered in a fine dusting of dark hair that clung to his wet skin.

Ingrid inhaled as she admired the strong male and prayed her cheeks did not turn bright pink.

"We'll take siesta, eat our late meal, and travel in the darkness. It is rare to find this heat so soon in the season. Maybe it is a good thing we are moving northward," Tiago called to the group as he rode to where she was.

Ingrid nodded. "Ah, but north also means colder in the winter. I have heard there is snow that piles higher than a man's head."

"That is true." He called to his men in Spanish and soon they were climbing under the supply wagon and the coach to escape the sun. "I will stand guard for now and then call one of my men. We do it in shifts."

She nodded again. "Alma is already taking her nap."

"Take yours. We will travel tonight in darkness. It will be cooler."

Inside the black coach, it seemed twice as hot. Her skin was red and hurting from the sun. She really didn't want to touch her face, but she poured a few drops of water on a lightweight cloth and covered her face with that fabric as she attempted to lie across the padded bench inside the coach.

Sleep eluded her. An occasional moo sounded more like a protest. A fly buzzed. Alma tossed and turned, fretful in her sleep. In the distance, she could hear Tiago keeping the herd together, then she heard him return and Marco, one of the younger men who had come with them, took Tiago's place. She wondered if Tiago would find sleep in the oppressive heat.

Far in the distance, there was a rumble. She sat up and looked out one of the small windows of the coach. All she saw was earth and sky, but on the edge of the western horizon was a shade of gray-green. Ominous. Her skin prickled. Suddenly everyone was awake. Tiago reached into the coach and grabbed his daughter.

"Ride! Now!" Tiago reached for Ingrid with his other hand.

"What is it?" Ingrid asked, as she took the horse he offered and climbed into the saddle. The stirrups were too short and she realized she was on José's mount. José had already taken the coach.

The men were shouting to each other and Alma

was holding onto her father's waist for dear life. Ingrid kicked her horse, and Tiago took off, too. In a way, it almost looked like they were riding into a column of smoke, but she realized they weren't. Tiago told her to ride as fast as she could. Her stomach knotted as she leaned slightly forward. Her fingers gripped the reins as though she could squeeze the leather into pieces. The funnel cloud looked more like a big wall raging towards them.

She knew the danger of such a thing, but she had never seen one. Unpredictable in its path, she galloped onward, concentrating on keeping her balance on the beast below her. The twisting wall drew closer and she could hear the wind. Tiago was on her heels with Alma screaming. Ingrid knew not to look at anything other than the terrain in front of her. She urged her horse onward. That monster was close, too close, and she could feel the wind from it. Dust and dirt blew around her. She pulled the neck of her shirt over her nose and tried to watch where she was going. The world had turned gray and there was an unearthly roar. She nudged her horse, but he was galloping as fast as his feet could carry them. No longer could she hear Alma's screams over the sound of the wind. Dear God, do not let the devil take me. Protect us.

She leaned forward in her saddle, her face only a few inches from the horse's neck. Dirt swirled -

blinding her.

In a few minutes, it was over. The air around her cleared and she saw nothing. She reined in lightly and looked to her right. She reined in again, held her breath and looked behind her. Everyone was stopped. Not a word was being said as the men looked around. Then she heard Alma's soft cries. She counted the men, but the coach and the supply cart were nowhere in sight. José!

Something inside of her broke. He was so young. He had given her his horse so that she could ride to safety. His fate should have been hers. The desire to cry was there, but her heart was still pounding too hard, and her breath was nothing more than a series of heavy gasps.

Tiago called to her, "Are you all right?"

She struggled to find breath useable for words. Gulping a heavy mouthful of air, she exhaled a yes and hoped he heard her.

He rode to her with Alma still in tears behind him. He turned around in his saddle and lifted Alma from his horse to Ingrid's, sending the child into an awkward position to make the transfer, but Ingrid appreciated the strength the move required.

"Stay with Ingrid. I have work to do."

Ingrid didn't need to ask. She knew by the look on his face as he turned his horse around that his next concern was for José.

Two of the men had wandered into the herd and she was certain that they were counting heads. Raindrops began to fall, first just a few, and then harder until she and Alma were drenched. For once, Ingrid didn't care that she was wet. The wetness felt wonderful after all the heat. She watched as Tiago rode south until the rain obscured him from view.

"José?" Alma asked.

Ingrid turned and reached behind her, knowing her words would not be understood. "Your daddy went to find him."

She saw both men in the herd holding up seven fingers. Another man shrugged, but a fourth also held up seven digits. Soon all five men were in agreement. She was certain that meant they had lost seven head of cattle to the twister - seven head, all her belongings, their supply cart, a cowboy, and José. She wanted to tell Alma not to cry, but Ingrid wished she, too, could shed tears.

The men pushed the herd onward and she fell into step with them. Her confidence was lacking, and if it weren't for the child whose arms wrapped Ingrid's waist, she would have dismounted, dissolved into a puddle and prayed for death to be quick. For now, she had nothing. Everything she owned was in that coach, and it was gone. There was no way for her to survive without money.

As evening progressed, the temperature dropped.

Not enough to say it was cold, but when wearing wet clothes, there was a distinct chill in the air.

Alma's teeth chattered in the cool air.

If Ingrid had worn a skirt like an ordinary woman, she could have given her petticoat to the child, but wearing the more modern pants had removed that option.

She called to the men, "Will anyone give up his shirt for Alma?"

-3-

Marco rode to her and removed his shirt. "Take mine."

The shirt was damp and stunk of male perspiration, but it was another layer to protect Alma from the cold. A few minutes later, Ingrid realized that Alma's hold was relaxing a little too much.

"Does anyone have anything that I can use to tie Alma to me?"

Ingrid saw the lasso in the air, and then felt the rope go over her head and tighten as two of the men laughed.

The one man brought her the end, looped it twice more around them, and secured it on the saddle's horn. "It's not perfect but it will help. It's best if you keep a hand on her arm."

"I will. Thank you. I'm also glad that I am not a cow, for that did not feel good falling on me."

He laughed and rode off.

Now she, too, wanted to sleep. There were neither stars in the sky nor a moon. The rocking motion of her horse kept lulling her and she fought to stay awake. Tomas, the oldest of the cowboys called for them to stop.

With a creek in front of them and the sound of water, it was a welcomed relief. Tomas helped lift the sleeping Alma to the ground and the child barely stirred. Then he helped Ingrid from her saddle. She tucked one arm under her head and with the other, she snuggled Alma.

"Wake up," Tomas said, "We're going to ride again. No food. We ride."

The sky had lightened to a pale blue in the east and stars twinkled overhead. Ingrid wasn't certain where they were riding or why. Without Tiago, there was almost no purpose. But the men pushed onward.

On the eastern horizon was a small town and two of the men took off in that direction. None of them had eaten since before the twister, and there were no supplies. The forward pace slowed until the heat became intense. Again they stopped, and this time Ingrid sprawled on the grass and closed her eyes to the burning sun, only to be awaken to the sound of cheers from the men. They had a cart and it was filled with all sorts of supplies, including bread and jelly. She cut thick slices for everyone and slathered each slice with jelly. They all had seconds.

Tomas started a fire and they made coffee. The one man bought Alma a glass jar of milk. Ingrid sniffed it and realized it was goat milk.

"It is strong, for it has come from a goat, but is good for you. Drink it all." She swirled the jar to mix the cream into the milk.

Alma took it, made a face, and drank it.

"Good girl." Ingrid attempted to comb Alma's long hair with her fingers.

The child smiled at Ingrid and she returned it. The precious little thing was relying on people who weren't her family. Virtually orphaned, she had no one else.

Marco rummaged through the supplies and handed over a dress for Alma. It wasn't much, just a calico with a pinafore and it was a wee bit too big, but it was better than nothing. He rummaged some more and found a newspaper for Ingrid. "What is here?"

"So you speak our language, but you cannot read it?"

Marco nodded. "Only a few words."

The torn newspaper was several days old and from Oklahoma. She scanned it for an ad by the railroad. At the bottom, near the center of the page, she found it. Certain it was the same one she had seen before, it listed several places including Creed's... The tear removed the rest. Not that it would do her much good now, for whatever money she had was in her bags in the coach. She sighed and read a little news to the men.

At least, she had some written words to show Alma the letters and how they formed words. It was better than nothing, but Ingrid found she was almost jealous of the men, for if she had gone with them, surely she would have found a McGuffey Reader for Alma.

A half hour later, the men began to move again.

Tomas said they were going to try to ride through the night this time. Ingrid nodded. Sleeping through the heat of the day helped, but her nose felt as though it had been kissed by fire.

Their progression was slow, and when they crossed the railroad tracks, several of the bovines refused. With much poking and plenty of protesting, the men got the herd across. A little while later, they watched a train come down those very same tracks. In so many ways, luck had been with them, except in one. Her worry had shifted to the fate of Tiago. It had been several days and nights with no sign of him returning. She waited until morning when Alma was asleep to ask Tomas.

Ingrid walked to where Tomas was standing and realized he wasn't much taller than she. But like Tiago, he had a powerful body for a man who was probably old enough to be her father.

"Do you think Tiago will join us?"

He looked around and then answered. "He might have lost a day or two looking for José and Luis." He referred to the other young cowboy who wasn't much older than José. "But once Tiago has some answers, he will catch up. It is much easier to ride without a herd or with just a few head. I know José and Luis turned around and rode south. They couldn't keep up."

"Do you think they survived?"

Tomas lifted a shoulder and let it drop. "I never saw one that big. I have no idea."

"I don't think I've ever prayed that hard in my life, and at one point, I was too terrified to even pray."

Tomas put his hand on her shoulder. "God understands. He was watching over us that day. He knew your heart."

She smiled at the man.

Three more days and nights and another rainstorm got them. She huddled under the cart with Alma and attempted to sleep through it, but thunder and lightning kept her awake. As evening came, the rain abated and the sun began to disappear, they made the decision to stay where they were.

Tomas, the oldest man in the group had taken charge and began to make a fire. It wasn't much of a fire and, with all the wet sticks, it took forever for it to catch and stay lit. The whole process was compromised further because her skills over the open flames were lacking. She managed to cook some chunks of squash and some chunks of potatoes by placing them on sticks for everyone. There was barely enough heat to do more than warm the vegetables and create a pot of weak coffee. Alma wouldn't eat the squash, and Ingrid wouldn't chastise the child for turning her nose up at food. The poor little thing was missing José and her father.

Two of the men scouted the area, while others sat around and talked. Alma thought it was fun to stay up at night and sleep during the day and had fallen into the easy pattern, but with almost no light, it was nearly impossible to teach her much of anything. The child had learned the alphabet and could count to thirty-nine. It was progress.

Ingrid knew her words were still falling on ears that did not really understand. But each passing day seemed to add to the child's vocabulary.

When Ingrid spotted one of the men with a deck of cards, she almost leapt for joy. Reluctantly he handed over the deck, and Ingrid proceeded to teach Alma the printed numbers. Then it was as though a light had shined on the child. Alma figured out the numbers and what they meant. She took off with the deck and wanted to play cards.

Ingrid rolled her eyes at the thought of what was happening, but she gave the child credit for learning the numbers so quickly. Or did she know her numbers in Spanish and knew how to add and subtract?

Tomas played long enough to placate the child and then sent her back to Ingrid.

There was a town almost straight ahead of them. They would drive the herd around it, but Ingrid wanted to stop in the town with Alma. Marco would go with them. They rode into town. Using the little bit of change that was still in her pocket and the few dollars that Marco had given her, she bought several things that she and the child needed including a beginner reader. As she paid for her things, she asked. "Do you have a newspaper for sale?"

The woman made a little puffing sound between her lips and put several sheets on the counter. "How much of it do you need?"

She had meant a real newspaper, but she wasn't going to turn down the chance to buy only the page with the ad. She picked up several pages and found the advertisement. "I only need this."

The woman huffed but didn't charge her for what she must have considered wrapping paper.

Knowing that the ad might run well beyond the lands availability, she mentally crossed her fingers and prayed that Tiago would catch up with them.

44

Ingrid was certain that he would at least pay her for teaching Alma. But what will he pay if Alma hasn't learned enough to suit him?

The child spotted the stick candies in the jars on the mercantile counter and wanted one. Ingrid was willing to buy the peppermint for her, but Alma pointed to the brownish horehound flavor and almost cried when the woman behind the counter opened the wrong jar. "Let her have the horehound."

She looked at the bathhouse and decided that no matter how much she wanted that bath, it was a useless luxury. After making several more stops in town for food supplies, and with only a few pennies left to her name, they returned to their horse and rode through the town to meet the herd.

The men were thrilled to discover that Ingrid had bought more bread and jelly, cheese, and some ingredients to make cornbread.

The following day, they came to a river and Tomas came to her. "We will wait here. We can get the animals across, but the cart will not be easy. If we veer off course, we make it more difficult for Tiago to find us."

"I agree. I'd also like to wash."

Tomas looked at her and chuckled. "For your safety, you will stay where we can see you."

She looked at Tomas and wrinkled her nose. "I suggest that you and the rest of the men wash, too."

She stripped Alma down to her under things, washed her clothes, and placed them on a bush to dry. "Now I need help."

Alma giggled as Ingrid slipped into the water and removed her clothes.

"Here." She handed the child her blouse and her pants when she'd finished washing them the best that she could. Lounging in the cool water felt wonderful.

Tomas kept a respectful eye on the two females as they played in the water, then apparently must have ordered the men to turn around long enough for Ingrid to get out of the water and dress for the men lined up like soldiers with their backs to her. She would have liked to have stayed in the water a little longer, but the men needed to bathe, too. With only a bar of soap, she washed the clothes for the men and then handed them the soap.

"Come, Alma. It is time for our rest." She spread a blanket on the ground.

The two of them climbed under the small supply cart with the sounds of the men frolicking in the water. For Alma, sleep came easily, but Ingrid couldn't stop worrying about Tiago. She had grown used to his attention. She missed the handsome man who was a good father to little Alma. Inside, she could feel her heart breaking. Wiping tears from her eyes, she convinced herself that sleep was necessary.

As evening came, the men made a fire and Ingrid boiled potatoes and eggs, and made a yeast starter for bread. She also made several batches of cornbread, and then washed the pans and utensils in the river.

"It is good," Marco said when everyone was done eating the eggs and the cornbread laden with honey.

"I'm glad you like it."

Tomas said, "You have done well. We were all afraid that you would be a problem on this trip. You are not like the women in the Colima house. They would whine and we would be forced to take them back." He shook his head. "Very rotten, everyone keeps them happy."

"Thank you. This has not been easy, but I have no choice." *No choice if I want to live and not be murdered like my brother and father.*

Before the sun vanished from the sky, she started to teach Alma to read. Often Alma needed a word translated, but she went right back to her book. Mathematics seemed to come naturally for the child and, although Ingrid wasn't certain if Alma was doing the math in her head in Spanish or English, Ingrid figured it didn't really matter. Using a small slate board she had bought when she bought Alma's book, she'd hand the child several problems, and the child would do them in record time. For being so little, Alma was doing extremely well.

As morning was breaking, the men shouted to each other and Ingrid discovered the reason for their concern. A wolf had come for a drink in the river. They let the animal drink and then fired a shot to scare him off.

Another day passed and then another. The men took turns sleeping and scouting the area. But when two Indians rode to the river, the men seemed more concerned over these visitors than they did over the wolf.

The Indians were young and rode to the supply cart.

With Ingrid's father being a doctor, she had ridden with him onto a reservation on several occasions, and she had no fear of Indians, but she didn't want to lose her supplies. As they lifted a pan of cornbread, she went to them.

"You are hungry?"

The one looked at her.

She took his arm gently in hers and brought him to what was left of the evening's fire. The Indians sat and stared at her as she fixed a meal for them.

"You are loco," Tomas said in a low voice.

"No. They are men, and they are hungry." She fixed a pot of coffee and everyone drank some. She smiled at the Indians and they returned it.

"They sneer at your hospitality," Marco said. "Then they will slice you to pieces."

"They have smiled at me. The smile on many Indians is often flattened. It is not a sneer."

When they were done eating, they indicated that they wanted one of the cattle. Knowing they were not hers to give away, she turned to Tomas. "They want one of our bulls."

"No!"

She put her hands on her hips and walked over to Tomas. "Is that not a small thing compared to trouble?"

"We shoot them now."

"You are loco! They probably understand everything we are saying. You will make trouble for us."

"No!"

She walked back to the two Indians. "The men do not understand. If you were asked to take care of your tribe's herd and someone asked for one, would you give it away if your chief was not there to approve it?"

The men looked at each other and Ingrid knew they understood every word she said. The one pushed her towards a horse.

"Where are you taking me? Is it far?"

The one shook his head. "To our chief."

"May I ride and come right back?"

The same one nodded.

She turned and called to Marco. "Come with me."

Marco grimaced and saddled two horses.

A little ways upstream, they crossed the water as though it was nothing more than a small stream. They continued to ride until they entered a reservation, there the one Indian took them to a tipi. They stopped Marco and pushed her to enter.

A combination of fear and curiosity filled her as she entered and was presented to a man who wasn't much older than her brother should have been.

The three men talked.

"You do not fear us?" the seated man asked.

She shook her head. "My father was a medicine man. He taught me that all people are the same and should be respected."

She held out one hand and took the hand of the other young Indian beside her. "We have the same fingers and our blood flows the same. So why am I here?"

The men chatted in their language.

"We want your man cow."

"They are not mine to give away." She chewed at her lower lip. "A cloud." She held her hand up and mimicked the movement of the twister. "It came and separated us. The owner is someplace behind us. He is the one you need to ask"

They talked again among themselves.

"When will this owner return?"

"We have waited several days for him. The men

say if he does not return in a few more, they will turn around and go back."

The men talked some more and she waited.

"You will stay here. We will trade you for man cow."

She frowned. "A man cow is a bull. A lady cow is a cow. They are all bovines or cattle. And why should I stay here?" She took the Indian's hand beside her. "He comes with me so he can ask for a bull."

"No."

"Yes! You cannot keep me. Do you know how much trouble you would be in if the Bureau of Indian Affairs found out you were holding me?"

Again the men talked between them.

She squared her shoulders and stuck her chin out. They are not going to keep me! "There is a child and you are keeping me from her."

They talked some more. The one man said, "If we let you go, how do we know you will give us a b-b..."

"Bull." She stared at him. His eyes were dark and his skin was a rich shade of mahogany. "How do I know you won't hurt me?" She took the one Indian's hand. "We will take him with us."

"No. White men kill us."

"I will never allow that to happen! He is safe with me." She looked up at the young man standing beside her. Knowing that they had reached a stalemate wasn't helping matters. Then a thought hit her. "There are more of you than there are of us. You are welcome to watch over us. We will not harm him."

The men conversed and the one man said, "I go with you."

She nodded and smiled. "That is good. You have my word and my word is good. May we leave now?"

"No. First we eat."

The meal was simple, fish and some sort of berry. She and Marco ate it, but neither one liked it. The fish was bland and the berry was tart. And then she thanked everyone and they left.

As they made the trek back to the camp, she discovered the Indian's name. It was long and difficult. She smiled and said, "I will call you Trader, for you have traded with me."

It was almost dark when they arrived, and Tiago's men were pleased to see they had returned in one piece. Alma was so happy that she ran, threw her arms around Ingrid and refused to let go.

"Ah, my good girl." Ingrid ran her fingers through the child's hair. "Do not fear. I am fine."

Two more days passed. Ingrid contented herself with knowing there was a stream and plenty of trees to protect them from the sun. She spent part of each day working with Alma, teaching her mathematics and English. But Trader was getting anxious and Ingrid knew he was concerned.

On the third day, two of the men returned from their scouting, and the talk among the men was enthusiastic, but she didn't understand what they were saying in Spanish. Trader looked at her and she shrugged. "I do not know."

A few minutes later, she heard noise. The distinct sound of wheels sent her from the protection of the trees. Tiago! He was driving the supply cart, and behind him was the coach. For the first time in weeks, she relaxed as joy flowed like blood through her system. "Alma, it's your daddy!"

The child scurried from where she was sitting and ran as fast as her legs could carry her towards her father.

Ingrid looked at Trader and smiled. "He has come. You will talk and tell him you wish one bull."

Tiago jumped from the cart, grabbed his daughter and spun her around. But when he put her down, his gaze settled on Trader.

"Why is he here?" Tiago snarled.

Ingrid couldn't understand much of what the men were saying, but she knew it was disparaging. She took Trader's hand and walked him to Tiago. "This is Trader. He has been waiting for you to arrive. His tribe wishes to have a bull."

Tiago said something in his language.

"Please work out a deal with his tribe. They have been most kind to me and to us. They are all around us."

Trader called to his fellow tribesmen and about twenty of them appeared.

Ingrid smiled at the Indian. "They have been kind to us. Provided us with fish to eat while Trader is here."

Tiago spit on the ground.

"No, Tiago. They could have killed all of us, but they didn't. They only want a bull. Consider a fair trade. They will listen." She turned to Trader. "Call the young man who took me to your chief."

Trader called and the other man appeared.

"This is the man who took me to his chief. They wanted me as hostage, but I convinced them to allow Trader to come here with me. They are good people."

Trader looked at Tiago. "She said I must ask you for bull. I ask. We want bull."

Ingrid reached in her pocket. "I have the advertisement for the land. We only need to safely get there. I think they can help."

Tiago pulled a map from his pocket. "Where is the land?"

She showed him the newspaper and he pointed to the map. "He speak English?"

"About as well as you do."

Tiago frowned and she knew she'd hurt his

feelings.

She patted his arm. "Your English is better."

Trader took the map. "We want bull."

Ingrid removed the map from Trader's hand. "We know you want a bull. I am making a deal."

"We are here in this area, and according to the newspaper we need to get here. We stay here." Tiago ran his finger over the map. "Until we reach this area, and then follow the river."

"Most tribes will trade. We could trade for protection and help."

Tiago looked at the red-skinned man standing next to Ingrid. "You trust them?"

"I trust them more than you do. They have been kind to us."

Tiago grimaced. "Let Marco go and tell them what we want in trade."

"I will go. They trust me." She turned to Marco. "Please saddle a horse for me and cut out a bull."

Tiago frowned. "You will not go alone. I will go with you. We don't need to give them a bull until we have some sort of pact."

"We will take one with us."

"You are a very demanding woman." Tiago spit on the ground.

She walked to where he was standing, while he barked orders at his men, and tugged on his sleeve.

He turned to her. "What?"

She stood on her tiptoes and kissed his cheek. "Thank you."

A delicious feeling spread through her system. Please keep us safe one more time.

4

Tiago stood stunned at Ingrid's kiss. It was no different than the kiss of a familiar family member, but it didn't feel that way. He felt it to his toes and to places in between.

He and Tomas chose a bull. Trader nodded and they set off for the reservation. When they arrived, Ingrid and Tiago went into the tent to greet the chief.

"We brought you a bull now we want--" Ingrid's elbow intersected with his ribs. "What?"

Ingrid smiled at the chief. "I have kept my promise. This is Tiago Colima. But we would like something in exchange. We must travel far." She turned and asked, "May I have the map?"

Tiago unwillingly handed over the map.

She turned back to the chief and pointed to where they were. "We are here. We need to go..." she pointed to a spot, "up here. We could use some scouts if you know the area."

She kneeled in front of the chief with a big smile and handed him the paper. "These are the mountains. This is the river and here is the railroad."

The men talked among them and Tiago didn't like not knowing what they were saying. But he definitely disliked Ingrid usurping his command.

Ingrid was now sitting beside the chief pointing to things on the map and smiling at the Indians. She looked up once at Tiago and grinned. Two men stepped forward. Ingrid nodded and pointed at Trader. "He is a good man."

A woman stood slightly behind him with a baby.

"Oh. I am sorry. She needs you more than we do." She pointed at Tiago and held her hand off the ground. "Alma."

Trader nodded and his wife stepped away.

The chief called another man who wasn't more than a young teenager.

And Ingrid nodded while offering her hand to the chief. "It is good."

Tiago and Ingrid were fed fish placed into a corn batter. From the look on Ingrid's face, she didn't like it anymore than he did, but she ate it as did he. When they were done, Ingrid went to Trader and shook his hand. Then she went to Trader's woman and gave her a hug. "You are a lucky woman. He is a good man, always kind to us and a great fisherman."

The three Indians, taking a fourth horse with them to carry a few supplies, left with Tiago and Ingrid. It was late when they arrived at the camp. Tiago dismounted, tumbled to the ground, and didn't want to move. But as soon as morning broke, his mind began to churn with thoughts. He jumped bareback on a horse and stood there counting the number of head he had left. He figured he had lost more, but he hadn't. Just two and those were accounted for and now, a bull in trade for three scouts. He wasn't certain how Ingrid had done it, but she had given him more men - scouts to make the journey safer. That also meant more mouths to feed.

He looked at his map and realized they were far from another town. The aroma of breakfast tickled his nose. Ingrid was fixing a solid breakfast of goose eggs and smoked bacon.

After breakfast, Ingrid called Alma and they bathed in the water. It was apparent that Ingrid had taught his daughter to swim. Watching them frolic and play stirred more than protective feelings in him. And when she chased the men to take a bath, he wasn't thrilled, but decided the cool water did feel wonderful. Yet it didn't seem to cool the heat brewing inside of him.

The next few weeks went by uneventfully. Then a wheel on the small cart broke, and before they had figured out what to do about that, a scout informed them that they could not get through the canyon. They would have to retrace two days back to a stream and go east. The only good thing about all of it was watching Ingrid bathe in the tiny stream one more time. Just knowing she wasn't dressed was enough to stir feelings in him. And she never missed an opportunity to bathe.

But he had caught her admiring gazes towards the Indians who wore almost nothing in the blazing summer heat. She would catch one showing more of his body than was respectful and discreetly look away, but a pink blush would cover her cheeks as she smiled. A feeling of anger pricked at him, for he, too, was a handsome specimen of male, but he was civilized and knew how to behave in the company of a woman. Proper men didn't walk around virtually naked in front of a female, and the Indians only wore a little flap that left too much showing.

Ingrid had given the Indians nicknames and they responded to them. In fact, even Tiago's men seemed to be at her beck and call. She had cast a spell over all of them, and Tiago was determined that he wasn't going to fall under her charms. But he appreciated her cooking and the clean clothes she provided. He was also thrilled with Alma's studies. Ingrid had proven herself to be a good teacher.

Pouring rain delayed them. Ingrid cut cornbread left from the previous night and dribbled honey on the pieces. It was better than nothing, but the rain soaked it before they could finish eating it. He climbed into the carriage and consulted the map. When will we be there?

***

Alma was bored and Ingrid tried to think of something they could do other than schoolwork. The child was tired of doing it, and it was no longer a game. It was stifling hot in the carriage, but it was dry except for the perspiration that dripped down Ingrid's neck, ran down her back, and made the fabric of her shirt stick to her skin.

"Oh, Alma. Maybe we should just try to sleep. With luck when we awaken, the rain will have stopped."

"No! No sleep. I'm not tired."

"Fine. Get your slate."

"No. No school!" the child whined.

"No. I don't want to play school either. We'll play a game of dots and boxes." She made several dots and showed Alma how to connect the dots to form boxes. "There was a man from Savannah, Georgia who taught me how to play this. He said it was very popular in the east."

Ingrid wasn't trying to lose, but her heart and mind weren't into it. Every game they played Alma won. Ingrid began to wonder if maybe she'd forgotten something or was the child just very bright. Alma was bright, and it showed in everything she was doing. This time, Ingrid paid attention and tried harder. She still lost, but won the next game and the next before losing again.

The game whiled away the afternoon and Alma announced, "I'm hungry."

"While it is raining, we cannot make supper."

"I'm hungry!" Alma protested.

"Try not to think about it." Ingrid's own stomach protested. "We're getting closer to our destination."

"But where are we going?"

"Your father wants to find land and start a ranch. I just want a house where I can live in peace."

"Are you and Daddy going to get..." Alma scrunched up her nose.

"Get what?"

"I don't know your word." She shrugged. "You and Daddy. You be my mommy."

"Your daddy does not want me. He will build his ranch and then find a beautiful woman with dark hair like yours."

"But I want you!" She crossed her arms over her chest. "I love you."

Ingrid giggled. "I love you, too. Your father does not have to marry me for me to love you. I think I will always love you." She brushed a lock of hair away that was stuck to the child's face. "You have become very special to me."

The sound of horse hooves made Ingrid open the flap on a window and look out. The rain was subsiding to just a few drops. Tiago jumped into the carriage with them and the one Indian followed him. Tiago pulled out his map.

The Indian pointed. "Here."

"No. It is too far." Tiago shook his head.

"Yes. Here. I see the railroad. Here. We are here, not here."

"Oh please let us be that close!" Ingrid said almost in a whisper.

"Before the sun sets tomorrow, we will be here," the Indian said.

Tiago pocketed the map, looked at Ingrid, and kissed his daughter. He started to leave the carriage, but stopped and looked one more time at Ingrid. She smiled at him, but part of her wanted to reach out to him and run her hand up his arm. The desire to feel his lips on hers made her blush. She wanted to see him as she had seen the Indians, to see his broad chest and to touch him as a lover.

He stared at her and the heat in her face grew, but it was the heat that glowed between her legs and made her heart pound that she wasn't expecting. Her father had told her what it was to be with a man. He had taught her about those body parts just as he had taught her about all the body parts. She knew, but she didn't know. She only knew that she had never had such delicious feelings. Her gaze never left Tiago's.

"I will see to a fire." He broke the spell with words.

"Yes. That would be good. Alma is hungry." She stared into his black eyes, unwilling to let go of her feelings. "I am hungry, too."

"We all are." He stepped from the carriage.

She closed her eyes and tried to compose herself. A few deep breaths helped, but seeing Alma brought her back to what she needed to do.

Ingrid went to the door. "I'm going to the wagon for food. You will get wet but not too wet if you want to jump rope."

"It's more fun when you jump with me."

"Ask the men to turn the rope for you." She sprinted to the supply cart and hoped that cooking would put an end to the feelings inside of her.

The rain had brought in much cooler air. But it had also soaked all the available wood, making it difficult to get a fire going. After several tries, Tomas had succeeded in creating a small but hot fire. Ingrid made a thin batter with oatmeal and fixed what Tomas called flapjacks to go with the smoked ham. With the last of the batter, she made a small one for herself and then scraped the bowl to create one more, which she offered to the youngest Indian, Soaring Bird. He grinned at her and devoured the small second helping.

Tomas made coffee as she washed the pan and plates in the tiny stream. She laughed to herself as her cooking skills were limited. Yes, I can cook when there is something to cook. But evenings such as this one tested her ability to feed so many hungry men, yet not one of them grumbled about the limited provisions.

The clouds had parted and she knew that stars would begin to twinkle in the late evening sky. She looked around her and admired the countryside. The air was scented with bovines and that wonderful fresh smell of newly washed earth.

She returned to the campfire and Alma sat on her father's knee, proudly reading to him from her book. It was a nightly ritual between father and daughter. Tiago's face beamed with love for his daughter, and he seemed delighted with her progress. But when the child began to yawn, Ingrid knew it was bedtime for Alma.

After settling the child into the carriage for the night, Ingrid tossed her shawl over her shoulder and went back to the men. She poured a cup of coffee that had been made with coffee beans, wheat berries, and a scraping of cinnamon. It wasn't quite the same, but it stretched their supply of coffee beans, and the men didn't complain. It had been Tomas who suggested that she add the cinnamon to the coffee, and it did make it more palatable to her. With her cup in hand, she walked away from the fire and the men sitting around it.

A small stream that was barely a trickle, even after all the rain, ran next to a small copse of trees and thorny bushes. A bird overhead flew away as she wandered near the thicket. Dreams of her own little house wandered through her mind.

She touched her nose. It had been burned so many times and peeled so much that she wondered how she still had any skin left on it. Her lower arms and hands were almost as brown as the men's. She knew she was a terrible sight. Her father and her brother had always told her she was pretty, and even several of the women in Bluff Falls had remarked about her beauty over the years, but right now, she didn't feel very pretty. Certain that she looked like a scullery maid, she almost wished she could cry. But this trip had toughened her. Ingrid Smith was no longer Ingrid Svensen. This Ingrid was different.

She heard footsteps behind her and turned to see who it was. She smiled at Tiago. "I like this weather much better."

"Yes. It is good." He stood beside her. "You have done well with my daughter. She's learning so much."

"Thank you. She needs more books. When we get to Laramie, I will see that she has them. There must be a store there where I can buy her such things. Also, she's growing like a little blade of grass. Several of her dresses are tight on her and the hems are getting shorter by the day."

"Whatever she needs I will buy."

Ingrid put her empty cup on the ground and looked at Tiago. She tried not to think about what the child had said. But deep inside, something stirred and warmed her until the heat rose to her cheeks.

Like a proper gentleman, Tiago offered her his arm. "Ingrid, let us walk over here, away from the men, for I wish to speak to you."

She laid her hand on his arm and followed him across the stream and to the other side of the trees. There the mountains came into view. "Do you think we are that close?"

"I will believe him only when I see it. This has been a long journey for all of us. My men are used to driving cattle, but this trip has been full of challenges. And traveling with ..."

She looked up at him. "A child and a woman? I assure you we have not stopped the forward progression."

"No, you have not. And you have not whined. Tomas says you have made this trip good."

"I have tried hard. The men work hard."

"I also do not understand how you traded one bull for three scouts. They are good men. How did I get so lucky?"

She giggled. "My father did not know how to raise a girl, so he merely raised me to be a person."

"Our women are taught to do the things that women do."

She mimicked sewing with a needle.

"Yes. And they are taught to dance and other things that..."

"A woman in town taught me to sew and do fine stitching, but it's not what I prefer to do."

"What do you like to do?"

She held both hands palms up. "I have enjoyed teaching Alma. Even this trip has had many good moments." She put both of her hands on his arm and could feel her body warming. "These Indians are different from the ones I have known, but learning about them and their ways is good. Maybe I have liked learning and being part of this adventure."

"Do you like me?" Tiago asked.

She prayed the darkness hid the heat that had rushed to her cheeks. "Oh, yes. You are a good father and you have taken care of your men. You treat everyone well. But you must learn to treat all people with respect, even those you do not know."

"You have taught me much that I did not know about Indians."

"You have fallen victim to the white man's prejudices. You have come from a family of wealth even by white man's standards. But in many places, you are considered to be unworthy because of the color of your skin, and many more hate you because you have color and are wealthy."

"Ah, but my family was in Texas first."

"And the Indians inhabited the United States first. Yet we put them on reservations and keep them there like dogs. We could have done the same thing to you."

"No. My family is from Spain."

"With the name Colima?"

"Yes."

She had no desire to give him a lesson on geography, and maybe the Spaniards named the Mexican area Colima. She squeezed his arm. "It does not matter where anyone is from. All that matters is what is in a person's heart and you have a good heart."

"You do not know what is in my heart."

"Maybe not everything, but I know you are a good man." She looked up and a few million stars twinkled. "It is so beautiful."

"You are beautiful. More beautiful than all the stars in the sky."

She could feel the flush warming her cheeks. "Thank you. You are very kind to me." She gazed at the ground by her feet and then at the mountains, before settling on his face. "And you are very handsome."

He turned and faced her. She could almost feel his breath. Her heart pounded, drowning out all the night sounds. She closed her eyes. There was no way she could continue to look at him for fear he might see what her body was doing to her. His fingers touched her cheek and her knees weakened. Certainly she would turn into a burning puddle and melt into the earth. Instead, her heart beat harder, making it more difficult for her to breathe. He lifted her chin and his lips touched hers. Flames licked her entire body.

Never before had she kissed a man. Not like this. She didn't know what to do. She couldn't breathe and her lungs burned from lack of air. She pushed away from him.

"I am sorry. I meant no offense."

She gasped several deep breaths and realized she had her hands on his shoulders. His shirt was twisted in her fingers. She opened her eyes and saw eyes that matched his daughter's, except on him they were dangerously sexy. "Oh. I-I couldn't breathe. I never... It was... Oh..."

She looked back at the mountains. Their strange jagged outline matched the feelings inside of her. When she looked back, he was smiling at her.

"Was that your first kiss?"

She nodded.

His hand slipped to the nape of her neck. "Then let me teach you. Relax, and do what I do."

He drew closer to her until his lips touched hers. This kiss was softer, his lips more tender as they covered hers. She couldn't follow him because her body burst into flames. He pulled her tight to him and she clung to his shoulders to keep from dissolving.

His lips left hers. "It is best that we go back. I must not do more."

She couldn't open her eyes, and she couldn't let go, not yet. She held tight to him. Her feet weren't going to support her. "It is best if you do that again so I do not forget."

He chuckled and gave her a brief kiss. "If I do more, I will do much more. And if we stay here any longer, our status with the men will be gone. For they shall think I have done much more and that you are not a lady."

"Oh."

The sound of a twig breaking made them both look into the trees, but there was no one there.

The name Jezebel rolled through her mind. She didn't care. It felt much too wonderful. And she wanted much more.

5

Tiago offered Ingrid his arm and she took it. In the quiet of the evening, they walked back to the small stream that separated him from his men. He knew the journey to Wyoming would only be the start. It would take maybe weeks before he knew if he had the land and then he needed to build a house. His father had given him money for land and for a house, but he would need to make his own after that. He worried about Ingrid. Would she attempt to leave? Was this not her destination? Alma would be heartbroken. It was obvious that Alma loved her teacher. But what exactly was he feeling?

He was hungry for the company of a woman, and he knew it. It had been ages since he had been with a woman, except Ingrid was different. He pushed those thoughts to the side. His desire would show and he didn't want to suffer the baldy comments from his men. In an attempt to break the mood between them, he asked, "Did you know that the captains of ships sail by the stars?"

She stepped over the small creek and looked up at the stars. "Yes. But I do not understand how when they are constantly moving. It was the Greeks that named them, many for their gods." She pointed towards the southern sky. "Do you see how the stars make a house? That is Sagittarius." She blew out a breath. "They must have had a great imagination, because it's supposed to look like the archer Sagittarius, half human and half beast."

He patted her hand where it rested on his arm and chuckled. "I see a house and a second roof on the side as though the first one slid off from the wind."

She laughed. "You are right. And it is past my bedtime."

He watched as she picked up her cup and prepared for the evening. He would need his sleep and thinking of her would prevent it. She was as tough as she was beautiful, but still innocent. Don't play with the hired help. He shook his head trying to clear it of his thoughts, but they lingered anyway. He knew he would enjoy playing with her. She was more than hired help. She was much more and the feelings she stirred went beyond a few minutes of pleasure.

When morning broke, everyone was ready. The

men would want a few days off in the town. Yet it was still a day's drive away. He called to his men to round up and move.

He stayed behind and put the morning fire out, made certain Ingrid and Alma were ready, and then mounted his horse. Watching Ingrid and Alma made his morning brighter. But sleep had not come easily and now he'd pay for it.

As they came towards town, the men kept the herd off to one side as he and Ingrid continued onward.

He rode ahead and then came back to the carriage. "It's not Laramie. It is Cheyenne."

"Oh, but it is still a big town and maybe we can find answers there," Ingrid called back.

"I'll find a hotel. The men want some time off."

She nodded.

The stockyards were crowded and so was the town. He pulled to a stop in front of the largest hotel and tethered his horse. He stepped inside and looked around. It was a fine hotel with ornate gold moldings and trim. Men in red uniforms with lots of gold trim were stationed in various places around the large lobby. The soft seating appeared to be covered in red velvet with gold-colored fringe that matched the drapes, and the oil lamps all had fancy silk shades with gold fringe. It was a bit too much for him, but Ingrid would appreciate it. He strode to a polished counter of the reception desk. The wall behind it was filled with brass keys. He hit the small bell and waited.

Finally a man came. "We don't serve Mexicans."

Tiago looked around and then at the man. "Are you speaking to me?"

"Yes."

"I am not Mexican. I am American. My family hails from Spain."

"Just one moment." The man went through a door and then returned. "I'm so sorry. How long will you be staying?"

"I am not certain. That depends if I can conduct some business transactions here. I was headed for Laramie. Maybe three nights, maybe more."

"I will put you down for three. If it is more, please let me know the morning after your second night."

"I need two rooms: one for myself and one for my... governess and daughter. We will need a toilet and a bath. Is that possible?"

The man inhaled and looked at the keys on the wall. "We have a suite with three bedrooms and the other rooms that you requested."

"That will be fine."

The man quoted him a price, and he thought he'd die on the spot. Instead, he produced the cash. "It had better be nice for that price."

"It comes with meals."

It should come with part ownership in the hotel.

A few minutes later, Ingrid joined him. He handed her some money. "Go buy a few nice things for you and my daughter, you will need them while staying here."

"Do I get to wash up first?"

"No."

***

Ingrid took the money and went down the street where she had spotted a dress shop. She quickly chose two outfits for herself and two for Alma. They each got a new pair of shoes, and then they hurried back to the hotel. Now she knew why he'd given her so much money. She had never seen such expensive clothes. Even a plain dress for Alma was outrageously priced.

The hotel was beyond her wildest imagination. Alma chose a room and Ingrid took the remaining one. There was a room that contained an indoor toilet and another that contained a bathtub and a sink with hot water that poured freely from the tap. She washed her face in the warm water and looked longingly at the bathtub that sat on four fancy, clawed feet.

"Tiago, is there time for me to take a bath?"

"Yes. And bathe my daughter, too. When you are

done, we shall have supper. In the meantime, I will inquire about the land."

"Come, Alma. You take your bath and then you may pick which one of your new dresses you wish to wear this evening."

Quickly she bathed Alma, but leaving the child to dry her own hair was probably a mistake. Yet it gave Ingrid more time to relax in the tub. The water instantly turned muddy. She drained it and refilled it. Washed again and when satisfied, she left the warm water.

The lavender-blue skirt and matching paler colored blouse suited her. She pulled her still slightly damp hair into a braid and frowned. Turning it loose, she pulled it into a knot at the nape of her neck and held it in place with several pins. She tied Alma's hair with a ribbon and admired the child's dark curls against the pale yellow ribbon. "Do you need help with your shoes?"

Alma stuck her feet out and Ingrid used a long-handled buttonhook on Alma's shoes. Then Ingrid put her own shoes on and buttoned them. "What do you think?"

"I think you look extra pretty!"

"So do you. Now remember your manners. Don't put your fingers in your food, and don't talk with food in your mouth."

Alma smiled.

"Just a moment. Do you have a loose tooth?"

The child instantly stuck her tongue on her tooth.

Ingrid reached over and checked the front tooth. Not only was the tooth slightly forward from the others, it wiggled a little. "Seems you are growing up. You are going to loose that baby tooth and get a big-girl one."

Alma smiled and skipped off to visit with her father while Ingrid finished preparing for their evening meal.

Ingrid inhaled. Her own father had taught her manners and other such things, but he'd never taught her how to be a lady. She gazed into the mirror one more time before joining Alma and Tiago in the spacious parlor of the suite.

Tiago looked at her and the smile on his face said he was pleased with what he saw. "You look lovely, as does my daughter. Your choice in clothes is to be commended."

"And you look very handsome." She walked over to him and removed a hair from his black jacket. "Now you are perfect."

"Shall we go to dinner?" He gave her his arm.

The dining room looked like the rest of the hotel, overly ornate. And the food was delicious. It reminded her of the places she read about while visiting the homes where women received magazines on fashion and such. At her home, she and her father ate simple foods and their dining room was plain. She tried to memorize everything that she saw and decipher the spices and herbs used in the food.

"There is a land office down the street. I will check it tomorrow." Tiago sat back and stirred his coffee. "Maybe you should see to any books that Alma might need."

"Yes. She also needs writing supplies, but until she is settled someplace and can have a desk…"

"More books?" Alma asked.

"Yes, darling. You need more than your reader. Maybe you can help me pick them out."

Another young girl came into the dining room, holding a doll in her arms as she walked to a table with her parents.

"I want one of those!" Alma said, pointing to the other girl.

Tiago laughed. "You want a sister? I shall have to marry first."

The child looked confused as she answered, "Yes, I want a…"

Ingrid raised her eyebrows. "You mean a doll like the one that she carries? And it's not polite to point."

Alma looked at her father and then at Ingrid. "A doll."

Ingrid couldn't stop the bubbling inside of her that became a giggle, but she tried to keep the sound as soft as possible. "A doll is much easier to obtain than a sister."

Tiago grinned at Ingrid. "Sisters aren't difficult to obtain when everyone is willing."

Ingrid turned her attention to Alma. "Maybe it is best to wait until we reach Laramie before we buy a doll. I am certain such a doll is very expensive and will get very dirty on our trip."

Alma pouted.

Ingrid touched the child's shoulder. "But we can look at them so that you have some time to decide on just the right one."

Alma went back to eating her dessert.

But when Ingrid's gaze caught Tiago's, she could feel heat rushing to her cheeks.

The morning shined bright, and after breakfast, Ingrid took Alma shopping. It seemed as though everything cost more in Cheyenne. They stopped at one store that sold books and found several for Alma. Ingrid chose two and suggested they wait until they were further along on their trip to buy more. They stopped at another store where they found dolls. Alma ogled all of them and didn't want to leave when Ingrid suggested they make their way back to the hotel.

After dinner, Ingrid sat with Tiago, and he showed her a new map along with the land that was for sale. Slightly west of Creed's Crossing were several contiguous blocks of land tucked almost to the mountains.

"That's quite a bit of land."

Tiago nodded. "The question that remains is if it is worthy of a ranch or is it useless land? I can't raise cattle on dry land."

"So now what?"

"We check it."

"We? How would I know land suitable for cattle?"

He chuckled. "I will check it. There is also another strip of land here that might be better." He pointed to another spot on the map. "The cattle can freely graze here. But I have been warned that there are no hotels in Creed's Crossing."

"So we might have come all this way for nothing? And when we get there, there will be no place to stay?"

Tiago rolled his palms upwards. "Maybe."

6

After spending an extra day resting, they left the following day. There was no point in going directly into Laramie, so they continued on to Creed's Crossing. Tiago didn't want to tell Ingrid that it could be as much as another two weeks. The terrain would be rough, and with the cattle, he didn't expect to make good time.

He handed the three Indian scouts notes of employment and gave them some added cash for all their help. The youngest scout, Soaring Bird, didn't want to return to the reservation and refused to leave. The other two scouts nodded at his refusal, and Tiago understood. For this young man, it was the adventure of a lifetime, and the other men probably had responsibilities to the tribe. Six men, José, a young Indian, and almost a hundred head of cattle... It was going to be another hard drive.

Tiago kept a watchful eye on Ingrid and his daughter. The road was well traveled and quite clear. At least, the intense heat they had endured seemed to ease, even though the sun shone down on them the entire time. This portion of the trip both Ingrid and Alma wore straw hats with large flat brims. Alma's was trimmed with cloth flowers, but Ingrid's was plain with a black ribbon. It suited her.

When he had handed her money in Cheyenne, he figured she's spend all of it and come to him wanting more. Instead, she bought everything and returned half the money along with the receipts, apologizing over the cost of the purchases. She was frugal, and she was as tough as any man, but she was solid woman and he liked what he saw.

As they approached another town, she only asked to buy some things for Alma and didn't even ask for a hotel room or to spend a night or two. He handed her the money and stayed with her, as Tomas and the men drove the cattle around the town.

She bought boys pants for Alma and several used books for the child.

But when Alma spotted a doll, she fell in love. "Please, Daddy?"

He looked at Ingrid and she smiled.

"Is that a yes?" Alma asked.

Ingrid's grin widened. "We are almost there, are we not? And the price isn't what they were in

Cheyenne."

"Yes, Alma. You may have the doll." Then he spotted Ingrid looking at some hand mirrors. He turned to the saleswoman. "And we'll take whichever mirror set she chooses."

The saleswoman walked to where Ingrid was standing. "He said for you to choose one."

Ingrid turned to where he was standing with Alma and started to walk away. "Oh, no. You mustn't spend such money on me. It is only a childish whim."

"No, every woman wants such things, and you've not had them. You must pick a set. I insist."

She held up a hand. "Please, no. I am fine without such a silly thing."

"It's not silly. I'm not leaving here until you pick one."

She frowned and picked out a tiny mirror with a matching comb.

He shook his head. "That will not do." He went to where the sets were displayed. "Alma, which set suits Ingrid?"

Alma debated between a red painted set and the fancy silver set. "This one."

"That's what I would have chosen, too, if you had not been here to help me." He turned back to the saleswoman. "The silver set."

Ingrid did that female pout thing and he laughed.

A few more supplies and they were on their way to catch up to the herd. They stopped for the night. With fresh supplies, Ingrid fixed two chickens along with some garden vegetables. Everyone agreed it was the best meal of the trip.

"We should be in Creed's Crossing tomorrow night," Tiago announced and the men celebrated.

Tiago laid his head on a blanket in the supply cart and drifted off to sleep while two of his men watched over the herd. He awoke with a start.

***

Ingrid heard the noise outside and grabbed for the rifle under her seat. She woke Alma, put her under her seat, and covered her with a blanket. "Don't even stick your nose out unless I call you or your father does."

Peering through the flap that covered the coach's window, she could see three men holding most of Tiago's men hostage while a few more attempted to round up the herd. Oh no you don't. We didn't get this far to have you do this to us!

She cocked the rifle, looked down the barrel, and shot the man standing in front of Tiago. Sticking another bullet in the gun, she shot another man. Grabbing the pistol, she shot at a third man. The chaos outside was too much. She could no longer tell who was who. But the gunfire was unreal. A bullet whizzed past her and stuck into the far wall of the carriage. A man opened the door to the carriage. The unknown face stared at her. Her heart pounded, something at the nape of her neck prickled as though spiders crawled there, but her hands remained steady on her pistol as she pulled the trigger.

Suddenly the carriage started to move. Unsure who was driving, she peeked out the tiny slat at the naked backside of the driver. She knew who it was and breathed a sigh of relief. "Alma, you can come out."

Alma climbed from her hiding place. "What happened?"

"Men tried to rob us. Soaring Bird is taking us to safety." I hope.

The carriage slowed and finally stopped. Soaring Bird opened their door. "You are hidden here. I will go back."

"Please don't be long."

He shook his head. "Bad men."

"Yes, bad men." Too many bad men. Mucho. "Be careful!" But she wasn't certain he heard her.

She reloaded both guns and sat listening to all the sounds of the night. Through this whole trip, she had never felt or been so alone as she was this evening. She was Alma's only protector, and she had no idea where they were.

Minutes seemed like hours and hours turned into what felt like days. Holding tight to her pistol, she took her toilet with Alma. They were between two ridges in a narrow gully. She wasn't even certain which way the sun was rising, only that the sky was getting lighter and the stars had vanished.

The sound of horse hooves made her gut clench. She relaxed a little when she realized it was Soaring Bird. She jumped out of the carriage and greeted him.

He motioned for her to follow him. She climbing onto the seat and grabbed the reins. A few minutes later, she was back with Tiago and his men. Tomas had been shot in the leg. Another man had a bullet in his arm, and Tiago's side was bleeding.

She grabbed her father's medical equipment and started applying her medical knowledge. What she had was limited.

"Tiago, can you hold Tomas and keep him from moving?" She handed Tomas a stick. "Put this between your teeth."

Even with Tiago holding the man, Tomas still jerked as she dug for the bullet. She looked through the bag and realized she had very little to wash the wound and seeing beyond the semi-clotted blood was impossible. She lifted a bottle of Lysol that her father always carried in his bag. He had used it for wiping things clean, but she had nothing else. She

E. Ayers

poured some into the wound, and Tomas passed out. She fished for the bullet and found it. Blood poured, but it wasn't spurting so she knew the main blood vessels were fine. Quickly she stitched him up and covered the wound with a bandage that had been splashed with more Lysol. Hope this works.

She did almost the same thing to remove the bullet from the one man's arm. She asked him lie on the ground and she immediately poured the Lysol into the wound. He, too, passed out, giving her a short window of time to do what was needed. Then she turned her attention to Tiago.

"Oh, no. This is nothing."

"I decide what is nothing and what is serious." She lifted his shirt as he attempted to back away from her. "Stop that, right now! Is this the example you want to set for your daughter?"

He snarled at her.

"You don't scare me. Take your shirt off."

She helped him remove the shirt. Beautiful light golden skin was covered with dark hair and across his side was a deep scratch. She splashed Lysol on his shirt and wiped the wound.

"Dios!"

"Be still. It doesn't need stitching, but it still needs to be cleaned." She grabbed a pair of tweezers, removed several threads from the wound, wiped some more in spite of his protests, and then she bandaged his side. "You're going to have a wide scar."

He looked at her and snarled again.

She picked up the instruments she had used. "I need to boil these." She tore his shirt into long strips. "And your shirt. You will need more bandages, as will the men."

One of the robbers lying on the ground moaned. The amount of blood around him told Ingrid he wouldn't survive. She walked over to him and realized he was the one who had held Tiago at gunpoint.

"Guess my aim was slightly off. I must have missed the heart." She leaned over him and listened to him breathe before feeling his ribs. She walked over to the supply cart and grabbed a heavy pan with a good handle and then came back to him. She smiled at Tiago. "A lot goes on during a battle. I do not remember much, do you?"

Tiago looked at her.

She held the heavy pan over her shoulder and slammed it into the dying man's chest. Gurgling could be heard and blood poured from the sides of his mouth. "He's not going to recover."

Tiago rolled one man over and saw that he'd been shot in the face. Tiago looked at her, and she shrugged.

"He tried to climb into the carriage with Alma and

me. I shot him."

The other men were dead. One looked as though he'd been trampled to death rather than shot to death. Altogether they found five men, and Ingrid was certain there were at least seven, maybe eight. Part of her quaked and part of her basked in the fact that she had managed to shoot four of the men.

She helped Soaring Bird start a fire and began to boil water. With the passage of time, normalcy returned, and she found herself shaking.

The herd had scattered in different directions, and it took the men awhile to round them up, recount the number of heads, and look for the strays.

"Fifteen," Marco shouted in Spanish.

Tiago shook his head. "Whoever was left has them. They must be hiding in a canyon around here." He walked to where Ingrid kneeled by the small but hot fire. "Can you write a little note to the sheriff in Creed's Crossing? We need help."

She nodded and found paper and pen. But holding the pen steady was near impossible. Inhaling several deep breaths, she dipped the nib into the jar of ink. A moment later, she handed Tiago the letter. And watched Tiago send José and another cowboy to Creed's Crossing.

Three hours had passed before the sheriff and a posse came to the rescue.

Tiago scratched some marks into the soil with his

heel. "They are all branded and the brand is registered to me." He walked over to a nearby cow and traced his fingers over the mark. "This is my father's and this was added for mine. Both are registered. My father is Sergio Colima."

"Sergio Colima? I know that ranch. Is that not one of the largest ranches in Texas?"

"Yes, sir. But I have come to start my own."

The sheriff nodded. "Let us get your cattle back."

Tiago got onto his horse but not with his normal ease.

She went to Tomas and he would barely look at her. She reached for his thigh and he backed away. "I'm just checking for heat in the area."

"No touch my leg."

"Fine." She reached for his weathered cheek and still he backed away from her. She stepped to him and grabbed his arm. Then she reached for his cheek. He didn't feel the least bit warm. "I'm worried about infection. You've received dirty wounds and I have no way of properly cleaning anything. I did the best that I could. But you need to be watched."

"I'm good."

She smiled at him. "I want you to stay that way."

She didn't understand these men and she didn't want to fight with them. She'd tell Tiago when he returned.

Part of her had wanted to eat in town tonight, but

the sun was starting to set and the men would be hungry. She looked through the supplies and made a meal by mixing bits of things into a big pot. Just as she added the last of the potatoes she had cut into squares, gunshots could be heard in the distance. Her stomach clenched. Had she come this far only to lose Tiago? Her heart ached and the feeling surprised her. They had become friends. She'd seen his highs and his lows. He was passionate in everything he did.

She looked in the direction of the gunshots and tried to steady the tremor inside of her. The luxury of giving into emotions was something she couldn't afford to do.

***

Tiago's side burned as he and a member of the posse took off after the one thief. The chase had led them to another gully that was divided a few times. A man could hide in there for days.

After a short discussion, they turned around and returned to the herd and the sheriff. Night was falling and it was dangerous to pursue the lone man. When they returned, three more of the thieves were dead. Two had scatted and gotten away, but the sheriff seemed happy. They collected the dead bodies for the posse to take to town.

The sheriff stood near the campfire. "Certainly

smells good."

Ingrid smiled. "Would you care for a cup? It won't be ready for a while, but you are welcome to stay."

"That's mighty nice of you."

She brushed the back of her hand over her cheek and forehead. "I'm hoping I can find a house in town. I'd like to buy something not too large."

The sheriff looked at her and then at Tiago. "I thought you wanted some land."

"I do. But she's looking for a house."

The sheriff knitted his brows. "So you only need someplace to stay until you can build a house on the land?"

"Yes, true. But she needs a house."

"Sometimes the widow Ritter takes in women, but she's real particular."

Tiago frowned. "I've got several men and myself to house, and Señorita Smith needs a place to stay."

"Señorita?" The sheriff looked towards Ingrid.

"Yes. She's my...governess. She will be keeping my daughter until I have my own house." He said a silent prayer that Ingrid wasn't going to pick up one of her pans and hit him with it. He could keep Alma with him, but it was better if she stayed with Ingrid. "What can you tell me about the land the railroad has for sale?"

The sheriff laughed. "That's a sorry piece of land

if there ever was one. Ain't nothing around here worth the price. Might as well keep going north."

Tiago blew out a breath. That's not what he wanted to hear.

Ingrid ladled some stew into a cup and passed it to the sheriff. The man gobbled it up and asked for more. Tiago nodded at Ingrid and she put more in the man's cup. The sheriff ate his fill and left.

Tiago spit on the ground.

"Don't even bother to waste your energy on him. We came this far, we'll find some land." Ingrid dished up what was left of the stew. "We will find land. A boarding house is fine with me, if she'll have us. We'll find a place for your men. Certainly there are a few bunk houses around with extra beds in them."

Tiago nodded as he pulled out the map he obtained from the land office in Cheyenne. "I don't think it is bad land. There are several streams."

Ingrid looked over his shoulder. "You won't know for certain until you actually see it."

***

The following morning they drove the herd towards town and Ingrid took Alma with her to see if they could find a place to stay. She made a few inquiries and found the widow's house.

A redheaded woman who was probably no older than Tiago opened the door. "May I help you?"

Ingrid smiled. "I hope so. I am the governess to Alma, and her father wishes to establish a ranch in the area, but in the meantime, we need a place to stay. Please forgive me. We've been traveling for days...for months, and it has been days since I've been able to bathe. I'm hoping the widow Ritter will take pity on us until I can find a house to buy."

The woman laughed. "I am the widow, Cora Ritter. My husband, Carl, died very suddenly last year. I manage by renting rooms."

"How many rooms do you have available?"

"Four, but I only rent to women." She looked at Alma. "I've never had children as guests, and I don't want my other tenants to be disturbed by a child in the house. The saloon has rooms."

"No, please. I'd sleep under the wagon before I would stay in such a place. Alma is from a good family. Her mother died after her birth and her grandparents have raised her until I took over. I promise you, she's extremely bright and well bred."

Cora frowned. "Bring her in. Let's see how well she can do. Would you like a cup of tea?"

"We would love such a thing, but I'm not dressed to even sit in your parlor. We both need baths."

"Then come with me to my kitchen. We can talk there."

They walked down the hall, through a passage, and into a large room. At one end sat a very ornate woodstove with eight burners. Ingrid wiped the sweat from her forehead. Near the stove sat two laundry tubs. Opposite the tubs was a cabinet with a sink. Beside the sink stood a pump. A glass-fronted china hutch, a pantry, and a primitive linen press lined the walls, and a large oak table sat at the far end of the kitchen with an odd assortment of chairs.

Cora opened a small door near the stove and retrieved several pieces of wood. The windows were wide open and so were the transoms, but the heat collected in the still room. The thought of more heat was almost too much. "It'll just take me a moment to make tea for us. I do love a cup around this time each day." She added water to a kettle. "And I will admit, I've been known to take an afternoon nap on very warm days."

"The Colima house always took afternoon naps through the heat of the day, and even while traveling, we stopped for naps and traveled in the dark to avoid the heat. But some days were even too hot for napping. As we have traveled north, it has been easier."

"Where did you start that was so hot?"

"Texas. The Colimas have one of the largest ranches, but Tiago is the third son and needed his own place."

"How did you wind up here?"

"I had dreamed of such a place where I could teach many children or even find a job as an assistant to a doctor."

"A doctor?"

"Yes. I-I had worked for one for several years, but he retired and a new doctor came with his own assistant." She was surprised at how easily she lied. "I started teaching instead. I discovered I love teaching." She reached over and fingered one of Alma's dark curls. "She's been a total joy to teach, and this trip... I feel as though I have a daughter."

"She is very young. What can you teach her?"

Alma smiled.

Ingrid returned the smile. "First I had to teach her English, and she's learning to read, and do mathematics. We need more books so I can add subjects such as history and science. She's a very good student."

Cora put two china cups on the table and handed Alma a tin cup.

The child frowned and whispered, "I am not a baby."

Ingrid smiled. "You are not. Cora, she does not need a child's cup."

Now it was Cora's turn to frown. She took the metal cup away and rummaged for an old china cup. "Here. I don't want my things broken."

"Thank you, señora...um...ma'am," Alma said, and then held up her hands to indicate that she wanted to wash them.

Ingrid showed hers to Alma and winked. Both sets of hands were filthy, but Ingrid's were probably worse. Alma giggled.

"What?" Cora asked as she brought the tea to the table and joined them.

"Nothing." Ingrid answered. "We both thank you for your kind hospitality."

As soon as Cora sat in a chair, there was a knock at the front door. Cora huffed as she stood and left the room.

Ingrid put her fingers to her lips. "I'm sorry, darling, but it's obvious that she's not fond of children, and she has no clue what a child does."

Alma pointed to the big chip in the rim.

"Turn it around and drink it left handed."

"Why do your people think that children should not speak at the table?"

Ingrid shrugged. "Tradition. Maybe because it was the only time the family was together and important things were discussed between the adults."

"Why would they do that in front of the children?"

"Very good point. Let us leave it with tradition."

"What is tradition?" Cora asked as she stepped

back into the kitchen. "There's a dirty Mexican waiting for you at the front door."

"Oh dear, excuse me." She wondered why Tomas would be looking for her.

As Ingrid stood, Alma looked at Cora. "Do I get to answer your question?"

Ingrid bit the insides of her cheeks as she left those two in the kitchen. Alma would either make friends with the woman or destroy all chances of them staying at the boarding house. And so far, Cora's attitude assured a very unpleasant stay. Ingrid opened the door to find Tiago standing there.

"Oh, it is you." She stepped onto the porch. "I hope your news is better than mine."

Tiago started to spit.

"Don't!"

"There is a livery in town. I can stay there. I am not good enough for the saloon. Did you know I am considered a dirty Mexican?"

Ingrid giggled. "Forgive them, for I, too, thought you were Mexican, and you are dirty." She waved her hand in front of her face. "You smell worse than a dead animal that is rotting in the sun."

He opened his mouth and closed it before letting loose with a string of Spanish words that she didn't care to interpret.

She moved, hoping she'd be upwind from him. "Please, try the bathhouse. If that doesn't work, find a stream and then come back. I'll see what I can do to find you a place to stay."

Tiago's anger showed in the set of his jaw as he turned to leave.

"Tiago." She grabbed for his hand.

He looked back at her, but his eyes were narrowed and fire burned within them.

"I love you." The words spilled from her lips and she couldn't believe she had said them. She'd only meant to tell him that she was sorry, but she was more than sorry. Her heart ached for the man. Her words now hung in the air between them.

Part Two

7

Tiago stared at Ingrid. Wisps of long light-colored hair hung over her cheeks and clung to her moist skin. He should have known. Had she not looked at him with hunger in her eyes? Had he not returned those looks? But she was a lady, and in an odd sort of way, she was innocent. He had already stolen her first kiss. A kiss that was as sweet as the nectar of flowers and as soft as ripe cotton fresh from the boll. His lips curled at the thought of his lips on hers.

Soft pink flowed up her neck to her cheeks as she let go of his hand and covered her mouth with her fingers.

He turned and faced her. Taking her hand in his, he brought those fingers to his lips. "Good day, my lady. Do not worry about me."

"Come back when you are clean and in fresh clothes. I will do my best to find you a more suitable place to stay."

He stepped away from her and let her fingers slide from his. "I have kept you too long to be polite."

He stepped off the front porch and went to his horse. Her three little words had buried into his very fiber. It was one thing to lust over a woman and another to love her. He'd spent many days and nights during the drive with lust on his mind. Now everything had changed.

He rode to the bathhouse and prayed they would not turn him away. Squaring his shoulders as he dismounted, he walked through the door of the tiny building.

A woman of some age greeted him.

"I am the younger Señor Colima of the Colima Ranch in Texas. I've driven cattle with my men for weeks to inspect and buy land to start my own ranch here. I am in need of a bath."

"O-o-oh, we do not--"

"Yes, I saw your sign, and I am not Mexican. I am Spanish. My family sailed here from Spain. For generations, we have been ranchers."

"O-o-oh."

"A bath!"

A few minutes later, he was shown a filled tub. When his injured side hit the hot water, he inhaled at the searing pain. He washed until the water turned a pale shade of brown. Wrapping the towel around his waist, he called to the woman. "I need a fresh tub."

She stared at him. "That will be another ten cents."

He gave her twenty. "Make certain to rinse the tub. I have no desire to climb back into a dirty one. And it doesn't have to be as hot this time. And take my suit and press it."

"That's another ten cents."

He fished for more change. He added a Barber dime to the other coins on the table, leaving him with only a few pennies and a couple of nickels. "Don't burn my suit."

The woman drained the tub and wiped it out before refilling it. This time he sank into tepid water and cleaned the rest of the dirt from his skin. He soaked until the grime was gone from under his nails and his fingers and toes were wrinkled.

When he stepped out, he found his razor and trimmed the beard from his face. A haircut would be nice. He ran his fingers over his clean-shaven face and admired the man in the mirror. Dirty Mexican! What is the difference? We are all the same. The Spanish and the Mexicans have intermarried for years.

His thoughts went to Ingrid. She, too, had thought he was Mexican, but she never treated him any differently. She never treated Soaring Bird differently than she did any of the men. Maybe he had read too much into her actions. Then her three little words rang through his mind. Did she really mean them? Had she not told his daughter that he would marry a woman with dark hair like his?

***

Ingrid joined Cora in the kitchen and discovered that Alma was conversing with the woman. Inwardly she cringed as Alma spoke about their long trip, and how Ingrid had cared for the wounded men.

"I am sorry to take so long, but that was Alma's father, and he is dirty, but he is a Spaniard. He's going to get a bath and then come back. I fear that I smell as bad."

Cora stared at her.

"Tiago Colima brought me here. I wanted to come to Wyoming and he wanted to buy a large piece of land to start his own ranch. We both wanted to come to the same place."

"You traveled alone with him?"

"Never alone. He brought several men and one hundred head of cattle. Then he hired a scout." She smiled at Cora. "He needed me to help with Alma, so it was perfect for both of us. He is a man of honor, and we were quite safe until yesterday when several men attempted to rob us."

"I heard they had put together a posse."

"Yes. Several men escaped with a few head of cattle. We got the head back, but not all the robbers. It was terrifying." The look on Cora's face was not positive. "I'm most anxious to settle someplace quiet where I can relax and teach."

Cora looked at Alma and then at Ingrid. "She seems quiet enough. But if she creates any noise, you will have to leave immediately. I charge a dollar a week, and an extra fifty cents if you want meals. That's three dollars for both of you. Non-refundable."

"But Alma will be staying with me."

"Three dollars."

This woman wasn't stealing cattle, but she was robbing Ingrid.

Ingrid inhaled. She didn't have a lot of money. "Is there someplace cheaper in town?"

"You may stay at the saloon."

Ingrid shook her head.

Alma looked at Ingrid. "Why can't we stay in the coach? Daddy will protect us. Three dollars is the wage for a whole week on the ranch."

Ingrid wanted to laugh at the child's bluntness. She was right, but Ingrid knew that the widow was probably desperate for money. "Alma, that was in Texas. And what was paid to ranch hands is different from living here in Creed's Crossing. It is only until we can find a house for me to buy." She smiled at Cora. "We want a big house, such as this but with more modern things to make life easier. Miz Cora does not have a husband to support her, or any other way to make a living."

Alma looked up and asked, "But why won't she let Daddy stay here?"

"She would rather rent to us alone than allow your father to stay here, too. She is fearful of men. Yet he is an important man. She does not understand that he could buy her house and pay for half this town to be at his beck and call. If your father finds the land he wants, he will have a thousand head of cattle here by next summer. Your grandfather is anxious to expand his ranch and to make certain that you are provided for in the lifestyle in which you came." She gave Alma a little frown to keep her from opening her mouth. "Once your father builds a house, he will be hiring people to cook and clean. People who can make certain you are well tended and that you are dressed in the finest of clothes. You will only need me for a few hours a day."

Alma rolled her lower lip out and a tear slid silently down her cheek.

"Do not cry. Be thankful that you will have a clean place to stay, and I'm positive that Miz Cora will provide good food." She turned back to her hostess.

"Tiago Colima will remember who treated him with the respect he deserved."

"I'll show you to your rooms as soon as I am paid."

Ingrid glanced sideways at Cora as she reached into her pocket and withdrew a pouch. She placed four dollars on the table. "Make it four and give her father his own room."

The woman stared at the money and picked up three. "Right this way."

Ingrid left the other dollar and followed the woman up the stairs. The room was lovely. Pristine white curtains fluttered at the open windows. A crocheted bedcover topped white sheets and crocheted doilies sat under the two kerosene lamps. In an alcove, tucked by a window, was a small narrow bed, not quite a miniature of the large one, but only large enough to hold one person. A washbasin and pitcher sat on a marble topped table, and there was a large wardrobe that was ample for anything that had been brought with them and plenty of room for more. There was also a desk with a chair.

Ingrid turned to the woman. "Laundry?"

"Take it to the bathhouse. I will not be a slave to anyone's clothing."

Cora turned to leave.

"Excuse me, but we both need a bath, and where

is the toilet?"

"There is a privy in the backyard, and you may use the bathhouse. She charges ten cents."

Ingrid's blood boiled and she fisted her hands. "Alma, let us retrieve our bags. We don't have many choices."

A few minutes later, with clothes placed in the large wardrobe, Ingrid took off for the bathhouse. Clean and properly dressed, they returned to Cora's. Along the way, they stopped in the general store. As much as Ingrid wished to buy some new things for both of them, the store carried virtually nothing in stock in the way of clothing. Even though Ingrid knew how to sew, she didn't like to sew. She picked up a magazine that contained the latest fashions and sighed. "This is not what I want."

"What do you want?" A young woman asked. Her blonde braid hung over her shoulder.

"A split skirt that I can use while riding. I have no desire to confine myself in a corset."

The woman picked up another magazine. "Ja. Like this?"

"Yes. But I have no sewing machine, no way to make anything, and I don't see anything advertised where I can just buy it."

The young woman smiled. "I am Adie Coleman. I can sew. Pick out the material and I will make it."

Ingrid smiled. "But how do I know you will do a

good job?"

"I made what I am wearing. I will not charge and I will give you back the cost of the material if you do not like it. Is that fair?"

"Yes. That is more than fair."

Ingrid picked out several things and Adie suggested not using certain fabrics. "This is not the big city. Durability is important."

Alma wanted a yellow fabric, and Adie suggested a different fabric that was also yellow. "This is much better for a young girl, I promise."

Adie asked the store clerk for a tape measure and measured Ingrid and Alma. "Where do you live?"

"For now, I'm with Cora Ritter until I can find my own place."

"I will bring you everything on Saturday."

"Thank you." Ingrid held up a single finger. "Before I leave, is there any place where eight men and a hundred head of cattle can stay?"

***

The carriage was still parked in front of the widow's house. Tiago stepped inside of it and realized that Ingrid had removed her bags, along with Alma's. They must be staying here.

He cursed the empty carriage. He wanted a pen so that he could write home. He stepped onto the widow's porch and knocked on the front door.

When she opened the door, he asked for a pen. "Ingrid has several."

"She is not here. And why would you want a pen?"

He looked at the redheaded woman. "I'm sorry to disturb you. I forgot that many women are not properly educated and cannot read or write, much less do it in several languages. I shall be on my way. Obviously you are not aware that pens are used for writing. Forgive me for jumping to conclusions."

He turned and walked off the porch. The door slammed behind him. He laughed as he continued towards the street.

At the far end of the street, he spotted Ingrid in her pale purple outfit. What a beauty.

She smiled and waved to him.

He walked to her and they met halfway, not far from the post office. "I need to borrow a pen."

"No problem. They are in my room. I have also found a place where you can take the cattle and your men. The Coleman ranch. It is up the road. Frank Coleman will meet you in an hour in front of the post office. They have a bunkhouse and plenty of water. But I've yet to find you a place. Although you are welcome to stay with your men."

She watched him make that face too many times. "Don't spit. I know you are angry, but that is a terrible habit. You must stop it."

"Right now I am hungry, and the most I can eat in this town is a plate served from the back door of the saloon."

"That is insane." She looked around. "But I did pick up some good news. Frank Coleman's ranch backs up to the area that you wish to purchase. He took what he could under the Homestead Act, and the next checkerboard is railroad land. Adie Coleman said that it is excellent land, but there are some deep gullies on it, plenty of water, and good grazing areas."

"Then why would the sheriff tell me otherwise?"

"I do not know. Will you ride out tomorrow and look at it?"

He nodded. "I'd take you, but I'm sure you are tired of traveling."

"I am. Maybe. I would like to see it, but I do not know. It might be best if I took a day to recuperate from such a long trip." She grinned. "They had books for Alma at the general store, and I'd like to spend some time perusing them. Also I need to make inquires for a house."

"You do not need your own house. I will build a grand house for us." He held out his elbow and she took his arm.

He looked at Alma and smiled. "And how is my darling daughter? You look lovely in your yellow dress."

"Ingrid is going to have more dresses made for me. There was a nice lady in the store who is making them. She's going to make me another yellow one. It's my favorite color."

"That is wonderful news. And I know yellow is your favorite color. You always want your hair tied in yellow ribbons." He looked at Ingrid and pulled out his money sack. "You will need this for her things." He passed her several dollars.

"Thank you."

"How is your room?" he asked.

"Lovely and much too expensive."

Alma jumped at his side. "Carry me, Daddy?"

He swooped the child into is free arm and grimaced at the pain.

"I want to see your side. And I want to check your men." Ingrid said in a flat tone.

"I am fine."

She shook her head. "I will decide that. I am the one with medical training."

He walked to the front door of Cora's house and Ingrid led him into the house.

"Come to the kitchen. I need to see your wound."

He stepped into the house, and in the hallway, he came face to face with the widow. "Good day, ma'am."

She blushed slightly and acted as though she

didn't recognize him.

He made a slight bow. "I will only be a minute."

Ingrid frowned. "That depends on your wound. Alma, please find a pen for your father." She turned her attention back to him. "Do you need paper?"

"No. I bought some earlier at the general store."

He watched Alma scurry off. "No running in the house. You know better."

"Sorry, Daddy." She slowed her pace on the stairs.

Ingrid turned to the widow. "He and two of his men were hurt yesterday. I need to look after their wounds."

Tiago followed Ingrid into the kitchen where she tugged at his shirt.

"If you can keep it clean, I won't wrap it again. Aside from the one spot where it is deeper, it is looking very good."

"Here, Daddy." Alma handed him a pen and scrunched up her nose. "Do you still hurt?"

"It is nothing, my darling, but a scratch. Ingrid is only being cautious. She is fussing like a mother cat with newborn kittens." He took Alma's hand in his. "Now that we are here, you must remember that you are not wild weed. You are a young lady. I am sorry you are tanned like a piece of leather on the fence."

He turned back to Ingrid. "If the land is good, I will file the claim immediately. It shouldn't take more than a week to have my answer, and I can begin to build a house."

"Daddy, where will you sleep tonight?"

Ingrid poked around the edges of his wound.

"In the field with our men," he answered.

"Why can't you stay with me and Ingrid?"

"Ouch! What are you doing?"

"Checking your wound. It's doing well." Ingrid frowned. "Alma, please say 'with Ingrid and me'. You must remember to keep the order of your words straight."

Alma blew out a breath.

He tried to keep from laughing at her, but a chuckle rolled out. "Did they have any books in Spanish? She must learn both languages."

"I didn't see any. But I did spot one on Latin."

"Then I shall ask my mother to send Spanish books. We can look for a Spanish tutor once we are settled. Until then, I have much to do." He peeled his daughter off his hip. "Kiss me goodbye, my darling little girl. Smelling food cooking is only making my empty stomach rumble."

Alma's lower lip rolled out. "I don't want you to go. I won't be able to kiss you goodnight."

"Well kiss me now and I shall keep it for later."

"No."

He laughed. "Starting at one hundred, count backwards for me by four in English."

She scrunched up her eyes. "One hundred, ninety-six, ninety-two, eighty-eight, eighty-four, eighty, seventy-six… must I? This is too easy."

"Keep going."

She rattled the numbers off and he listened to each one.

"I am proud of my darling, for learning English so quickly. Now do I get my kiss?"

"Can you come back and tuck me in bed?"

"Ingrid will do that tonight, and for as long as it takes until we can be together."

"Then I don't want to stay here."

He kneeled in front of Alma. "I am sorry that you must endure being treated like a worthless person. Be thankful that you have a bed and food. That is better than what you have been forced to abide on our drive here. You are strong like all the Colimas. This will not last. But we are strangers here, and people do not know us. You will be fine."

"Sir." The widow turned from where she stood by the stove stirring a pot. "Maybe it is best for your daughter's sake if you stay with your family. Only once did I have a family stay with me, and the child was not very good. I never wanted to repeat that situation again."

"Ah, but I would need a separate room. Ingrid is not my family, and it would not be proper for me to stay with her. She is a lady and I am a gentleman."

"I am certain I can find another room for you."

Ingrid pulled her watch from her pocket. "You are to meet Frank Coleman in just a few minutes."

He walked over to the sideboard and lifted a roll from a basket. "I shall return shortly. Let me settle my men first."

Frank Coleman was easy to spot waiting for him.

"I am Tiago Colima. You will take my herd and my men?"

"Yes, sir. We have room in the bunkhouse for the men, and a field where your cattle can graze for a few days."

"Two of my men were shot yesterday. Their wounds have been dressed, but is there someone who can look after them?"

"Yes, my mother."

"And one of my men is an Indian."

"No problem. All men are equal in our eyes."

"That is good. I will not ride with you, but I want to know where my men will be."

When everything was settled, he returned to the widow's house. He was tired, and he was tired of the attitude that people had towards him. Seeing Ingrid and Alma sitting at the kitchen table instead of in the dining room bothered him, but he only wanted to eat and tumble into a soft bed.

The meal was simple and he devoured it. If the widow or anyone else said one more nasty thing to him, he wasn't positive that he could hold his temper.

8

Ingrid put Alma in her nightgown and then opened the door for Tiago.

"Do I get to enter?"

Ingrid nodded. "We will leave the door open, besides it is cooler."

He strode to where his daughter was lying.

Ingrid listened to Tiago and Alma saying their prayers in Spanish, and watched him leave.

At the doorway, he stopped and turned to her. "Goodnight. May we both sleep well."

"Yes. I don't think anyone slept last night."

"I didn't. Goodnight."

He walked across the hall to his room and her heart fluttered for a moment. She closed the door long enough to prepare for her night. Just the thought of the bed called to something deep inside her. She couldn't even remember her head touching the pillow.

She opened her eyes to Alma sitting on her bed.

"Hi. You are a sleepyhead."

Ingrid stretched her arms over her head. "Oh, you are right." The bright sun sent large beams of light into the room. "I must get up. Put your clothes on."

As Alma skipped off to dress, Ingrid stepped behind the small screen and slipped into fresh clothes. The dark cream pants with light cream blouse, and both trimmed in black, looked sophisticated, but were comfortable. She smoothed the fabric of the full pants and tied the black bow at the collar.

She loved this new fashion. The pants gave the appearance of a skirt, but were comfortable. She was thrilled when the young woman in town knew exactly what they were and had made them for her sister. She sat at the vanity, combed and braided her hair, and then swirled the braid into a bun.

Alma danced beside Ingrid as she attempted to button their shoes.

"Please hurry." Alma wiggled.

She finished Alma's. "Go, and no running! I'm right behind you."

Not having a toilet in the house was a disadvantage, and by the time she finished buttoning her shoes, she knew she didn't want to wait another moment. Leaving the beds unmade, she hurried down the stairs and out the back door. Alma was sniffing the herbs growing in a small dirt bed by the kitchen.

The privy was quite modern, complete with a porcelain toilet. It flushed by pouring a bucket of water into the back of it. Fortunately it had a sanitary paper dispenser, a very elaborate thing that held a small oil lamp, matches, an ashtray, and another slot that appeared to be large enough to hold a book. The fancy wrought iron holder looked out of place in the generous but plain room made from pine and oiled to a high shine. And a pump stood over a deep polished copper sink. She washed her hands, splashed her face, and flushed the toilet.

"Alma, come brush your teeth."

Alma dashed in and pulled her toothbrush from her pocket. "See. I did!"

"That's good. How wiggly is that tooth?"

Alma put her tongue on it.

"You need to pull it out before it comes out in your food."

Alma made a face. "It hurts when I touch it."

Ingrid smiled and picked up a clean washing cloth. "Let me see."

Alma made a face but opened her mouth for Ingrid to get a grip on the tooth.

"Just one little wiggle. I want to check it." A quick push and the tooth was free. "There. It shouldn't hurt anymore." She dropped the tooth into her hand and wet the cloth in the cool water. "Here. Bite this for a minute."

Alma took the cloth. "What is the cold water going to do?"

"Make your mouth feel better. Your grown up tooth is ready to fill in the hole from your baby tooth. You can probably feel the new points in your gum."

Alma took the cloth from her mouth, and stared wide-eyed at the tinge of red and pink. "I'm bleeding. What did you do to me?" Her little tongue shot forward into the empty space. "My tooth is gone!"

Alma looked at her cloth.

"It's not there. It's here." Ingrid held out her hand with the tiny tooth. "See the mark here? That's where your new tooth was pushing against this tooth and pushing it out of the way."

"May I save my tooth for Daddy?"

"Of course. He's going to be very excited for you. This is your first real step away from childhood and into adulthood. You are no longer a little girl."

Alma started to skip off but Ingrid called her back. "Give me your toothbrush and I will return it to our room. Don't wander off. I'll see about breakfast."

As she walked up the stairs, she realized that Tiago's door was still closed. She placed her ear against it and heard the soft sounds of a snore. For once, he feels safe enough to actually sleep. She returned the brushes to the room and quickly made the beds before making her way to the kitchen.

Cora wandered in. "If you want breakfast, you'll have to get up earlier."

"I'd appreciate a cup of coffee or tea. Is there any place where I can buy milk for Alma?"

"The Haggers' have milk. They are the fourth house in that direction." She pointed away from town.

"Thank you. I shall go now."

"You might want to drink your coffee first. It's a long walk."

"Oh."

"I'm not even confident they will still have milk. They deliver it early. I'm not paying for her milk."

"That's quite fine. I will pay for it and make certain there is milk in the house. I happen to like it in my tea."

"And where is your gentleman?"

"I believe he's still sleeping. Not one of us slept the night before. We were all exhausted."

Their chitchat continued as the coffee percolated in a series of burps behind them. From where Ingrid sat, she could see Alma as she played in the backyard.

Cora removed the coffee from the hot stove and poured them each a cup. "Would you like a roll?"

"Yes. Thank you. I actually enjoy baking. If you have a potato I could make a delicious starter."

"Help yourself." She pointed to the pantry closet. "I only keep a few in here. The rest I store under the house."

"You have quite a garden."

They both turned as Tiago walked into the room. "Toilet?"

They pointed to the door and he strode out.

Ingrid stood and went to the pantry. "Would you like me to boil potatoes for supper, since I will be boiling one for my starter."

"Go right ahead."

Ingrid didn't like the woman's attitude about anything, but she also figured Cora had probably withstood plenty since her husband had died. After months of cooking over a fire, a stove and oven were total luxuries, and this was a nice stove.

Tiago reappeared looking a little better.

"Get dressed for the day. I'm going to take Alma and see if we can buy milk for her. I know you wanted to check on your men and see the land. I was wondering if I might go with you."

"Yes. I would enjoy the company."

Tiago went upstairs and returned looking more normal. He went back to the privy and shaved before joining them in the kitchen for coffee. By then the potatoes were boiled and Alma had come in from her explorations.

Ingrid found Cora on a side porch washing clothes. "We are leaving now, and I suspect we won't be back until supper. I've put the starter in a jar and the potatoes are by the stove in a bowl. We can eat them tonight."

Cora only nodded.

"Milk?" Tiago asked as he brought two horses for them to ride.

"Yes, and maybe some cheese since we've not had any breakfast." She put her foot into the stirrup and mounted the horse.

Tiago lifted Alma and tucked her behind Ingrid. "Hold on tight."

They walked the horses to the Haggers' farmhouse.

The family promised daily milk for Alma and a small container of sweet cream. Then they produced some cheese for the three of them. They even gave the child a cup of sweet milk to drink before they left. Alma curtsied and thanked them. Ingrid paid them for the week and then left with Tiago and Alma.

The ride to the Joseph Coleman ranch took longer than expected and it was noon when they arrived.

Alisa Coleman, Joseph's wife, greeted them. "Welcome to our ranch. Frank is my son. He and Adie told me you would be coming. We were just getting ready to sit for dinner. Please join us."

"If you have enough we would appreciate the meal," Ingrid answered. We didn't expect it to take so long to come here."

"We are quite a ways from town. Virginia, find more chairs," Alisa ordered her youngest daughter and then turned back to them. "There is a toilet with a wash sink upstairs."

Ingrid took Alma upstairs and when they finished using the small room, Tiago went in. As Ingrid and Alma entered the dining room, she was surprised to see Tiago's men sitting at the table. "How are you?"

Alisa laughed as she brought in a bowl of food. "Seems Tomas doesn't like having a woman tending to his wound. But he's doing quite well. I made a poultice last night for him, and it looked much better this morning. He said you got the bullet out."

Ingrid nodded.

Tiago looked around the room and said, "I was not expecting to see my men at your table."

Joseph chuckled. "This is a family ranch. We treat everyone as family."

The meal was delicious. The stewed chicken was tender and the thick noodles smothered in gravy were heavenly. Ingrid ate every morsel on her plate and then turned her attention to Alisa. "You must give me your recipe for these noodles. I don't think I've ever had a noodle quite as tasty as these."

"Thank you. I will give you a list of the

ingredients. The trick is to knead the dough enough to mix it, but not too much. You want a soft dough ball, and then quickly roll the dough and cut it. Then I cook everything in potato water."

"This was delightful."

Joseph smiled. "My wife is a good cook."

When the time came to leave, Virginia begged for Alma to stay and play. Alisa agreed that it would be faster if they weren't taking Alma.

"Tiago?" Ingrid asked.

"She may stay."

This time. Tiago and Ingrid set off at a steady clip and soon they could see Frank Coleman's house. He joined them and showed them where his property ended.

"From what you showed me on the map, as far as you can see would be yours."

Tiago withdrew the map from a satchel on his horse and handed the map to Frank.

Putting his finger on the map, Frank said, "We are standing here."

"This is excellent land."

"Yes. It is. We can help you drill a well. We have the equipment. But I promise you might be dropping several holes before you hit water. And we can help you build a house. If you start it in the next few weeks." He pointed to the mountains. "Once the snow begins to hit the mountains, we have to bring the cattle in and no one will have time for anything else."

"I understand." Tiago reached over and took the map from Frank, and then pointed to the northernmost spot of land on the paper. "What is here?"

"Crow Reservation. And here is the Bozeman Trail. There's another Rez over here - the Shoshones. This used to be a fort. And there's another town here. Your land would go to here. You have natural barriers. We run the cattle north after calving and bring them back before it gets too cold. I'll be honest, our cattle are often over here. Fencing is expensive."

"Hard to explain to animals where they belong."

Frank laughed.

Tiago turned to Ingrid. "Do you want to see more?"

"I will go wherever you want to go."

"I have seen enough." He held out his hand to Frank. "If all goes well, we'll be neighbors."

"Yes. It is good."

Ingrid listened to the men talking about wheat production and the number of head per acre. It was all very interesting, especially when Frank talked about overproduction of the land. Apparently a few years back, a drought almost put the entire cattle industry under. The land had been overgrazed.

"So no matter how much green you see, don't

count on it. No one can foretell the future. We keep a steady amount and we do well. Prices fall and prices rise. In good years, we save our money for the bad."

Tiago agreed. "My father's ranch is large. This one will be small, but I am the only one to run it."

"You'll be fine. Talk to my dad."

They stopped at Frank's house and had a cup of coffee with Adie and Frank before picking up Alma. Adie showed off the clothes she was sewing for Ingrid.

"This is lovely. I can't believe you've managed all these tiny pleats." Ingrid held the front of the blouse to her.

"I took the liberty to cut a jacket for you. I had some leftover gabardine that I knew would work well with the colors you chose." She showed Ingrid the pattern. "But I will not have it ready by Saturday."

"It's beautiful. I'm thrilled."

Adie blushed. "Frank bought a sewing machine for me before we were married. It is fun to use it, but I dread the hand stitching."

The cry of a baby could be heard.

"They are awake. Come with me."

Ingrid was introduced to Adie's twins, Emma and Anna. "How do you find the time to sew with young babies?"

Adie laughed. "I make time. They are easy babies.

Sometimes Frank's younger sister, Clarissa, comes over and helps me. She adores them, and if she is here, I can sew."

Tiago called and the women came down the stairs, each carrying a baby.

"You look very good with a baby on your side." Tiago grinned. "You need a few of your own."

"That's not going to happen anytime soon."

He raised his eyebrows. "A new woman in town? I might have to fight to keep my governess."

"You shouldn't tease me. I will be an old maid."

Frank took Emma from Ingrid. "I'll agree with Tiago. He's going to have a heck of a time keeping you to himself."

Ingrid thanked them for the lovely visit and left with Tiago.

They cantered to the elder Coleman ranch and picked up Alma.

"Please let her come back and play. She's a good child, and Virginia had so much fun."

"Thank you. We may take you up on that as I start to build my house." Tiago placed Alma behind Ingrid on the horse. "We're going to have to get her a pony to ride."

"We have several that we keep just for the children. When you are ready, come back," Frank's father, Joseph, suggested.

"I'll remember that."

The ride into town didn't seem as long, but the whole way Ingrid contemplated why the sheriff would have suggested that the land wasn't good. Something is very wrong.

***

The following morning, Tiago filed the papers for the land. He opened a bank account and wrote to his parents requesting the necessary deposit. Each step put him closer to owning the land.

Three times that week, he rode to the Coleman's and talked to Joseph Coleman. The history of the ranch was there in ledgers and other records. Over the years, they had seen plenty. Tiago knew it would be a few years before he had the ranch running successfully.

One evening as they sat on Cora's narrow porch, they allowed Alma to play in the front yard. The child had wanted to catch fireflies in a glass jar, but there weren't any. Tiago turned to Ingrid and asked, "Would you be willing to live with me and continue to care for Alma? She's grown very close to you."

"I know she has, and I know it is not proper for me to live there."

"Because we are not married?"

"Yes. I came to make my own life here."

"You want to be an old maid?"

She giggled. "No. But no one will have me. And I probably don't want them."

"Because you are educated and from a good family?"

"My family is gone. I have only what I have, and that is all."

"But the town has a teacher, and Alma needs you. One house is cheaper than two, and you won't have to split wood for your stove or take in boarders to survive."

Ingrid sucked in her lower lip for a moment. "There is a sadness about Cora. I feel sorry for her."

"And you will be in the same place in five years if you do not marry."

She looked at him with such sadness that he wanted to take her into his arms.

"Will you send for a wife once you are settled?"

"An arranged marriage? A mail order bride? Never! I have everything I want right here."

"So you have no plans to marry?"

"I didn't say that. Alma, it is time for bed." He turned his attention back to Ingrid. "Wait for me. I will put my daughter to bed and return. The night is too pleasant to miss."

"Must I go to bed?" Alma whined and then stifled another yawn.

"Yes. You will sleep well in this weather. Kiss Ingrid. She will be up later. The adults need to talk some more."

Alma threw her arms around Ingrid and kissed her before taking his hand. It didn't take long to get her snuggled into bed and return to the porch.

"Here." He handed Ingrid the shawl he spotted on the chair in her room. "I don't want you getting cold."

"Thank you, but I am fine for now."

He stood on the edge of the porch and looked up into the sky. Several stars began to appear. Something prodded him, told him to turn and ask for her hand in marriage, but he wasn't ready to do that. He still didn't know if he had the land. "It's a beautiful night."

"It is and I haven't seen you this relaxed since before we left your parents' home."

"Driving cattle is hard work even with good men."

"How will it be with your own ranch?"

"Better. The Colemans homesteaded and we are buying. Frank and Joseph have offered to help. Everyone works together. We didn't have that back home. It is different here."

"Yes. It is. Even the town is different - friendlier."

He turned and stared at her. "Maybe to you, but not to me. They think I am a dirty Mexican."

"I was raised to think that all people were the same. My father used to quote Shakespeare, 'If you prick us, do we not bleed? If you tickle us, do we not laugh? If you poison us, do we not die? And if you wrong us, shall we not revenge?'"

"He is right. And my blood is tinged with Mexican. I know that. My father's grandmother had Mexican Indian in her. But I am mostly Spanish. My mother came from Spain to marry my father."

"You are a handsome man and your daughter is beautiful. Any woman would be grateful to have you as a husband based only on your looks."

"Ha! Not here. My skin is too dark and so is my hair - and my eyes."

She came and stood next to him. "You are not only handsome, you are a good man."

"Back home, people stared at us, but they knew we were prominent ranchers. They didn't dare say a word against us. They were the newcomers. My family has been in Texas for over two hundred years."

"It will be different here."

"I know. They already think I've robbed a bank to buy the land."

Ingrid frowned. "That is ridiculous."

"You know differently, but the name Colima means nothing here."

"They will learn."

He turned to her. "When I said I have everything I want right here, I meant it. That includes you."

***

Ingrid gasped as he lifted her hand to his lips and kissed her palm. Heat surged through her. She looked up at him hoping she'd feel his lips on hers, but he kept a respectable distance. Her heart pounded in her chest. She didn't know how to tell him that she wanted him or that she would love to be more than a governess to his daughter - that she would be proud to be his wife. "It is time for me to retire."

"Yes. I understand, but I don't want you to go...not yet."

"But Alma will awaken early and Adie is to bring me my new clothes. I am hoping we can buy more material. Alma and I both need coats."

He took money from his pocket and gave it to her. "For you and Alma. I do not give you enough for teaching my daughter or putting up with me."

"This is too much."

"I could never give you enough money. You are worth the world to me and Alma."

"To Alma and me. How do you expect her to learn correct English when you say it wrong?"

"I do not care. I care about you. I would give you the world if I could. I would give up everything for you."

"You are being ridiculous. It is time for bed."

They stepped inside and closed the door. Together they walked up the stairs, and when they reached their rooms, Tiago stopped and squeezed her hand. "I will build my house and you will stay with me. I don't care what is proper."

She could feel the heat rising to her cheeks, and she hoped it didn't show in the darkness. "But I do."

In the morning, Adie came to Cora's with several things for Ingrid. She tried them on and was pleased with each one. The blouses were beautiful - each done with tiny tucks, and one was cut with a bib and gathers below.

Adie passed another to her. "This is a skirt. It needs a belt."

Ingrid tried it on. "Yes, I think I will need a skirt or two, but for now I need pants. I'm riding so much. But tomorrow, Tiago was hoping to go to church and a skirt would be more appropriate for such events."

"I had enough left to make a few things extra for Alma, but I haven't finished her last two dresses. I thought you might want to try them on her."

Alma smiled up at Adie and she handed over the things she had sewn. Two of the dresses had pinafores, and two more were plain. "Ja. She could use some pants, too - ones like the boys wear. Virginia often wears pants that belonged to her brothers. On a ranch, Alma will need them."

"I'm not certain Tiago would approve. I did buy

her a pair when we first reached Wyoming. He was not happy with me."

"Tell him you know what is best."

"Maybe ones such as mine?"

Adie shook her head. "No. Pants. I will make her overalls. They will protect her clothes."

"What are overalls?"

"You will see. We can pick out more fabric."

"I will need a coat and so will Alma."

Taking Alma, they walked to the general store. Adie chose several fabrics and suggested that Ingrid have overalls, too, if she was going to help build a house.

"Me? I cannot imagine what I would do."

Adie shrugged. "I keep a pair just in case. But Frank does not allow me to do much other than tend the garden."

Ingrid found some skeins of wool. "I've not knitted in ages, but I used to love to knit. I just do not know much about it."

Adie asked, "Do you know Mrs. Hagger?"

"Yes, I met her when I came."

"You buy the pattern and the wool. If you have a problem take it to her. Her knitting is beautiful. Alisa can knit, but Mrs. Hagger is just as good and closer to you."

"She will help me?"

"Ja. She is a very kind lady."

Based on the pattern, Ingrid bought needles and the number of skeins needed to make a shawl. It would give her something to do in her free time.

There weren't many choices in wool for a coat and Ingrid settled on a dark blue for her and Alma.

"Does Tiago need a coat, too?"

"Yes, but I have no idea of his size."

"If I can measure him or his jacket, I can make one for him." She pulled at a bolt of red plaid wool.

Ingrid shook her head. "He will not wear such a thing."

Adie pointed to another bolt.

"Maybe this one." She pointed to a fine black wool.

"No." Adie grabbed a bolt of dark green. "Will he wear this?"

Ingrid nodded.

"As a rancher, he will need heavy coats."

Adie chose several more things and Ingrid paid for all of it.

Ingrid and Adie returned to Cora's house where Frank met them. Soon Tiago joined them and they had a picnic lunch on Cora's porch.

"Where are the twins?" Ingrid asked.

Frank laughed. "Clarissa has them. We are lucky she does not steal them."

Adie insisted on measuring Tiago. "Your shoulders are broad."

Ingrid smiled. "Yes, they are. And he is covered in strong muscles."

Adie helped Ingrid start her knitting and then left. Pleased to have something else to do, Ingrid immersed herself in her new task.

Tiago stood and watched what she was doing for a moment. "I thought Alma needed some new books? You did not buy her any?"

"She needs some time off to play and be a little girl. Once you start construction, she will need to keep busy."

Tiago frowned.

She caught the look on his face and giggled. "Let her be. Adie says that in another few weeks there will be all sorts of used books available."

"How does she know that?"

"The new school year will be starting and people bring in their books and buy new ones. Not every child goes to school because it is too far to travel into town."

"Do not children--"

A man rode up on horseback. "I'm looking for a Mr. Cool-lima."

"I am Tiago Colima."

"Well, this must be for you." The man slid from his horse and handed Tiago a telegram.

Tiago tipped the man and walked onto the porch before opening it.

Ingrid peered at the page as he opened it. Land purchase approved. Part of her was thrilled and the other part of her knew that the next few weeks would be more than hectic.

Tiago grabbed her and kissed her.

Her heart fluttered, and her cheeks grew warm as she pulled away from him.

***

Tiago could not contain his excitement, but he had to wait until Monday to complete the transaction. He immediately wrote to his father knowing that by the time the letter was on its way, the paperwork would be completed.

Sunday morning, the tiny town, except for the saloon, was closed. Tiago, Ingrid, and Alma went to the only church in Creed's Crossing. Apparently, there was a Catholic church slightly west of the town's church, but the priest only came to Creed's Crossing on occasion. Tiago discovered the difference between the types of worship, but decided that God would be pleased that he attended and set an example for his daughter. Immediately after the service, they had an invitation to join the Colemans for dinner.

Ingrid took her knitting with her and seemed excited about the visit. Alma was happy to visit with her new friends, and Tiago was pleased to share his good news.

That evening he and Ingrid studied several house plans he had obtained from the farm supply store.

"This one." Ingrid picked one from the pile.

"But the rooms are too small."

"Maybe that does not matter to a carpenter. If you tell him you want larger rooms."

"You like the turret."

She grinned. "Yes. It looks very modern, yet it looks like a castle. You want something that will stand out. This one does."

He took the plans and looked at them carefully. "All these little rooms. What are they for?"

"Alma needs a school room. We could use this room for her. And you will need an office."

"What about you? Do you not need your own room?"

"Why would I need a room in your house?"

"Because it will be your house, too."

"I cannot live with you and Alma."

He stood and strode to the edge of the porch. "You will live with me." He stared at the sky, which was quickly turning dark. "First we build a barn and a bunkhouse. Then we will build the house for us."

"Alisa said that building would stop as winter descends on us."

He nodded. There is not much time. "Frank told

me he has a brother-in-law living on a reservation who will provide the lumber. He owns a sawmill. When the Colemans go for the herd, he will go ahead of the men and visit. But we must pay for someone to bring him the trees. Frank said it will be cheaper than ordering it through the farm supply store."

"So you will do it?"

"Yes. But for now we order the lumber for the barn from the store."

"How do you know what lumber to order?"

He turned and stared at her. "Frank said to give his brother-in-law the plans."

"But if you change the plans--"

"I know. My head is filled with so many thoughts. I am not a draftsman, yet I will have to redraw the plans. I am not a carpenter, but I will be building my own house. So many things are different here." He hoped his worry did not show.

"Yes. Because we do not know everyone here, and back home, if you needed something, you knew who could do it."

"That is true. But I wanted our house built before winter came."

She put her knitting down and stood next to him. "You cannot make everything happen in two weeks, just as you could not move a herd here in two weeks."

"That is true. I also promised I will help them

move the herds and my men will also help."

"Then you will be gone."

He nodded. "And you will be alone."

"I will be fine."

Her sweet scent drifted to him. He wanted her and wanted to kiss her as he had that one time. The thought of her lips on his and the slight tremble of her body warmed his body to boiling. He took her hand in his and brought her fingers to his lips. "You are beautiful."

She closed her eyes and he could see the tremor as it ran through her. Rolling her hand over, he kissed her palm and then her wrist. He was certain she was willing, but he didn't feel right about kissing her in the open where everyone could see them. He needed to control the burning sensation building inside of him, for now was not the time or the place.

She tugged on his hand and this time she returned the kisses to his fingers.

Explosions went off inside of him. "We must stop before I forget that I am a gentleman."

She giggled softly. "You have always been a gentleman."

"Do you think Cora would keep Alma long enough for us to select a spot to build our house?"

"I could ask."

He nodded. If he could be alone with her, where no one would see them, he had no intention of remaining a gentleman.

9

Tiago beamed as he came through Cora's front door. "It is ours, four hundred eighty thousand acres."

Ingrid blew out a breath. "That many acres? That is almost a half million acres."

He laughed. "My father has over a million. But my land is better. Are you ready?"

She held up a finger. "We need to eat first."

He laughed. "Yes. We shall eat. Did you ask Cora?"

Panic seized her. "Not yet."

"Ask me what?" Cora turned from the stove.

Ingrid sucked in a breath. "We would like to check the land for the placement of his house. I wondered if Alma could stay with you. It would be easier if she were not riding with me."

"Oh, I do not know. I've never had to care for a

child."

Alma walked over to Cora and tugged on her sleeve. "I am not a baby. She only wants to be certain that I am not alone."

Cora looked at Alma. "And what would you do while they are gone?"

Alma looked at Ingrid.

"Play with your doll, read a book, play in the backyard, maybe Cora will show you how to weed the garden and you can work on it with her." Ingrid looked at Cora. "Maybe you will let her pick herbs and set them out to dry for the winter."

"She may stay."

After their meal, Ingrid and Tiago walked to the livery and collected two horses. Tiago was determined to saddle her horse for her.

"I can saddle my own horse. I've been doing it since I wasn't much older than Alma."

He ignored her and did it anyway. Then insisted that he give her a boost into the saddle.

"You are the most obstinate man I know."

He laughed and finished saddling his own horse. "Our land comes to the road."

They rode slightly out of town and then onto the property.

"I thought building near town would be better. It will be easier to pick up supplies or whatever else we might need," Tiago said, as he nudged his horse.

E. Ayers

"Shall we?"

She took off after him and in a few minutes, he reined in. "This is my land. We build here, near the road."

"No. Not here, up there."

She went a little further to a slight rise. "Oh, this is lovely. The view is spectacular."

"Yes, I agree. We shall build here. A beautiful house for my beautiful woman." He dismounted. "Come."

He helped her down and she could feel her lips curving upwards. "Why do you say that? It will be your house, for you and Alma."

"For the three of us." He lifted her hand to his lips.

His very touch sent waves of heat through her body and they settled deep inside of her. She tried to control the feeling but could not. Melting was not something she wanted to do, but she was certain she would.

He pulled her close. His breath was on her face. She sighed. "Please don't. You will find someone else. You are only doing this because I am near."

"What am I doing?"

"Taking advantage of me."

"I might be a gentleman, but you ask for the impossible. You are there every day around me. Your sweet scent and laughter haunt me every night and

148

make it almost impossible for me to sleep. Why would I not want you?"

"Because men don't want women like me."

"You think I want some foolish woman? You are more worthy of the name Colima than all the women in the world."

His lips found hers and he drew her tight to his hard body. Her knees weakened as his mouth nibbled its way to her ear. His warm breath filled her ear as he kissed her earlobe. She gripped his shirt and clung to him.

"Please no." She forced the words out.

"Do not talk. Allow me to kiss you as I have wanted to do a million times." His hand cupped a shirt-covered breast.

"No. Please no. I am a virgin. Do not take that from me."

His lips traveled down her throat. "And I am a man."

Mustering all her strength, she moved her leg and brought her knee up between his legs.

He growled and grabbed for her wrist. "Why did you do that?"

"I will not be ruined." She yanked hard and freed herself from his grip then took off in a full run for her horse.

He tackled her, sending her to the ground. She screamed, but he covered her mouth with his.

"You are a little spitfire. Do you think I'm going to steal something that is not mine?"

Her chest heaved as she tried to breathe. "You brought me here." She heaved another deep breath. "Alone so you could..."

He finished the sentence for her. "Ruin you? No. I bought you here to find the location for our house, not my house. And I brought you alone because I wanted to kiss you as a man. Because you would never allow me to do that in front of Cora, Alma, or the town. You already told me once that you loved me. But you've never said those words again." He sat up and pulled her with him. "Did you mean them?"

Tears spilled down her cheeks. "Yes."

He blew out a breath. "I do not know how to be... I do not know your word to make you understand that I want you, too, because I have tumbled in love with you."

She wanted to laugh, but she knew precisely what he was saying. "I do love you. And I love Alma."

"I cannot ask you to be my wife when I do not have a house for you. I have land. The rest will come. But I would never take your ... A man does not talk of these things."

"Women are not supposed to talk about it either. I only had a father and he told me what I needed to know."

"I don't have the English words." He huffed. "I

was married. Evita was a beautiful young woman. Together we learned." He plucked a blade of grass. "I had another child. He died at birth, and I almost lost Evita with him. She was sick for a long time afterwards. We were warned not to have more children. But she became with child. I will spill my seed upon the ground for as long as I shall live, for I never want to go through that again."

"My mother died before I was born."

"Impossible."

"No. My mother was a nurse and was exposed to sickness. Her..." She held her hands before her to show a large belly. "She had a high fever. She was too weak. The doctor was there. So when she died, he used a knife and took me. She did not die in childbirth. She hadn't gotten that far. The doctor gave me to a woman who had recently had a child. That is why I am here, otherwise I would have died with her." She shook her head. "My father was protective of me. You are the same with Alma."

"As much as I would love to fill the house with children... I fear."

"I promise. I am healthy. But I want to protect my virginity and save it for my wedding night."

He plucked a seed from her hair. "I will not take you, but I want to kiss you and know that you are mine."

"Then promise that you will only kiss me."

"I give you my word before God." He leaned over and kissed her again, sending her back to the ground.

The sun beat down on them as he kissed her. His fingers unbuttoned her blouse and his lips followed his fingers. Her entire body glowed under his touch as his hands roamed her curves.

Her heart pounded in her chest. Each kiss left a trail of fire. She wanted more, but she didn't dare tell him. Her hips lifted as her womanly parts burned and begged for him.

He broke the spell when he stood and walked away from her. "Do not follow."

"I know what a man does."

"Stay there." He stepped into the shaded area between a small stand of trees.

She stood and buttoned her blouse and tucked it into her waistband, then attempted to remove all traces of grass and seed from her clothing.

When he returned, she helped remove whatever bits of debris had clung to his clothes.

"Your hair. Can you take it down?"

She nodded and turned it loose.

He plucked quite a few seeds from her locks. "I think I have everything."

She re-braided it, pulled it into a bun, and put the pins back in it. "Do I look the same?"

"No. You look like we've spent most of the

afternoon kissing." He put a finger to her lips.

A slight breeze blew as he retrieved her hat. "I will kiss you again, and I will kiss you often."

He plopped her hat on her head.

"Wait." She pulled the hat off and properly pinned it. "You are lucky I did not lose my pins in the tall grass."

He shook his head. "Women!"

"Are you going to start complaining about my being a female?"

"Never. I love that you are a woman."

"I would have never guessed."

He gave her a leg up, and she slipped into the saddle. From her perch, she watched him climb on his horse. His movements were stronger and she was certain that he was well on his way to being healed.

The sky darkened as clouds rolled over the mountains. They left the horses at the livery and ran to the house as drops of water began to fall. Lightning lit up the sky. And they laughed as they ran into Cora's house.

"Alma! Cora! We're home!"

Panic gripped her throat and Tiago ran up the stairs. The kitchen was filled with the aroma of bread baking. She stuck her nose out the back door and called again. This time the door to the privy opened.

"We're in here. Alma needed a bath!"

Instantly she put her hand to her chest and

relaxed, but she couldn't stop shaking. "Tiago! I found them."

Alma dashed into the house wearing only a towel. Grinning at her father, she ran up the stairs, leaving droplets of water in her wake.

It was hard not to smile at Alma's toothless grin. But as Ingrid thought about how she had spent the afternoon, all the delicious feelings ran through her. Her smiled tugged at her cheeks as she looked at Tiago. You have no idea how much I want you.

***

Cora, who was more than disheveled, came through the back door laughing. "We were in the garden, and Alma became quite a little dirty little bird. I hope you don't mind."

Tiago looked at Cora's bare feet. "What were you doing?"

"We started out...and then...but we... Please excuse me. I need to dress so I might finish dinner. Will you check the bread for me?" The woman hurried down the hall.

Tiago's brows knitted. "Is she sound?"

Ingrid laughed. "You forget that Alma is a little girl. I can just imagine what happened. And it looks as though any herbs that were picked for drying have blown away or been soaked."

"I do not want her growing up like a waif without a proper home."

Ingrid shook her head at him, washed her hands, and pulled the bread from the oven along with the second half of the day's chicken. "She needs time to run and play. That does not make her a child of a tinker. It makes her a child. You seem to want to keep her from running and playing like a normal child. She needs time to fall on the ground, giggle, and get dirty." Ingrid took the dishes from the china buffet. "Your mother let you run and play on the ranch. You rode your pony, and probably managed to get into all sorts of trouble. And when you came in, you were bathed and scrubbed clean. Only then were you reminded of your manners."

"Yes. It is true. And no one told me no because I was my father's son."

"Allow your daughter to do the same."

He set his jaw.

"And that is a very nasty habit. Spitting is not befitting a gentleman."

"I wasn't going to spit."

She laughed at him. "No, but you wanted to do it."

The following morning, Tomas, José, Marco, Luis, and Soaring Bird met him early to start drilling. The previous evening's rain brought in cooler weather, but drilling for a well wasn't easy. Two men, taking turns, worked hard before passing it to the next team of two. As Frank had said, they dropped three unsuccessful ones, one had produced a trickle but they kept drilling and went to nothing. A fifth one seemed to work for a few minutes, and it, too, quit. Frustration was building as they stopped for their midday meal.

Frank rode over with his father.

Joseph looked at the equipment on the ground. "No luck?"

"None. It has gone as Frank predicted," Tiago answered.

Joseph looked around. "You are putting the house up here on the hill?

"Yes."

"Did you buy your windmill yet?"

"No, because I wasn't certain how high I'd need to go."

"Good." He walked off the hill. "Down here. The only problem is you might need a second windmill to get the water from here to there."

"I will do it if it means good water. Besides, I thought I'd put the barn and bunkhouse down there."

José groaned as he stood for his turn, but Marco slapped him on the back and laughed. "It makes you a man."

Frank and Tiago set the next hole, and Marco and

José grabbed the cross pipe and began to turn. Soaring Bird and Frank took their turn drilling until Frank called it quits.

Joseph counted the pipe they had left. "Keep drilling." He took Frank's place and Tiago took Soaring Bird's. Another twenty feet and they hit water. Water gushed and Frank and Marco managed to get it capped. Drenched, everyone packed up and went home.

Dirty and wet, Tiago went straight to the privy to wash up. Feeling only slightly cleaner, he walked through the back door of Cora's house and went into his room. Pulling off his wet clothes, he climbed into bed. Bits of the morning flowed through his mind. With each attempt, had they stopped drilling too soon? Questions that had no answers plucked at his confidence. Had not his father prepared him to do this? This ranch would be nothing more than a puddle compared to his father's, yet he felt as though he had five million acres with the experience of a ten year old to run it.

A knock on the door awakened him. "Yes."

"Want some supper, sleepyhead?" Ingrid's voice was clear and as sweet as ever.

"Yes, my darling. I'll be right there."

He pulled on dry clothes. Wearing socks without boots, he joined everyone at the kitchen table. "I'm sorry. We all worked hard. I was cold and wet."

Ingrid touched his cheek. "A nap was the best thing for your body."

She passed him a bowl of squash and onions, and he put a spoonful on his plate. "I miss my tortillas."

"Ask your mother to send me the recipe and I will learn to make them."

"You would do that for me?"

"Of course." She smiled at Cora. "We both like to try new things." She took a slice of bread and passed the breadbasket to him. "Did you drill your well?"

"Yes. Tomorrow I will begin to order the other materials that will be needed, including a windmill." He looked at his daughter. "And you will have plenty of room to run and play." Then he turned back to Ingrid. "Joseph said to bring her tomorrow and he'll bring Virginia. We will stake out the squares for the foundations."

"I think she wants to tell you something."

"Yes, my little darling."

"Ingrid and I took your horse to the livery and then we stopped to see if there were any books for me."

"Thank you, both, for taking care of my horse. Did you find any books?"

"May I show you now?"

"No, eat your dinner, and then you may show me."

As soon as they were finished eating and the

adults were drinking coffee, Alma took off to gather her books. With her arms full, she returned and stacked them on the table next to her father. He picked up the first one. "Geometry? Is she not too young?"

"She spotted it and wanted it. She's only begun her multiplication and division. And she must learn fractions and decimals, but I told her if she studies hard she could do some things in that book next. There are many simple mathematical things for her to learn in there. But I have another mathematics book for her. It is on her level."

He flipped through the remaining books. "Can she read this?"

"Not really, but if she's willing to try, I'm willing to teach her. You will notice she has a simple speller and another book on her grade level."

"Maybe you make her do too much?" Maybe I ask you to do too much?

10

Ingrid smiled. "Alma likes the challenge. I think she's very much her father's child. She still needs some other books, and they told me to come back next week. The woman who works there said she will save a few for me that I want, including a dictionary."

Tiago picked up the one book, "Come, my little darling, show me what you can read."

Ingrid watched him leave with his daughter and then she helped Cora clean up the kitchen. "He needs a bath. I will fix it for him tonight."

"Yes." Cora responded. "He might have washed up, but he still smells as though he's been wallowing with pigs."

"Men are like that. If you don't mind, I will take my bath in the morning after Alma leaves. And I will launder our linens and other things." Ingrid was pleased that she had convinced Cora to allow them to use her bathtub, and Cora agreed not to charge if Ingrid cleaned the tub each time. It was an arrangement Ingrid could handle.

While Tiago bathed, Ingrid changed his sheets so everything was fresh for him. Then in the morning, she chased him and his daughter out of the house so that she could relax in the tub. She had to force herself from the warm tub and face the laundry. She shared many chores with Cora and she enjoyed doing them. But the thought of a day without Alma nearby meant she had time to do some serious reading.

As soon as the last item was hung on the drying line, she went upstairs. Hidden away, she found the letters that her brother, Lennart, had written to her father. She stifled her tears and began to read them.

Train robberies, stagecoach robberies, and bank robberies were all documented in the letters. Lennart believed they were connected. He had figured there were about fifteen men who were considered dispensable, mostly two-bit petty criminals who had been hired by a small, select group of men. He knew those men actually hiring the criminals were working for someone more powerful. Lennart named those that he knew. He suspected quite a few others, including a riverboat owner. Lennart wrote about how the thieves seemed to have had inside knowledge about what was being transported and where, and he knew that his supervisor at Red Hall Security was involved.

He wrote about overheard bits of conversations and suspected that it went clear up the ranks of Red Hall. He wrote detailed accounts of those who were caught and virtually walked out of the jails that were supposed to hold them.

Millions of dollars over a period of a few years had been stolen and none recovered, and the amount was escalating. People were being paid off for their involvement.

But why come after our father? That doesn't make sense. She bundled the letters and hid them away. She had intended to write to her aunt and decided against it. What if someone was watching her aunt's mail? Would they know where a letter originated? Would they come after her aunt? The sheriff back home didn't do much when her father was shot, other than tell her that he was sorry. Was he in on it?

I am far away and no one knows me.

She looked though several of Alma's books and began to write lesson plans to go with them. She never dreamed she'd end up teaching a child, but she loved teaching Alma. In many ways, Alma reminded Ingrid of the child that she once was. Anxious and eager for knowledge, she'd read almost anything she could, and her father supplied her with tons of books. From whaling adventures to romance, she read them all.

Wuthering Heights...Heathcliff... So brooding and an... She stifled the derogatory thought.

Now I have Tiago and his lost love, Evita. A man with ways and traditions I cannot understand. A man who makes me want to do things I shouldn't.

A thought struck her. If she had graph paper, certainly she could redraw the floor plan of the house to suit Tiago. She would check at the general store to see if they carried such paper. Using the ruler she had bought for Alma and the preprinted lines... I can do this. It will help him.

She picked up her knitting and went downstairs. She sat outside and talked to Cora as the woman washed her rags and hung them on the dry line. Cora had confided that she was hardly more than a mail order bride. The youngest of seven girls, her mother was anxious to be rid of the youngest child. Cora's father was a fisherman and had drowned. Her mother wanted to remarry. Cora was sent off to marry Carl Ritter, a surveyor for the railroad.

They had lived in Laramie while he had her house built. Every paycheck he did more until she could move into it.

"He never was home very much. But I didn't lack for anything." Cora pushed her cedar red hair from her face. "He had everything budgeted. Another two years and I would've had a grand house complete with running water."

"You're doing fine, Cora. You are still young. You'll remarry."

She waved her hand through the air and sat next to Ingrid on the step. "So far I don't want them." She frowned. "The Cade's youngest son is marrying and I know he's looking for a place to stay. I was hoping maybe to rent to them. I have enough rooms. And it would give me a nice income."

"I know Tiago is hoping to leave before winter, and I'm assuming he'll take Alma with him."

"He's very handsome, if you like them dark."

Ingrid giggled. "He is ten shades darker than when I first met him. The Mexicans often would remove their shirts or unbutton them in the heat. The Spaniards keep their shirts on in the summer heat, but the Indians... They are almost naked with no modesty in front of a woman." She waved her hand in front of her face. "I saw more of them than I should have."

"Were you not afraid?"

"No. Never. They were all good men. Just different."

"The Coleman's keep a pack of Indians as workers. Everyone knows them and knows they are good workers. They are welcome everywhere in town. They often come with Frank or Joseph, or sometimes with the women. But they are always dressed as proper men."

"All people are the same. They have different customs, eat different foods, and do things differently, but inside they are the same. There are good people and, unfortunately, bad ones, no matter what their color."

"You are kinder than most."

"Uh-oh, I think I made a mistake. I should have four stitches here, and I only have three."

Cora shook her head. "Take it to Mrs. Hagger this afternoon. She'll figure it out."

"That's what I get for talking while I am knitting." Ingrid put her knitting in the bag. "I'm not very hungry. With everyone gone, why don't we eat something simple? I see another ripe tomato in the garden."

Cora buttered bread and Ingrid sliced the tomato and some cheese to go on the bread.

After their meal, Ingrid took her knitting and walked to town. Her first stop was the general store. "Do you have any graph paper?"

The woman shook her head. "We can order it, and it will take a few weeks. Why don't you check with the land office? They might sell you a sheet. They order a package of it every so often."

"Thank you. I will." Her eyes settled on a table stacked with wool fabric. "Did you receive a shipment of new material since yesterday?"

"Yes, some nice wools, imported from England."

Ingrid walked to where the bolts were stacked and fingered the brown wool. Having bought enough with Adie, she knew how many yards she needed. She didn't have much money on her. She picked up several bolts. "Will you calculate how much before you cut it? I wasn't planning on buying yardage today."

As the woman added it up, Ingrid reached into her pocket and counted her coins. She could do it if she didn't go to the livery. I can walk. The exercise will be good for me.

It was expensive material but worth it.

With her knitting and her fabric, she stopped by the land office. Uncertain if she should knock and enter, or just knock, she hesitated.

"I can't believe he bought that many squares."

"He's ruined everything."

"Watch what you're saying."

"Who has that kind of money anyway?"

"His father. They are almost as large as the King Ranch."

"I still say we need to run him off."

"We can just tell him we occasionally keep a few head there."

"That's not going to work."

"This is a sleepy little town in the middle of

nowhere. Why here?"

"Don't know."

Ingrid's heart pounded in her chest as her stomach clenched. She stepped away from the door. I don't need graph paper. Quickly she walked towards the farm supply store. Then she turned. She wanted to see who exited the land office, and she was willing to wait. She didn't know whom to trust. No longer did she know the good men from the bad ones.

Fear surrounded her, wrapped her in a cloying blanket that crackled like an impending lightning storm. Had she not moved hundreds of miles to escape trouble? Except she was facing a different form of danger, this time aimed at Tiago. A wave of nausea passed through her and she wanted to vomit.

"May I help you?" A middle-aged man asked.

"Oh, um. I was trying to decide. Do you have Pyrethrum Chrysanthemums?"

"We have mums, just these."

"Oh." She spotted the flat reddish bloom of the Pyrethrum Chrysanthemums with several more buds that were ready to open. These were not as showy as the new ones from Asia, but Pyrethrums were more useful. "Those. Will you save me two? I'll get them tomorrow morning."

"And you are?"

"Mr. Colima's governess."

The man's smile brightened. "Certainly, ma'am.

I'll hold them in his name."

"Oh, and one more thing. By any chance do you have graph paper?"

The man raised his eyebrows. "What is that?"

"Paper with little squares on it."

"I might, not sure what you call it - it's got squares, but I can't imagine why you would want it."

"I only need a piece or two..." Alma's name went though her head. "Maybe three."

"Follow me."

She didn't want to go inside. She wanted to stay where she was. But she followed him through the door. The place was crammed with all sorts of odd things from nails to what looked like pulleys. Against one wall were heavy sacks filled with seeds. Another wall contained shovels, rakes and other tools. Two men seemed to be examining a barrel filled with hinges. The place smelled like some bitter tonic and that wasn't helping her knotted insides. She attempted to flatten her pants to her legs and hoped the hem of her pants wouldn't touch anything along the narrow aisle as she followed him through the store.

She watched as he went into an office. He returned with some ledger paper and several other papers, but at the bottom of the stack was an old discolored open package of graph paper. "This. I only need a few sheets. How much?"

"Take it. Been here since I bought the place fifteen years ago. It's cluttering up my shelves. My son used to use it when he was learning his letters."

"Thank you, sir. Your generosity is most appreciated." She took the paper and hurried outside just in time to see the sheriff and two other men leave the land office. She passed two of them and smiled politely. "Good day, gentlemen."

Dropping her paper and fabric at the house, she headed for the Haggers' house on foot. The sun was warm as she walked along the narrow road. The grass in the field was green and almost two feet high. A distant field was filled with sunflowers looking like they might burst with their brown centers and yellow petals. A bird swooped low over the field, and another chirped from an unseen spot nearby. She inhaled the fresh scent of pure nature.

In spite of the overheard conversation, she felt good. She wished she had Alma with her so that they could run, jump, and skip along the road. Thoughts of the child and her bright smile lifted Ingrid's spirits further. And thoughts of Tiago and his kisses warmed her more than the bright sun.

No one was going to take away her chance at happiness. Her meeting Tiago was by total chance, her trip here had thrown them together, but her love for him had grown as naturally as the grass in the fields. Did she dare trust her feelings to commit for life to someone she still barely knew? Does anyone truly know the other when they marry? Yet I am the one with secrets.

***

The sun was hanging low as Tiago collected Alma and headed back to town. It hadn't taken them long to stake the barn or the bunkhouse. But the house... Tiago hesitated. Mentally he calculated the number of feet he wanted. His parents' house was large and sprawled with a courtyard in the center. Such a design would not work where snow fell. This house would go up rather than out. But he wanted the rooms twice as big as what they appeared on the floor plan. They marked it off, but Joseph had shaken his head the entire time.

Alma chatted the whole way to Cora's house. Tiago dropped the cart at the livery, and he and Alma walked the rest of the way home. "Wash up and change into clean clothes before supper. No dirty girls are allowed at the table."

He poked his nose in the various rooms of the house and didn't find Cora or Ingrid. The stove was cold. Do we not get a meal tonight? Where are they?

Cora appeared carrying a basket filled with dark berries. "Good day, Tiago. We'll have dessert tonight, and I'll make jam tomorrow."

He reached out, plucked a berry from her basket,

and popped it into his mouth. Fully expecting sweet, the berry popped, spilling the sourest taste into his mouth. It made the edges of his tongue curl and he shuddered as though he had bit into a tart lemon. "What?"

Cora laughed. "That's what you get for not asking first." She put the chokecherries into a container and then pumped some fresh water over them. She checked each one as she added them to a pan. "They need to be cooked with sugar. Then they will be tangy, yet sweet."

He watched what she was doing for a moment before heading to the privy to wash before supper.

After supper, he walked outside and waited for Ingrid to finish her chores in the kitchen. He smiled when she appeared and questioned her whereabouts this afternoon.

"I went to town and then to Haggers' dairy. Mrs. Hagger had to help me with my knitting. I made a mistake and missed a stitch, but I couldn't find where I had gone wrong. Is that a problem?"

"No, of course not, but I was concerned."

"I understand. Did you and Alma have fun?"

"Fun? Maybe she did." He chuckled. "She wanted to know what we were marking and wanted to help. Virginia couldn't persuade Alma to play until she figured out exactly what we were doing and how we made everything square."

"I told you. She enjoys anything with mathematics."

We marked all three buildings on the ground and tomorrow my men will start working on the foundations. I also increased the size of the house." He reached in his pocket and withdrew the paper that showed the house. These rooms are too small. I doubled it."

"What? Doubled? It will be huge!"

"I know. I will need more bricks than the plans say."

She looked at him and her mouth opened slightly. "You will build with brick?"

He wanted to laugh at her but refrained. "You want a modern house, not a poor man's house made of wood."

Her knitting needles stopped. "And where will you get brick? This is not the city."

"I will need to order it from a brickyard and have it shipped here. But I will need to recalculate everything for the house."

"You are loco." She put her knitting down. "I have something for you."

He watched as she walked into the house. She looked better than she had when she arrived in Creed's Crossing. She had grown thin on the trip even though she was eating. Now she had real color in her skin instead of being sun drenched. She was totally different from Evita, not just in coloring, but also in temperament.

His lovely Evita would have never withstood the long trip. He reminded himself that her horsemanship was excellent, but she didn't have the fortitude. She was a woman and her ability with a needle was excellent. Even his mother praised Evita's skill, but she was a delicate flower.

Ingrid returned and handed him some paper. "I was going to attempt to redraw the house for you."

Part of him wanted to leap for joy. "Will you do it? I will give you new measurements. Then I can concentrate on other things."

"I have never done such a thing, but I thought I would try."

"If you draw, I will make any changes needed, but I must put my efforts into the barn and bunkhouse."

She nodded. "I understand."

Light was fading and tomorrow would come too soon. There was much to do and the cold weather would be moving in. He had to start building as quickly as possible.

11

Using a pencil, Ingrid worked on the drawing between helping Alma with her lessons. Painfully challenging, she used the ruler to follow the lines on the page. She looked at the way it was originally drawn and tried to copy that to her page. Her appreciation for mapmakers and other occupations that required drawing skills increased tenfold. Even after she released Alma to play, she continued to work until she had all of the first floor redrawn. Then she walked into town to collect the two mums she had chosen.

The following day, she worked on the house plans again. And when she had managed to complete it, she gave it to Tiago. Two days later, it came back to her with changes. She redrew the whole thing.

Evenings were growing cooler and they often sat at the kitchen table or in the parlor rather than going outside. But night after night, Tiago retired to his room. Yet when she went to her room, she could tell he had a lamp lit.

The next time she saw her drawing, Tiago had a calculated list of materials with it. She had never looked at him as a man who was capable of such things. Never having seen this side of him, it surprised her, yet it didn't. Certainly his father had not become a wealthy man by tending to a few head of cattle. He was a businessman with an empire under him, and Tiago was determined to do the same.

So many times she felt inadequate. She had book knowledge, but her practical skills were lacking. Cora seemed to know so much more about living than Ingrid probably ever would. She tried hard to learn all the things that Cora took as everyday tasks. But for Ingrid, they were as foreign to her as Tiago's Spanish words.

After lessons in the mornings, she'd walk into town with Alma. The butcher had a daughter, Louise, who was slightly older than Alma, and the two girls loved to play with Alma's doll. They would sit on the bench in front of the butcher's store and amuse themselves until Ingrid would collect them. And with days growing shorter and becoming cooler, their days of playing would become fewer.

Ingrid would stop and chat with the folks on the

street while keeping a watchful eye on the children. But one day as she walked past the sheriff's office her ears picked up the name Colima. She slowed her steps and lingered by the bakery window.

"He's got to be running out of money."

"No one can keep up that spending."

"We can't let him mess up our operations. Mr. Douglass isn't going to like this."

Ingrid recognized that name from her brother's letters.

"He's not. We got to get rid of Colima."

"We'll kill him."

"Yeah, ain't nobody gonna miss his Mexican--"

Ingrid hoped no one could see the shock on her face. Her heart raced and her skin prickled.

"Can't do that, men. We'll think of something else."

"We'll burn him to the ground."

"That just might work, but we got to make it look like an accident."

"How ya gonna do that?"

"No point in doing it now. Wait until he gets it almost built."

"Then he won't have money to rebuild."

"That's an idea. But mull this over. Every time something goes down, we get a cut. Who keeps the rest?"

"Mr. Douglass?"

"Nope, even he's got a boss. What if Colima is the one keeping the money?"

Ice ran through Ingrid's veins. Even she hadn't thought of that.

"That sure would explain a lot of wealth."

"And what better place to hide out than Creed's Crossing? Maybe he knows, and that's why he bought so much land. Real clever, ain't it?"

Ingrid knew she had to leave. Her insides were churning.

"Miz Ingrid," Mrs. Welton stepped out of her shop. "What are you so busy looking at in my window?"

Ingrid forced a smile, reached for her pouch and produced a coin. "Cookies. May I please have a half dozen? I don't want to step too far from the girls."

Mrs. Welton gladly brought her the cookies wrapped in white paper. "Anytime. Anytime. Don't mind bringing them out to you."

"Thank you." She took the cookies and crossed the street. "Here, girls." She handed them each a cookie. "Eat your cookie and tell Louise goodbye."

"Thank you, Miz Smith." Louise took her cookie and munched on it.

Ingrid knew it was a treat that few children had, and that she had spoiled the dinner appetites for both girls. Alma collected her doll and Ingrid waved goodbye to Louise's parents.

"You're very quiet today," Alma said as they walked to Cora's house.

"Thinking about the house your father is going to build and about your schooling."

"Louise starts school next week," Alma said.

"So I've heard. Maybe we should pay the schoolmarm a visit this afternoon. If you are here in town, you should go."

"And what are we doing tomorrow?"

"I was thinking about visiting Adie."

***

Tiago listened to Ingrid's request to send Alma to school for a few weeks. "But what about all the books you bought her?"

"I'll work with her in the evenings. They will reinforce what she learns in school, and it will give her something different to read." Ingrid smiled sweetly.

"Well, I agree that she would enjoy the social part of going to school. She likes being around other children."

"When the weather gets too snowy, she still has her schoolwork here. She won't fall behind."

"I thought they had to be six to go to school."

Ingrid nodded. "Miz Wade, the schoolmarm, said that she would make an exception because Alma is already so far ahead."

"And she is allowed to attend with the other children?"

Ingrid nodded. "That was never questioned."

He stood to leave the parlor.

"Please, before you go... I was wondering if we could take the cart and go to Adie's house tomorrow."

"That is fine, but you will wait for me. I will pick up a few supplies before I take you. Then I must unload and you may go directly to Adie's, but you must return for me."

"Thank you."

"Ingrid?"

"Yes?"

"Is something wrong? You seem distant."

"This is a new life, and I must adjust."

"Very well then." He picked up a candle, lit it, and carried it upstairs.

Using the candle, he lit the oil lamp, and sat at the small table in his room. He wrote a letter to his father.

Ingrid wasn't the only one embracing new things. He was, too. It took Evita's death for him to realize he wanted more from his life than to be the third son with no real wealth of his own.

His parents had supported his decision. His father had financially backed him, but his father wanted half the money back in five years. The weight of that alone pressed on his shoulders. His daughter needed him and his attention, putting additional stress on him. There was no question in his mind that his exhaustion came from both physical and mental toil.

He put on his nightclothes and turned down the lamp's wick until the flame flickered and died. Instead of sleeping, his mind went to Ingrid. Her drawing was precise and had made his job easier. His men were brawn, but she was intelligence wrapped in the most beautiful package. A partner...a person he could trust and lean on for help. The packaging warmed every part of him and the memory of his lips on hers cranked his need further. I need you, Ingrid, but I want you more than anything else in the world.

***

Ingrid enjoyed her day with Adie. Alma played with Adie's twins, chased chickens, and took a turn at churning butter.

Adie picked up Alma's doll and took a few measurements. "I might as well learn how to do this. With two little girls, I will need to know."

Alma's new dresses were perfect and with her starting school, she would need them.

"Alisa sent these over for her. They were

Virginia's."

Ingrid looked at the pretty knitted jackets and realized how poor her skills were at knitting. Each row was perfectly straight as though a machine had done them. And all three had been decorated with embroidered flowers, fruits, or leaves. "They are beautiful. Please tell Alisa how much I love them and give her my thanks."

"Ja. I will. Now while the babies are sleeping. I want you to try on your new clothes."

Each outfit looked wonderful, as Ingrid gazed at herself in the long mirror.

"You've done a fantastic job. I feel as though I've stepped off a Paris Street in these."

"I don't get to make too many new clothes. Seems I mostly mend or alter something to fit Virginia. I had fun doing this. Living in town is more exciting then living on a ranch." Adie waved her hand though the air. "I could wear an old shirt and overalls for a week, and the only person who would see me is Frank." Adie handed over the coat she had made for Ingrid.

"Oh, it is so beautiful." She admired the heavy wool coat that was lined, and then trimmed in fur. "But I did not buy fur."

"I used scraps I had from making heavy buntings for the babies. I learned how to preserve leather and fur last year."

"I can see I will have so many things to learn. I keep wondering if I've made a huge mistake coming here."

Adie laughed. "It is fun learning to do new things. I will teach you."

Adie went to her wardrobe and pulled out another coat. This coat was made from sheepskins and was trimmed in fur. "It's not very pretty. I made it and it doesn't fit. I forgot to allow enough extra for the wool. My chest is too big, even when I'm not nursing."

Ingrid took the primitive garment. The outside felt like suede and the inside was almost a solid-black color of a lamb's coat. Uncertain, she tried it on, and it fit. "It's different."

"Pull the hood up. There's a leather frog to button it."

Ingrid did as she was told. It didn't take her long to peel it off, as sweat was beading on her forehead. "Oh, it's very warm."

"You will be glad to have it when winter comes. It is very cold here. You will see."

"Then thank you. I can't imagine it getting much colder. When I was little, we would see snow occasionally. It was so pretty."

"You will come to hate snow. And your stockings... You need some heavy wool ones."

"Oh."

"And boots." She walked to a window and looked out. "These are the nice days that have been warmed from the sun with cool nights that make you want to snuggle closer. But soon it will be cold and the winds will come from the mountains making it even colder. The winter I came here we had so much snow…" She shook her head. "Your barn is not near the house. You will have a long trek there."

"Why would I want to go to the barn?"

Adie's face drained of color. "Oh. I am sorry. Most wives go to the barn."

"I am not Tiago's wife. I am governess to his daughter."

"I thought you were his wife. I'm sorry." Adie's face turned a bright pink. "I know you said you were Alma's governess, but I thought you were joking."

"I think many people assume that I am. He is a widower. I suspect that one day when everything is ready, he will write to his father to ask for a new wife. But I will admit, he is a very handsome man and a fine catch. I am an employee." The words tasted bitter in her mouth. "He will want someone suitable to his station."

***

As Frank had promised, the men in the community joined Tiago on Monday morning. And by Monday night, the barn stood. Tuesday was a repeat and the bunkhouse was framed. There was still plenty of work to be done on both, but they were standing.

Each night, Tiago tumbled into bed and slept. He couldn't remember a time in his life when he had worked harder. Every muscle in his body ached. His ears rang from the sharp ping to the deep thud of so many hammers driving nails into the buildings.

So far the whole move to Creed's Crossing had been one long grueling venture. His men moved into the bunkhouse even though they didn't have any amenities. They were prepared to create them. By Thursday evening, they had running water and a toilet. Friday morning, his herd had been moved to his property.

Friday afternoon, every piece of wood had been used and cold air blew in from the west. Tiago came home to a daughter who wanted his attention. His entire body ached and his head pounded with each beat of his heart. He'd not seen her all week and her little smiling face made him realize that she was the reason he was trying so hard.

"Come here, my darling, show me what you have learned this week," he said in Spanish.

She climbed into his lap with a book and opened it. "Did you know that a man named Columbus came to America before anyone else?"

He listened as she rambled on about history until her eyes closed and her head rested on his chest. He leaned the sleeping child back in his arms and looked at Ingrid. "Who is teaching her this stuff? You or the school?"

"Both." She laughed. "She's reading ahead. I talked to her teacher yesterday and she doesn't mind that Alma is moving along faster than everyone else. There are fifteen children in that school ranging from Alma's age to fourteen. That's a lot to teach. If Alma stays in her seat and doesn't bother the other children, the teacher is happy. Seems Alma keeps honing in on the older children while they are learning mathematics."

"She is smart. That is good. But she is still struggling with her vocabulary. Remember that English is still a new language to her."

"She will learn."

He stood, carried his daughter upstairs, and tucked her into bed.

The thought of helping the Coleman's and several other ranchers move the herds down from the northern fields weighed on him as he climbed into his bed. It seemed as though he had barely closed his eyes when he heard church bells chiming and the sound of horses racing through town. Shaking the fog from his mind, he opened the curtain and looked out his window.

"Fire!" The word was repeated again and again.

He pulled on his work clothes and slipped his feet into his old boots.

When he reached the front door, he could see the glow in the sky. His heart fell into his stomach as he raced to the livery and grabbed his horse. His bunkhouse and the barn were engulfed in flames. His windmill lay twisted on the ground. And scattered around must have been two-dozen empty kerosene jugs.

Tomas walked over to him. "Everyone got out of the bunkhouse."

"That's what really matters." He spit on the ground. "No one is going to burn me out. No one!"

People were still tossing buckets of water at the barn.

"Stop. It is gone. Spitting on a bonfire will not put it out." He rode back to the hillcrest where he intended to build his house. His strings and stakes were missing. The world around him was nothing but a crackling hot glow filled with smoke and the stench of lost dreams.

One by one most of the town's people packed up and left. Many stopped to give their condolences as if he'd lost a family member. For most of these folks, such a loss would have left them devastated. He'd have to tell his father and probably ask for more money. It's not what he wanted to do.

Anger and frustration choked him more than smoke. As he watched burning beams collapse, plans were beginning to formulate. He'd rebuild, but this time with block and tile roofing.

Frank and his father walked over to him. Joseph Coleman clamped a hand on his shoulder. "When you are ready, we'll help you rebuild."

"Thank you. You are good men."

Joseph nodded. "We will stay with you until the last flame is gone. Your men are welcomed back on my land."

"I think my horses and my herd is gone."

"They are. I knew you would notice, but I did not want to add to your burden."

Tiago wanted to slump over and cry like a child, instead he straightened his back. "I will not be run off my own land."

12

Sunday morning, Ingrid awakened to an envelope with a note that had been slipped under her door.

There is something I must do before the cattle drive south. Taking a few men with me. If I do not return, take this for Alma's care until she can be returned to my family. Do not let anyone know that you have it. Keep it on you or hidden in your things. It is safe that way. Pretend nothing is amiss.

She counted the money twice and her hands shook. Never had she seen so much cash. All day Saturday, she had debated about telling him of the conversations she'd overheard. But in her own mind, she couldn't decide if he was part of the ring that had killed her father and brother. But if he were? What am I going to do? I no longer know what is expected of me or how to act. I haven't lived a normal life in months.

She stashed the money and note under her pillow and awakened Alma. After breakfast, she sent the child outside to play in the yard. Then she dashed up to her room and reread the important letters from her brother. This time memorizing the names he had mentioned. When she was done, she hid everything, made the beds, and took Alma to church.

By one o'clock, it seemed as though the entire community had gathered outside the small church for a potluck dinner. Alma played with her new friends and Ingrid chatted with the townsfolk. Many gave her condolences over the fire and others asked about the whereabouts of Alma's father.

She smiled sweetly and, without lying she simply answered, "I am Alma's governess. Mr. Colima does not tell me what he is doing."

As things began to wind down, she collected Alma, and they walked home. Part of her knew she needed more information, and with Alma in school on Monday, she'd have a better chance of snooping around. A thought struck her.

As a child, she and her best friend had developed a written code. For them, it was a game, but now she realized she could put it to use. Using her code, she wrote down what she knew and several possibilities.

It wasn't until Alma had retired for the night that Ingrid had time to think about what she wanted to do or how she could do it. Using the excuse of cleaning Tiago's room would give her reason to spend time searching his room for connections to the ring of thieves. But how do I eavesdrop in town?

As soon as she walked Alma to school on Monday, she returned to the house. Cora was sweeping and dusting the parlor.

"Good morning, Cora. 'Tis a lovely day. I thought since Tiago is not here, I would clean his room and freshen it."

"If it's not too much trouble. I really appreciate you taking care of your own things. Takes the responsibility off of me."

"No problem. It doesn't bother me. A good cleaning always brightens the day." She scooted up the stairs and opened his door. The stench of smoke-filled clothes permeated the entire room. Gathering his bedding and his dirty laundry, she took everything downstairs and left it in a pile by the back door. Then she returned to his room and opened the windows. She searched everything including his boots. All she found was more money and a ledger.

Most of the entries in the ledger were written in Spanish, but it didn't take much for her to decipher what the numbers meant by the amounts of money spent and the dates involved. Mentally she added up the cost of materials for the barn and the bunkhouse. He had paid dearly only to have it burned to the ground.

After sweeping his room and dusting, she cleaned the chimneys on his lamps and refilled the kerosene in them, and then wiped his floor with a wet cloth. Satisfied, she went downstairs and started on his laundry.

If maybe... She poured hot water into the washtub and added his clothes. Adie had one of those newfangled washing machines, but Cora only had a washboard and wringer. The clothes Tiago had worn the night of the fire required several washings before they smelled and looked clean. Even with the afternoon sun beating on her shoulders, it was getting too chilly to be washing clothes outside. As she finished each article, she hung it on the line to dry. She shook out one pair of overalls and... Yes. That's my disguise. It's perfect. His clothes. I'll borrow his shirt and these overalls. Then I'll sneak around behind the stores. Everyone will think I'm a young man.

As fast as the idea came to her, it popped like the bubbles from the soap. She knew that wouldn't work no matter how hard she tried. She had to find a different way. When she'd hung the last piece of clean laundry and emptied the tubs, it was almost time to meet Alma. She quickly changed her clothes and headed into town. Certainly I can spend a few pennies.

She lingered near the sheriff's door but heard

nothing. Then she went to the bakery. "Good day, Mrs. Welton. The girls loved your cookies so much, I thought I'd treat them today on the way home from school."

"How many do you want?"

She was about to answer when the bell over the door rang and she turned in time to see the sheriff enter.

"Afternoon, ladies." He looked directly at Ingrid. "I'm surprised to see you are still here."

She cocked her head and looked at him. "Why would I not be here, and where would I go?"

"Well, after your husband's fire, I thought you'd--"

"Forgive me, sir, but Mr. Colima is not my husband. I am the governess to his daughter." Her head raced with thoughts. "Mr. Colima is a widower. I was... I was hired by his parents, Alma's grandparents, to tutor and take care of her. And when his father sent him here to start a ranch, I was asked to take Alma so that she could stay with her father." She smiled as demurely as she could. "I am only an employee."

"Forgive me, ma'am."

She stuck her hand out to the man. "I'm Ingrid Smith from Victoria, Texas. And you are?"

"Sheriff Tyson Stone, at your service."

"Pleased to meet you under better circumstances."

"We met before?"

"Yes. When Mr. Colima was coming to town. You brought a posse."

"Ah, yes. I remember."

She wanted to snarl at him. "I just stopped for some of Mrs. Welton's delicious cookies. I thought I'd treat the girls as I walked them home from school. Abigail is your daughter?"

"Ah, no, she's my niece."

"She's a lovely little thing. Alma's enjoyed making friends in this town." She turned back to Mrs. Welton and pointed to the large cookies that glittered with sugar crystals. "Four cookies."

Mrs. Welton took her pennies and handed her the cookies wrapped in white paper. "Keep spoiling the children. They all adore you."

She smiled and turned back to the sheriff. "I assume that you are investigating the fire. It must be difficult with so little information. But certainly someone knows something about it. I can't imagine why anyone would do something like that to him."

"Why would you think it was purposeful?"

She raised her eyebrows and looked at him. "Why would you not?"

Ingrid collected the three little girls from the school. She dropped Abigail off first, and then allowed Alma to play outside the butcher's shop with her friend Louise, the butcher's daughter, for a little while.

As Ingrid stepped into the butcher's shop, she spotted a wheel of cheese that wasn't there last week. "Has Cora bought cheese today?"

"No. I haven't seen Cora since Saturday morning. The cheese came that afternoon."

"Then I shall buy some for us." She held up her fingers to show the size wedge she desired, and then turned her attention to the children in time to spot the sheriff with the gunsmith. She paid the butcher and took her package outside. Now she wished she had brought her knitting with her as it would have given her an excuse to sit longer as she took a seat on the edge of the porch to the gunsmith's shop. When she heard footsteps, she didn't dare turn around. Pretend everything is fine. She watched the girls.

"He's gone."

"We know."

"Well, there's a whole pack of ranchers went to collect head from up north."

"I can't drive them through town."

"Douglass sent me a wire this morning. He wants them moved out and sold."

"We'll do what we can."

"He also wants some protection on a job."

"When?"

"Next week."

"I'll try to reach Mason, but he's not happy that

Colima is still alive. He doesn't like obstacles in his way."

Inside her stomach knotted. Slowly she stood and went to Alma and in a low voice said, "Sorry, girls, but it is time we went home and prepared for tonight's supper."

She opened the butcher's door and held up her package of cheese. "Thank you. I know we will enjoy it."

"Do you feel well?" Alma asked.

"What makes you ask such a question?"

"You look pale."

"I am fine. It's been a long day for me, and I'm feeling the chill as the sun slips behind the mountains."

Alma shrugged and skipped ahead as Ingrid quickened her pace to keep up.

I'm doing fine. She glanced at the sky once and could feel her grin. Don't be angry with me for lying, Daddy. Ingrid Smith from Victoria is much safer than Ingrid Svensen from Bluff Falls. I will get to the bottom of this.

***

Tiago and Frank stayed in a hotel in Sheridan and then rode further to see Adie's father. Frank told of his first visit with his dad to the Reiner stockyard to pick out several lambs for his mother. He was still a child when he'd met Adie Reiner, and they had written letters for years. When the time came, he had returned to the Reiner house to ask Adie to be his wife.

It was a sweet story of young love. But years of correspondence had given them both a chance to really know one another. It was apparent that Frank dearly loved his pretty wife.

Tiago felt almost claustrophobic in the ornately decorated office in the Reiner house. He hoped this was not what Ingrid had in mind for a modern house. The leather seating was soft, but all the buttons and tufting was too much for his taste.

Tiago and Frank were served coffee, and with a cup half drank, Tiago opened up to Adie's father. "I don't know where to start or whom to trust. Whatever is happening is bigger than Creed's Crossing. From what my father said, it stretches from the Mississippi to Texas and probably all the way to the Chicago stockyards." Tiago gave the man some details. "Cattle rustling is big business and always has been. Land pirates."

"Albert Goddard might have been part of that ring." Mr. Reiner tented his fingers. "There is someone I know." He took out a piece of paper and wrote an address on it along with a name. "Do not ask questions. Just inform. Let Adie post the letter."

Tiago took the proffered piece of paper. "Lynda

Applegate. I will be sending information to a woman?"

Mr. Reiner shook his head. "No. Any posts go to Lynda Applegate. But don't be surprised if you hear from Andy Lyles. They are one in the same."

Tiago tried to clear the confusion from his mind. But Mr. Reiner was certain that all information would be kept confidential.

Mr. Reiner pushed back in his chair. "Our newspapers are filled with stagecoach and train robberies. But I happen to know there is more afoot. Did you get your deed?"

Tiago nodded. "Yes. And it was registered."

"Good. Protect that deed and all proof of monies paid. Land is an important commodity, far more than a few head of cattle. People are getting rich off of the land. Did you buy from the government or from the railroad?"

"The railroad."

"Good. They know what they own." Mr. Reiner arose from his seat. "Let us have some dinner before you leave. I will tell Cook to fix you a basket of food to go with you. And I have a package for my daughter, Malene."

Tiago ate the meal, thankful for the full stomach, but he wasn't certain he liked the pickled cabbage they called sauerkraut. He missed home and his family's meals. This was a different way of life, and somehow he was tangled in something that he didn't understand. He'd lost all that he had created and almost one hundred head of cattle.

He was willing to bet his cattle were still on his property. The head hadn't been run towards town. They didn't end up on the Coleman land, and nature had fenced the one side of his property. The only place left was north, and he was going to find them.

Frank had them cut through the Crow reservation to Mark Hunter's ranch where Tiago met Adie's older sister, Malene. He and Frank spent the night and then continued their journey south. Not far below Sheridan, he found his herd along with over a thousand head of cattle grazing lazily on his land. They cut out Tiago's head along with Coleman and the Lazy A + 8 head and Tiago returned to Sheridan and informed the sheriff who didn't seem very concerned.

Now they were driving head and their pace would be slower. Three more days and they were home. But that didn't mean anyone was safe. Whoever was out there was probably looking for blood.

Tiago wasn't thrilled about writing everything he knew in English. By far more comfortable in Spanish, it took him an entire evening to compose a letter to Lynda Applegate.

It was late morning when Tiago left the Coleman

E. Ayers

ranch and headed into town. The thought of seeing Ingrid and his daughter lifted his spirits to the sky, as he got closer to Cora's house.

A gunshot rang out and he looked around. Suddenly four men surrounded him. His skin prickled and he could feel the hair on his arms rise. Bandanas covered the lower halves of their faces, but it didn't hide the fact that most were dressed better than the average ranch hand. "Know your opponent." The sage words of his father sounded clear in his head.

He assessed each man, took in exactly what they were wearing, and the way they sat in the saddle. All four had guns drawn.

The one man spoke, and Tiago recognized the voice.

Another shouted, "Get off your horse."

"Why?" he answered in Spanish.

A fifth man rode up with Alma tied across the saddle of a sixth horse.

The one man laughed. "Because we are going to kill you and then your daughter."

Tiago's heart pounded in his chest and echoed in his head. His fingers twitched as his mind raced. He was outnumbered, but he refused to be the prey.

One of the men rode close to Tiago and shouted for him to drop the gun off his leg.

Only one man seemed comfortable with the

weight of the gun in his hand.

Time. I need time on my side. Tiago looked at his daughter. Her little brown eyes were like saucers - wide-eyed and pleading. He doubted the men knew more than a few Spanish words. There was no reason for them to learn them, but Alma could follow instructions. His words were in Spanish. "Listen carefully, my darling, and no matter what happens, do as I say." He looked at Alma for recognition in her eyes. "When I say now, scream and tuck your chin to your chest, flip your weight over the saddle, and dive for the ground. Don't open your eyes until I tell you it's over."

"Why bother with my daughter?" he asked, hoping to bide more time.

The one man laughed. "You just don't get the hint to leave town, do you?"

"Why should I leave?" He moved his horse so that he was sideways to most of the men.

"Because, we don't want your kind in these parts."

"Ah, but that war is over and I had nothing to do with it. My people have been in Texas for over two hundred years."

"Your people? You can't fool us. We don't want your Mexican--"

"Get off your horse, now!"

Not far off, he spotted Ingrid and two men with

her. In one swift move, Tiago shouted to his daughter, grabbed his gun off his side and the rifle behind him.

Alma's scream was piercing as gunshot blasts filled the air. When the smoke cleared, there were two more men and Ingrid staring at Tiago.

Ingrid slipped from her horse and ran to Alma. "Alma, Alma, are you all right?"

The child stared as if she'd seen the devil.

The other two men dismounted and began to collect the men on the ground.

"Clyde's dead," the butcher announced.

"So is Phillip," the man from the farm supply store answered.

The butcher nudged Tyson Stone in his side and the man moaned.

Ingrid left Alma's side and stepped to where the sheriff was lying on the ground. She kicked the gun that was lying near him out of the way. Her voice was cold as ice as she ordered, "Jeremiah, hand me your gun."

She took the gun from the man who owned the farm supply store and stood over the sheriff. "Your job was to protect the citizens, not kidnap an innocent child."

A second later, Tiago shouted, "No!"

The sheriff was dead.

Ingrid walked over to the man who ran the post

office and put her foot on his throat. He grabbed for her leg, but in a few seconds, it was over.

Tiago gathered his daughter into his arms and held her. Her eyes were still wide and not a sound came from her mouth. He rocked her and covered her face in kisses as Ingrid knelt by his side.

13

Ingrid held Alma's hand and Tiago took his daughter's other hand as they walked to the church. It seemed as though the entire town and most of the neighboring ranches turned out for this meeting.

Dressed in a suit, Jeremiah paced the front of the church, looking totally out of place as folks filed in and sat in the pews. Quite a few of the men folk stood to give their seats to the women who came with their husbands. Now those men stood at the sides and back of the tiny church.

The little drone grew to a din and people shuffled until finally Jeremiah stood still and raised his hand. "Ladies and gentlemen, I think we're all here."

The meeting shifted between those in favor of electing another sheriff and those who saw no need for one.

Joseph Coleman rose from his seat and walked to

the front. "There's no point in beating a dead horse, and that's what we're doing. The fact is, we never had a sheriff until Tyson came to town and convinced everyone that we needed some protection. What we needed was protection from people like him. When my father started his ranch, the only neighbors he had were on the reservations. If he needed something, he rode to Laramie. Then the McLaughlins, the McCulloughs, and the Barrett brothers came. The Barretts opened a mercantile and a farm supply. Then the Colburns came. Cody Colburn's son decided we could use our own post office, so he applied for one and thus started our little town."

Most of the townsfolk nodded, and a hum of agreement made Joseph wait for things to quiet down again.

Joseph looked at the saloon owner. "Mike seems to take care of things at his saloon and he's never had much trouble, until recently. I have a feeling things will get real quiet again." He cleared his throat. "Ezra Cade is getting married. He's already begun to volunteer at the post office, and he claims that the post office and the land office could be combined. I think we should let him do it. That postal job will give him enough money to start a family, and he can live over the land office." Joseph smirked. "Being it's been vacated."

Mr. Cade stood. "I'd rather lease to my son. If he don't pay, I can whoop his hind parts."

The room dissolved into guffaws and giggles.

Joseph held up his hand again, and when the room quieted, he spoke, "We don't need a sheriff. We've always handled things ourselves. Not saying people don't get upset once in a while, but when that happens, we let them cool off until we can talk some sense into them. There's not a man or a woman in this room who doesn't know how to use a gun. I say we go back to taking care of our own. If we need help, we ask for it."

Jeremiah stepped forward. "All those in favor of Ezra handling the post office and the land office say yea."

"Yea!"

"Do I hear a nay?"

The whole room quietly shifted in their seats as they looked around.

"The yeas have it. Congratulations, Ezra, you have a new job to go with that pretty little gal you're about to marry next week." Jeremiah looked around the room before continuing. "All those in favor of finding a replacement sheriff say yea."

The room was strangely quiet.

"All those in favor of living without a local lawman say yea."

"Yea!"

"Any nays?" He stood there and waited. "That settles it. We don't need a sheriff."

First one person began to clap, and then the whole room applauded.

Jeremiah held up both hands. "Please. Reverend Sawyer would you mind saying grace so we can eat?"

The part-time reverend who served as part-time undertaker to the small town came forward and offered thanks for the food that everyone had brought.

Tables were set up in the side room and someone made a bonfire. Louise played with Alma, even though the child had not spoken since that fateful day.

Ingrid put her hand on Tiago's arm. "Let her play. It's the best thing for her. Louise seems to accept Alma's muteness."

He nodded.

Ingrid knew he was worried about his daughter, but she also knew that the child had been scared out of her mind. Having read about such things, but never seeing it until now, didn't make the present situation any easier. Only time could heal the child.

Tiago also seemed nervous and slightly out of place in the friendly community. Questions streamed though Ingrid's mind. He hadn't overheard the men talking. Why would he have reason to kill them?

And if he were somehow part of the bigger picture, would he not know who they were? Yet she looked at him and saw a loving father, a good foreman, and a man who had been kind to her.

And then there was Alma, an innocent child. Ingrid wanted to flog herself for not speaking up and saying something to Tiago. *Have my secrets made Alma a victim, too? My life is becoming a whirlpool pulling me into Hell. Do no harm, yet I have hurt the ones I love. But if I tell, do I not put them in more danger?* Questions swam in her mind until her head pounded.

"Do you not feel well?" Tiago asked.

She forced a smile. "There are many thoughts in my mind - not all of them pleasant." She touched his arm. "Do you think it is over? That the violence against you has come to an end?"

He shook his head. "I must prove myself to the community because my hair is not light nor my eyes blue. I'm sure that many here think I killed for no reason."

"They knew what was done to you. They know the sheriff took Alma from school. I do not think they question your motives. Plus you did not kill alone."

He turned his gaze to her and stared hard. "And you are unlike any woman I've ever known."

She smiled at him. "'Vengeance is mine; saith the Lord.' But there's nothing wrong with helping him."

"He also says to repay evil with kindness."

"Oh, I was kind. I put them out of their misery."

His eyes narrowed and she could see the distrust within them. But deep inside, she knew the only person she could trust was herself.

***

Tiago walked his daughter to school and walked her home each day. There was nothing he could do but wait on the shipment of bricks. Yet every day grew colder, and he knew that if it grew too cold, he'd not be able to build.

The bricks arrived and so did winter's first cold blast. The frustration of the wait was now compounded by the frustration of not being able to build.

Time gave him the chance to think and reevaluate his entire situation. In the beginning, he had admired what he considered to be strength and independence within Ingrid, but now he realized that she was as cold as the ice that came from the mountains. She portrayed herself as sweet and innocent, but she was neither. He wrote another letter to be mailed to Lynda Applegate and took it to Adie Coleman.

When an unfamiliar man knocked on Cora's door asking for him in the middle of the day, his entire body clenched with fear as though he faced a wolf with nothing but his bare hands to protect him. Too many people know I killed those men.

***

Ingrid dried her hands and watched as Tiago went to greet the man in Cora's parlor. She didn't want to be obvious, but she wanted to know who the stranger was, and what he wanted with Tiago. She sat on the stairs, trying hard to listen to their hushed conversation. She knew Tiago recounted the attack on his herd as they approached town and his being burned out. She caught most of the conversation about the herd on the northern end of his property. And when she overheard Tiago say something about getting his copy of the deed, she scurried up the stairs to her room.

Whoever Andy Lyles was, he was important. And how he fit into the puzzle, she didn't know. As soon as she heard Tiago leave his room and rejoin the man, she tiptoed down the stairs to resume her espionage. Silently she cursed the fact that she couldn't hear much of anything they were saying, just bits and pieces, but when she heard the name Douglass uttered by Mr. Lyles, her heart dropped into her stomach.

She pressed her ear against the wall. Her heart beat in a frantic rhythm. Nothing. It was as though all conversation had stopped. Then it struck her. She turned and tiptoed up the stairs. In Alma's alcove of their bedroom, there was a grate in the floor that allowed the warm air to flow from the downstairs fireplace to the upstairs bedroom. Maybe there she could hear more.

She lay prone on the floor and put her ear to the grate. She heard movement and put her nose to the cold ornate brass covering in an attempt to at least see something.

"The last bank heist was successful, but the attack on the train outside of Laramie wasn't because you killed those men."

She picked up Tiago's voice. "So I made things more difficult."

"For everyone."

The man said a few more things, too hushed to hear, but she heard the name Lennart Svensen. Her heart pounded so hard she could barely breathe. She could tell something was being said about the fire and her disappearance. Again it was only a few words almost hissed.

More movement could be heard, and she tried to peer through the grate but a lock of her hair seemed stuck in the curlicues of the grate. She moved slightly and tried to free the tangled hair from the ornate brass. What seemed like a second later, Tiago walked into her bedroom.

"Stand up!"

"I'm stuck."

"What do you think you are doing?"

"I was looking for something."

"And what would that be?"

"Um, the tip for a pen. Um, it rolled."

Tiago reached down and lifted her and the grate off the floor. "Were you not spying on me? Listening to a private conversation?"

"No. Of course not."

"Don't lie to me. You ransacked my room while I was gone."

"I-I-I... What makes you think I did more than clean your room and your clothes?"

"Why should I believe anything you say, Ingrid Svensen!"

She froze.

He lifted the grate from her fingers yanking a few hairs with it. "You are not Ingrid Smith, are you?"

Wrath flared in his dark eyes and his lips curled like an angry dog's.

The fear that had coiled in her abdomen was sending bone-chilling cold through her entire system. She wanted to fight back, to say something in her defense, but she had nothing. She didn't know who he was anymore than he knew who she was. Except he seemed to know that she was Ingrid Svensen and from Bluff Falls.

He grabbed her wrist and forced her down the stairs.

"Good afternoon, Ingrid Svensen. I am Andy Lyles. May I call you Ingrid?" The man showed his badge.

The same badge her brother carried before he went to work for Red Hall Security. She wanted to melt on the spot.

Tiago pushed her into a chair. "Start talking. I can't wait to hear what you have to say."

She wanted to tell someone everything she knew, but she knew her life hung in the balance. Had she endured the journey for nothing? Was Tiago one of them? Was this man before her the one who had her father killed? Her voice froze along with her blood.

***

Tiago's mind whirled with thoughts. She had tricked him - betrayed him - almost ruined him and everything he was trying to do. Was she the kind of person... It didn't matter. She had caused him havoc. It no longer mattered what she said or did. He wanted her out and as far away from him and his daughter as possible.

Andy Lyles smiled and quietly said, "It is important that you tell us anything that you know."

Ingrid sat almost motionless.

When Andy asked for the third time, she finally answered that she knew nothing. She would not even admit to changing her name.

Andy stood and held out his hand to Tiago. "I'm glad we got to meet. Anytime… If you know or remember…whatever information you can give us. Thank you."

Tiago took his hand, "Thank you for coming."

The man left and Tiago returned to the parlor only to discover that Ingrid had slipped around the corner and was running up the stairs. He followed her and caught the door before she managed to slam it closed.

He let loose in a tirade of Spanish before switching back to English. "Get out!" He reached in his pocket and tossed some bills in her direction. "I don't care where you go, just get out. I don't want you near me or my daughter ever again."

Ingrid stood still, watching him as a mountain lion watches its prey.

"I don't want you here for four seconds more than necessary." He opened the wardrobe and began tossing her things on the bed. When he yanked on the last drawer, it came out in his hand and under it was a bundle of money and letters.

"And what is this that I've found? Have you been stealing from me or were you paid to destroy me and everything I've tried to do?" He raised his eyebrows.

"Is it blood money?"

She didn't flinch.

"Get out now! Before I do something that I might regret."

She attempted to snatch the letters, but he stopped her.

"Out!"

She took off and ran down the stairs. He listened to the bang of the front door. She was gone, yet anger still boiled within him. He splayed his fingers in an attempt to release the rage that made him want to wrap them around her neck. He leaned against the wall and surveyed the strewn clothing. It didn't matter to him. His chest heaved. Breath went in and out in hard gasps. The money he had tossed at her lay on the floor.

He leaned over and picked up his cash along with hers. Then the oddity of the situation struck him. She never dove for the money; it was the letters she was after. Three bundles neatly tied with ribbon. He picked up the letters and went to his room.

If I can prove that you are behind the fires, I'll have you arrested.

It took him a moment to decipher which letters he wanted to read first. But then it dawned on him that he had to pick up his daughter from the school. He shoved the letters between his clothes along with the money. He paused and thought about what he had done. Not trusting Cora to let Ingrid back inside, he re-stashed the money in several places that he was certain would thwart Ingrid. The letters, he put under his shirt, next to his body, before storming downstairs and into the kitchen.

"I do not want Ingrid inside this house. Do you understand?"

Cora was paler than white as she nodded acknowledgment.

"And clean up her mess of clothes. I want nothing belonging to her remaining in the house when I get back with my daughter."

***

Ingrid hid in town between the butcher's shop and the land office. Her entire body quaked. With the evidence left behind, she had to get away, far away. Cities and places ran through her mind, except this time she had no money. She hugged her arms to her body. Chill was quickly turned to cold. People die from cold.

She slid to the ground as tears streamed down her cheeks. I have nothing left. If the cold doesn't kill me, the men who killed my father will. I'm tired of running. Let me die here.

***

Tiago collected his daughter from the school. Without the details, he only told Alma that Ingrid had left, and it would just be the two of them until he could find a better governess. Silent tears slipped over Alma's cheeks.

"No, my darling, do not cry. When you are older, you will understand that people are not always who you think they are. They might act as though they care and love you, but they don't. Ingrid tricked both of us. Even her name is not real."

Alma cried and he knew of no way to comfort her. He let her cry.

When they reached Cora's house, Alma ran to her room and threw her little body across her bed.

Tiago let out a breath and covered the tiny thing with a blanket. "When you are done crying, I will be in my room."

He looked around and Cora appeared to have hastily removed Ingrid's things. In his room, he removed the letters from his shirt, lit the lamp, and sat to read. The handwriting wasn't much more than a pitiful scrawl often punctuated with droplets of ink. These were letters from a son to his father. But as he read each one, it became apparent that Len was Lennart, Ingrid's brother.

Reading English in a book was a hundred times easier than reading handwritten notes. He finished one bundle and started on the next. It became obvious that Red Hall Security, a company that was supposed to be protecting bank notes and US mail, had hired Ingrid's brother.

Tiago finished reading that bundle and started on the next. This group of letters had an odd language written in Ingrid's penciled hand along the margins, and in places, names were circled in pencil and often underlined. He stared at the odd notation that often lacked vowels and realized it was written in code. Two pieces of paper were entirely in code. He kept reading the letters. Names of men that Andy Lyles had brought up were often mentioned, and the letters were disturbing. Ingrid's brother knew certain mail runs were being targeted for robberies. And he also hinted that certain men within the agency were criminals. The last letter in the stack told of her brother's determination to stop what was happening, and his concern over how far above him he'd have to go to find an honest man.

Tiago put the letters down and looked at the code. The two notes written in pencil varied. One appeared to be a list and the other broken into paragraphs. What was she doing?

Now he understood her reluctance to talk to anyone about anything. Andy Lyles said her brother was shot and killed during a robbery of a train, but the man also said that Ingrid's father, a much loved doctor, was found dead just outside of town with several bullets in his body. Then Ingrid's house had been burned to the ground and that she had narrowly escaped with her life. Little Ingrid Svensen wasn't but seventeen, and had left to stay with an aunt in Delaware, except she never caught a train. She had left driving a rickety cart that her father occasionally used. The family carriage with all her belongings had burned with the house.

It didn't take much for Tiago to decide that Ingrid Smith was Ingrid Svensen, nor did it take much for Andy Lyles to cross that very same bridge. That young female was determined to travel hundreds of miles by herself in a cart that wouldn't have survived more than a day or two without breaking down. Except José had inadvertently interceded on her behalf. She wasn't a criminal. She was running for her life.

He looked at the coded notes. LHRRHRRHOOH. There weren't many words with doubled letters. The pattern. M-I-S-S-I-S-S-I-P-P-I. Yes! He looked back through the letters. Found it! The Nile Queen of the Mississippi.

As quickly as he could, he tried to decipher all the words, but each one he had to think about. They were names - the names and places that had been mentioned in the letters.

He looked at the second note and deciphered

Lennart, a DOD, but the numbers confused him. Lennart DOD 0787 same pattern back up one, Lennart DOD 1898. That one letter that was written within days of his death but what did DOD mean? Date of Death. DOD. A few more sentences and he knew the money had once belonged to her father.

Tiago continued to decode and realized she had doubts about him. Worried that he was somehow tied to the ring. She does not trust anyone. And I can't blame her.

He had to find Ingrid. She wasn't much more than a baby. She's out there someplace and scared out of her mind.

"Cora, take care of Alma. I've made a huge mistake."

14

He practically flew out the door. She couldn't get far on foot, she'd have to use a horse. He ran to the livery.

"Did Ingrid take a horse?" He could see all of his horses, his coach, and his cart.

"No, señor. I have not seen her today."

He grabbed one of his horses and jumped on bareback. No cart meant she hadn't attempted to head for the Coleman's house, not on foot. He rethought that. She was so determined she would attempt it. He took off in that direction, but then doubled back into town. He checked his property. There were enough chars to start a small fire to keep warm, but she wasn't anywhere to be found. He headed for the dairy. She had mentioned Mrs. Haggar on several occasions. He galloped to the house and beat on their door.

"Ingrid is here. Yes?"

"No. I've not seen her today."

"Don't. She has to be here. We had a disagreement and she left. I must tell her that I am sorry. I must. Please let me speak to her. If she still doesn't want to see me, I will go away."

"Mr. Colima, she is not here. I have not seen her since the other day."

He took off again. The night air was cold, and without a coat it bit to his bones. He came back to town and looked around. There were few people she trusted.

The little girl, Louise. He knocked on the butcher's door and the butcher answered.

"Please I must speak to Ingrid. I've made a terrible mistake. Please, let me see her."

"She's not here. We've not seen her once today."

Tiago cursed in Spanish. "Please help me find her. I know not where she might be. I've checked the roads, she has not taken a horse from the livery."

The butcher looked at him. "Walk around the building. I'll meet you by the back door."

Tiago left his horse in front of the butcher's shop and stepped into the narrow space between the buildings. Deep in the shadow, he saw what might be a slumped body. "Ingrid!"

He ran to her and she was cold. She was still limp, but her eyes did not open. He put his ear to her mouth and listened for any sound. He grabbed at her neck and couldn't feel the strum of her heart. "HELP!"

The butcher and his wife came running.

"Oh dear God in heaven, bring her inside," the butcher's wife instructed.

As Tiago stepped across the threshold, the butcher's wife wrapped Ingrid in a blanket.

"Bring her here by the stove." The woman began to warm a towel and heat water. She turned to her husband. "Take the quilt from our bed." She unbuttoned Ingrid's shoes. "Her feet are too cold."

Tiago watched as the woman wrapped Ingrid's feet in a warm towel and then tucked the quilt around Ingrid and her feet.

The butcher pulled up a chair for Tiago to sit close to the stove.

"Hold her tight." The woman scooted away and then returned. She held a mirror to Ingrid's nose and mouth. "She's barely alive. I've seen this happen with kittens that had been abandoned. My father was sure they were dead and made me leave them in the tinderbox by the fireplace. A few hours later, I had three little kittens looking for milk. We just have to make her warm again. Where are her hands?"

Tiago fished under the quilt and found one. The other hand was tucked by his side. "Here. I have them."

The woman wrapped a warm towel around Ingrid's hands and stuffed them back under the quilt.

Tiago looked at the fair-skinned woman in his arms. Oh, Ingrid, I am so very sorry. Why did you not confide in me? Why did you let me think that you might be one of them? Please do not die. I love you too much to lose you. He held her head under his   chin.

Someplace behind him, a clock chimed. The butcher was living in a house that was mostly his shop. The private area was nothing more than a tiny kitchen and their bedrooms.

The butcher put more wood in the stove and the room heated to the point that sweat beaded on Tiago's brow.

Then Tiago felt it, the slight heave of a breath that Ingrid took. Oh, my darling Ingrid. He felt it again. "She's coming around."

"I praise you, Lord, for sending her back to us." The butcher's wife put her hand on Tiago's shoulder. "What happened? A lover's quarrel?"

"I wish it would have been that simple. For maybe if she had been my lover, she would have stood up to me, and prevented me from being a fool." He shook his head. "I was wrong, and I made a huge mistake." He looked at the woman standing beside him. "I dismissed her and told her to get out. Told her that I didn't want her near Alma. I was so wrong. She is everything to Alma…and to me."

"She is young to be a governess."

"She is. But she has not been a young girl for a long time. She had to grow up quickly, for she had lost her family at a young age." He wasn't certain what she might have told this family. "My family is very lucky to have found her for Alma."

Ingrid began to stir in his arms. If he had been alone with her, he would have covered her face in kisses, but that wasn't possible. Instead, he whispered little endearments in Spanish.

Ingrid's eyes fluttered open. "Where?"

"Shh. You will be fine. Be still."

A moment later, the butcher's wife handed him a cup of tea. "See if she will drink this."

She attempted to grab for the cup, but with her hands wrapped in towels under the quilt, Tiago put the cup to her lips and she drank all of it. She looked at him as though bits and pieces were coming back to her.

He smiled at her and in Spanish said, "Not here. Not now." And then continued in English. "We must talk, for I made a huge mistake. Forgive me."

The butcher's wife refilled the cup.

She freed her hands, sat up, and took the cup from him. "What happened?"

***

A few minutes later, Tiago carried Ingrid, wrapped in a blanket, back to Cora's.

He grabbed his own coat and went to take care of his horse.

Cora tried to feed her, but she didn't feel hungry. She nibbled on a few morsels and pushed her plate away. This time she drank tea with milk and honey, and then asked for more. Cora fixed her another cup as Tiago came through the back door.

Cora smiled. "Tomorrow I shall put all your clothes back in your room. They are safe."

It was all Ingrid could do to nod.

Tiago carried her upstairs and put her in her bed. Then he sat next to her on the bed.

"I am so sorry. I was the fool. I made a terrible mistake. I suspected that you were hiding something from the very beginning. And I was right. You were hiding the truth. You forgot how to trust because you didn't know who you could trust." He ran his hand over her cheek. "I was almost jealous of Trader because I could see the trust you had in him. You trusted him since he was so far removed from our world."

"I--"

"Shh. Do not talk. You need your sleep. I almost lost you forever tonight. I will stay with my daughter, but I will be here if you awaken."

Ingrid opened her eyes to the bright morning light. Her body ached and yesterday seemed like a bad dream. Her attempt to stand almost sent her to the floor, but she caught herself on the bedpost and groaned.

Tiago flew into the room from across the hall. "What are you doing?"

"What does it look like I'm doing?"

He scooped her into his arms and carried her downstairs.

At the bottom of the stairs, she pointed. "Outside for morning rituals."

He carried her to the privy and insisted that she give him a minute to prepare things for her. The little Franklin stove in the corner had made the room toasty warm and there was plenty of hot water in the kettle that sat on top of it. "I will be outside if you need me."

As soon as she finished brushing her teeth, she called his name and he instantly came to her. Tucked in his arms, he carried her upstairs.

"But I'm hungry."

"Cora will bring you food. You must stay in bed for a few days."

After three days of being treated as though she was an Egyptian queen, she put her foot down and demanded some exercise. "And where is Alma?"

"She's in school. She knows you are ill."

"I'm not ill, but I will be if I'm not allowed to do anything. Where is she sleeping?"

"In my room and I've taken her bed. I've been concerned."

"You weren't concerned when you threw me out. What has changed?"

"I'll show you." He left and returned with her letters. "I read them and translated your notes. I understand why you did not trust me to tell me the truth. I wish you had." Tiago's eyes were wet with tears. "I wish I could undo the other day. By keeping secrets from me, it made you a suspect."

"How can you say that? Why would I want to hurt you?"

"Because you thought I was the enemy."

She turned her head and stared out the window. The desire to cry or maybe scream rampaged through her as emotions flooded her. She still couldn't let go of the idea that Tiago might be somehow tied to the violence. His seemingly endless money supply was something she could not ignore. "How do I ever trust anyone?"

"That is like asking how I know my name or how do I know that Alma is my child?"

"Why would they be otherwise?"

"Do not be such a fool. Could not a woman have another man's baby?"

"Oh, but that would be wrong."

"Maybe not. What if her husband wanted a child but failed to produce an heir? Is it wrong for her to give him one?"

"Yes. It is wrong to deceive a man."

He raised his eyebrows. "Every family has its secrets."

A chill ran through her. "Alma?"

He chuckled. "No, not Alma. I have two sons, Ramon and Ricardo Colima."

Another chill came with some confusion as she remembered his family at the table and the two sons of his oldest brother. "Colima? Are they not your brother's children?"

Merriment danced in his eyes. "He will always think they are his. And now you know my secret that I must take to my grave."

"But your brother and his wife are so happy together."

"Another reason to take that secret to my grave."

"It is still wrong." The image of him with another woman stabbed at her heart.

"No. My sons are the heirs to my father's wealth and they are loved." He chuckled and his eyes danced with his laughter. "I was more than happy to oblige such an arrangement by my brother's wife. Juliana is a beautiful woman and I was very young with much to learn. She was a good teacher."

Heat rose to her face.

"I have shocked you?"

"Yes."

"So you are appalled that I would give my brother sons, yet you believe that I am a criminal?" He shook his head. "But you must keep my secret even from Alma. The only ones who know are Juliana, you, me, and God. Not even my brother knows." He stood. "If you feel up to dressing, I will take you downstairs today and let you sit in the parlor."

"I am well. And I am not a little girl like Alma. You do not need to carry me down the stairs."

He paused at her doorway, turned, and grinned. "You are not. You are soft and curvy like a woman. And how shall I cope when my daughter is no longer a little girl? How do I protect her from men like me who want to make love to a beautiful woman?"

She tossed her pillow at him and he left laughing. The rich warm sound did something wonderful to her and made her tingle. Yet the knowledge of what he had done played through her mind. Such scandalous behavior, the risk of being caught, the destruction it would cause within a family.

The image of those two sons and their mother, Juliana, flashed in her mind. Yes, you must have been very young and she is beautiful. Heat flowed to her cheeks as she imagined them together. A proud and very virile man.

Why do I still not believe that he is innocent? Why can I not trust him? Has he not shared his deepest secret with me?

The time it took her to dress gave her time to think. And no matter what she did, she could not shake the feeling. Had she spent so much time living with fear that to try to rid the suspicion was impossible?

Sunday they went to church together. She knew he was Catholic, but there was no other church in the area. There was only the small community church in Creed's Crossing run by Reverend Sawyer. In Tiago's parents' home was a small shrine and she wondered if he would have one in his home. After the church service, everyone congregated in a side room. There was coffee for the adults and the Haggers had milk for the children. She was thrilled when she saw Adie. "Where are Emma and Anna?"

"Frank's sisters have them."

Ingrid smiled and looked around. "I almost never see you without them. They are such beautiful little girls."

"Thank you. But they are becoming spoilt with all the attention from Frank's family." Adie looked over her one shoulder as if to assure herself that her twins were still fine. "My sister, Malene, and her husband, Mark, will be visiting next week. If the weather holds, I hear Tiago intends to have another barn raising. Her husband will help. He knows about brick."

Ingrid tried to keep the surprise from showing on her face. "He mentioned another attempt at building, but I don't remember him mentioning a date."

"Ja. Frank told me, but when Malene wrote to say she was coming, I did not know if Tiago would be rebuilding. Mark is very good." She dropped her voice to a whisper. "He is a Crow Indian."

"Your sister married a Crow? Is that not illegal here?"

"Ja. It is illegal here. She must be very careful if they are off the reservation."

"Oh my."

"It is often difficult for her because she loves Mark dearly, but she knew what she was facing when she married him." Adie smiled. "You will love him, too. Everyone does."

Tiago came over to where they were standing. "Are you ready to leave?"

Ingrid nodded.

Adie reached out and touched Tiago's arm. "Before you go, I will come to town tomorrow. Maybe we can visit?"

"Please come for dinner and bring the twins. We'd love to have you," Tiago generously offered.

"Clarissa has already volunteered to watch them. I will think about it. If they are with me, I will have more time."

Getting out had felt wonderful, but Ingrid was tired. She bid her friend goodbye and left. Once outside, she asked about another attempt to rebuild the barn.

"Who told you? Adie?"

"Yes."

"If the weather holds I will have two men who know how to lay brick."

"You can do that in a day?"

He shook his head as he helped her into the cart and then placed Alma on the seat beside her. "It will take several days. But if we can get some of it ready… 'Tis better than nothing."

"I thought it was too cold."

Tiago raised a shoulder and let it drop. "They seem to think we can do it. And extra help is coming." Tiago climbed up next to Ingrid and took the reins. "A man by the name of Mark Hunter is coming to visit the Colemans and he will help build. They say he knows how to lay brick."

"Yes. He is married to Adie's sister. He is a Crow Indian."

Tiago turned and looked at her. "Yes. I met him when we went north for the cattle."

"Adie said everyone likes him."

"Then we shall see."

The following morning, Adie stopped at Cora's

house early. "Frank said he will leave me and return for me later, if you don't mind."

"No. It will be fun to spend the day together."

Adie put the twins on their feet and waved to her husband. "He has supplies to pick up and will get some extra canning jars for me." She looked at the twins toddling in the front yard. "If they can play in the fresh air, they will take a nice nap for us."

"Better idea. Shall we go to town now? The walk up and back should wear them out."

"Ja. That will be good."

A few minutes later, they walked through the tiny town and Adie asked about Tiago.

"He took Alma to school and went to mark the land for the buildings again."

Adie shook her head. "I cannot believe such a terrible thing happened. We were shocked. And now Alma has quit talking."

"She will talk when she is ready. She suffered a great ordeal."

They stepped into the mercantile, each holding the hand of a toddler. Ingrid went straight for the books. "Adie, come look, there's a Royal Baker and Pastry Cook book."

"My sister would love such a book. Is there more than one?"

Ingrid looked through the stack. "Yes, two more."

"Good, one for you and one for my sister. Now come see the material they have."

As they looked over the bolts, Emma hollered, "Pa-pah!"

Frank came over and picked up the twins. "Are you two ladies buying the entire store?"

Adie giggled. "Will you wait for me to select some cloth? Then I will not have to carry it."

He nodded. "I will take the twins outside while you decide."

Freed of the children for a few minutes, they both selected several things.

"Malene will want me to sew for her while she is visiting. You must come and meet my sister."

Ingrid looked through the stack of folded cloth on a table. "Remnants. Aren't some of these big enough for the girls?"

Adie selected several things and Ingrid looked at several knitting patterns.

When they had finished, they had both spent more than they had intended, but Ingrid was pleased with her new books and the pattern she had purchased for making a man's sweater. It would be her Christmas gift to Tiago.

Feeling happier than she had in a few weeks, she and Adie walked back to Cora's with the twins. But as she approached the front porch, she noticed her pots of flowers had been knocked over with such force that the pots were broken and the dirt was spilled. She looked at Adie and saw the surprise on her face. They opened the front door and were confronted with an even larger mess.

"Cora?" Ingrid called. "CORA!" She dashed to the kitchen and then ran up the staircase. Everything in the rooms had been emptied onto the floor. Smeared in ink on her wall was DIE SVENSEN. Ingrid screamed and ran downstairs and out of the house. "To the butcher! Now!"

Ingrid ran ahead of Adie and asked the butcher to take Adie home. "Please, now! It is an emergency!"

"I can't leave my shop. I'll take her when we close. What's wrong?"

"Never mind."

Panicked, Ingrid ran to the livery and got the cart. Common sense set in and she knew she didn't dare travel with two females, two babies, and no guns. She'd have to go to Tiago.

"Adie, quick. Climb in. We must find Tiago."

As soon as Adie was settled with the twins, Ingrid slapped the reins and raced out of the town towards Tiago's property. She prayed he'd be there. Fear was choking her. The only person who knew her real last name was Tiago because that man told him. But she still wasn't certain if she were running to the enemy, except she had no choice.

"Tiago! Please take Adie home. Someone... It's

horrible. I can't stay. It's not over."

15

"Stay in the cart. Follow me." Tiago jumped onto his horse and they cut across the property to Frank's.

"What is wrong?" he asked, as they pulled to a stop in front of Frank's house.

Adie answered, "I never ventured beyond the foyer, but that house has been ransacked. She screamed and ran down the stairs and we got the cart. Cora didn't answer her calls."

"I'm not leaving you here alone. All of you, go to Joseph Coleman's. There are more people there. You will be safer." They took off again and made their way to Joseph Coleman's ranch.

Tiago managed a little more information out of Ingrid, but not much. She tended to close her mouth and say nothing when she was upset, and he knew that. "Stay here. I'm going to get Alma and bring her to you. Then I want you to stay here until I come for you. Do you understand? Adie don't let her take off."

Adie nodded, but Ingrid looked as white as the snow. And he truthfully didn't trust her not to run away. He went to the barn and spoke to Joseph.

"I will talk to Alisa," he said, referring to his wife. "She will keep Ingrid safe and at her side. You two have had too much trouble."

Tiago nodded. "Ingrid has seen the devil and he follows her. It is not her fault. And if you don't mind, I'm going to bring Alma here until I can figure out what is happening."

Leaving his horse, Tiago took off in the cart for Alma. And as soon as he had her at the Coleman ranch, he raced on his horse into town. He went into the house through the kitchen door. The place was a mess. But when he walked upstairs, he saw what made Ingrid fear for her life.

He checked his room and found his stash of cash. That made him think, and he returned to Ingrid's room. Her room had been ripped apart. Whoever had been there missed the letters and her cash, yet it looked as though they were hunting for something. Cora. "Cora! Where are you?"

He checked her room again and then every room in the house. He stepped into the backyard and called her name. There was a faint sound.

"Cora? 'Tis Tiago. Come out." He opened the door to the root cellar. "Cora?"

Nothing. He looked at the privy and knocked. This time he heard a thump. "Cora? I'm going to open the door." He drew a gun, praying it wasn't a trap.

Standing to the side, he pushed the door open and then jumped in front of the open doorway. He checked the first corner and then the one that held the stove. Assured there was no one other than Cora in there, he stepped inside to rescue her. She'd been gagged and her hands and feet were tied together. "Dios!"

As he was untying her gag, he realized someone had done more than just tie her. The dress and chemise she wore had been ripped, exposing her body, and there were the signs of a man's... He grabbed a towel and covered her. "Cora, I am so sorry."

Tears rolled down her cheeks. "They said they will kill me if I tell."

"These men are not men, they are filthy beasts who will kill for no reason. I know you do not want to talk about it, but please tell me, how many men touched you and how many came into the house."

"Four men came into the house. One brought me here. Only one... Another was going... but the one man said they were out of time."

She clung to Tiago and cried.

"I will start the stove. Take a warm bath. I will

bring you clothes. Lock the door behind me and do not open for anyone but me."

He lit the light in the privy. "Stay here."

He heard her drop the latch as he headed back into the house. In the kitchen, he lit another lamp and carried it upstairs with him.

He looked in Cora's room and picked up a dress that had been sent to the floor. Then he spotted a chemise and a pair of ladies panties. He blushed as he picked them up, but he knew instantly they were not in good shape. Patches had been sewed in several places and the lace was torn. He looked through the pile for better garments, but could not find any. Many times he had seen clean laundry hanging on dry lines at home and knew his mother and sisters wore only the finest silk imported from Europe.

He stopped and looked in Ingrid's room. Hers weren't made of silk, but each was bright and in good repair. Shaking his head, he left the room, went downstairs, and out to Cora. "Cora, it is Tiago. Open the door so that you may have clean clothes."

He passed her the items and she glowed red as she took her things from him.

He reached out to her. "Cora, you have become like a sister to me. Please do not be afraid to tell me the truth. If a man has... I will kill him. Did he put his...? Did he, um... inside? I can see that he, but did he...?"

She nodded.

He swallowed and closed his eyes. "I will not forsake you or allow you to face...without help." He leaned to her and placed a kiss on her cheek. "It is my promise to you. But please, I beg you, tell Ingrid the truth. Lock the door and do not come out until I come for you."

He returned to the house. Too many things were wrong. There was no way to start any sort of cleaning tonight. His fingers twitched over his gun with every sound. He went upstairs and collected his money and Ingrid's, along with her letters. She was holding onto something that would get her killed, but she did not know what, nor did he. The fact that whoever it was didn't find them... They would be back. And that thought raised his hackles.

Two hours later, he put Cora on his horse's rump and rode out to the Coleman ranch. Just short of being in view of Joseph's house, Indians stopped him. He recognized the one and called him by name. "Falcon. I am Tiago. I have brought Cora with me. She needs protection, too."

"We are trying to keep everyone safe. We heard what happened."

"No, you only heard part of what has happened. It is worse, and Cora is now tangled in this."

Falcon rode beside them as they approached the house. The warm glow of lights shone through the windows as if welcoming Tiago to their home.

When he reined to a stop, Falcon jumped off his horse and helped a very scared Cora from Tiago's horse.

"Will you take care of my horse? I want to talk to Ingrid and the Colemans."

The Indian nodded, and Tiago took Cora's hand and led her into the house.

Alma threw her arms around her father.

"I love you, my darling, but you must stay with Virginia, as I have much to discuss with the adults," he said in Spanish, and then looked at Alisa Coleman who had joined them. "Please, may we have a moment with Ingrid, and then I will explain to you and your husband."

Alisa nodded. "Come, Alma."

"Is there someplace we can talk privately?"

Ingrid showed them the way to the room where Alisa taught her children lessons. "Will this work?"

Tiago nodded and seated Cora and then Ingrid. "Cora was home when they came. I found her tied and gagged in the privy."

He could see the color draining from Ingrid's face as she said, "Oh no!"

He looked at Cora. "Do you want me to tell her or do you?"

Cora shook her head.

"Cora was... I do not have your word for it. A

man forced his body on her."

Ingrid gasped.

"I have promised Cora that I will not abandon her. It is not her fault, nor is it yours. This evil must be stopped." He looked at Cora who was shaking. "I will leave you two alone so that you are free to talk. For such things are not discussed in front of men. I will tell the Colemans."

He found Joseph and Alisa in the parlor along with several family members. "Señora, maybe it is best if you join Cora and Ingrid."

Alisa rose and he put his hand out to stop her.

"It is important that you know that the men... They... Cora... They forced themselves on her."

"We shall discuss this outside," Joseph said, as he stood.

He followed Joseph onto the back porch. "I am not sure of the word."

Joseph answered without looking at him. "Rape."

Tiago nodded. "It is not a word that is used very much."

Joseph looked up. "Thank God."

Tiago leaned against a porch post. "I know you are thinking that trouble is following me. It is not. Trouble is following Ingrid." He scuffed his foot on the porch. "Her brother was killed during an investigation of some criminal activity. Someone believes that she knows what her brother knew. They will do anything to keep her quiet, including kill her."

"Does she have information?"

Tiago raised his shoulders and let them drop. "I know what she knows, and it's not much. But someone must think it is more." He shook his head. "She is too scared to talk to the one person who can help. There are times she is not sure about me."

"You are the man. Make her talk."

"I am a man, but I am not her family or her husband. She does not trust anyone."

Joseph chuckled. "She might not completely trust you, but I think she loves you. I can see it in her mannerisms."

"I no longer know what to think when it comes to her."

***

The following morning, Adie and Alisa, along with Alisa's two older girls, Issy and Clarissa, took off for town with several of the men from the ranch. Ingrid knew they were going to the house. The little bit of conversation at breakfast told her that they would clean up so that she and Cora did not have to face the mess. But that didn't make things easier. When Tiago said he wanted to talk to Ingrid, her heart fell someplace in her abdomen.

After supper, Tiago knocked on her bedroom

door and opened it, as though it was a normal thing for a man to do.

"You don't just enter my bedroom."

He laughed. "You are dressed and I would not care if you weren't." He strode to where she was sitting. "I would enjoy seeing you naked."

She took a swing at him.

He caught her hand. "Don't bite the dog that feeds you."

"It is don't bite the hand that feeds you."

"I do not care. You know what I mean." He sat on her bed and looked around. "I need to talk just to you. We will go outside."

She followed him downstairs, onto the porch, and into the bleak darkness of early winter in Wyoming.

Tiago paced in front of her as she sat on the porch swing.

"I read those letters again last night. You are sitting on information or they think that you are." He paced a few more times and stopped. "If they didn't think you had something against them, they wouldn't be coming after you."

She nodded.

"I agree there's nothing much in the letters that makes sense to us. But the letters need to go to Andy Lyles. Let him figure it out."

"No!"

"Yes. He is very high in the U.S. Treasury

department. If he could figure out who you are, so could plenty of other people who are looking for Ingrid Svensen. I wrote him last night and told him about your letters and what has happened. This has to come to an end before you are killed."

"I feel so horrible that they hurt Cora."

"Think about it. If Cora becomes with child, I will be blamed as the father because I have lived there."

Her hand went to her mouth and even in the darkness she could see the sadness in his eyes. "I did not think of that. It is true."

He nodded. "She cannot afford a child... I could marry her, but she is not the wife I want. I want you. I want to marry you."

"Me? How can you say that?"

"Because I have grown to love you. And Alma loves you as a mother. You are perfect for us." He shook his head and frowned. "I wanted to ask you after I had the house built - to prove that I was worthy of you. Now I am caught in a strange position. I do not want Cora to suffer the insults of a child born without marriage. None of this is her fault."

Inside Ingrid began to tremble. "So you will marry her?"

"I want to marry you, not her. I am torn."

Ingrid covered her face with her hands. She wanted to cry, scream, or do something other than sit on the Coleman porch and look at Tiago. Her heart went to Cora, but she knew it belonged to Tiago. "Yes. I can see how your reputation is at stake with the community. I should leave you. There is no place here for me. Maybe I could become lost in San Francisco and be safe there."

"You will never be safe while those men are alive. You need to give the letters to Andy Lyles."

"No. I cannot trust anyone with them. You read what my brother said. Even he did not know how high up...powerful men are behind it."

"Do you still think that I am or my family is part of it?"

Tears rolled down her cheeks and she brushed them away. "I do not know."

Ingrid turned away from him and walked off the porch. She turned back once and looked at Tiago. Her heart was saying one thing, and her head was saying the opposite. She wanted to make love to him, wanted to strip him naked, and see his glorious body. Her insides trembled with the thought that he might marry Cora.

She walked to the back of the house and tried to get a grip on her emotions. As she stepped into the kitchen, she spotted Alisa at the stove. Then she spotted the parsley. "What are you doing?"

Alisa turned and smiled. "I am making a very special tea just for Cora. In three days, she will feel much better."

"That is dangerous - poor man's medicine."

"Not so dangerous and it works." Alisa stirred the parsley into the water. "I am a woman helping another woman. I have the herbs and the knowledge. She does not need to find herself with child."

Ingrid shook her head and ran up the stairs to the room where she and Cora were staying. The desire to warn Cora of what would happen if she drank the tea was replaced by the thought of Tiago marrying Cora. The need to run away overwhelmed her. "I am sorry, Cora, I'm not ready to sleep."

"I understand. I doubt sleep will come easily for me."

Ingrid nodded and slipped out of the room, down the stairs, and to the kitchen. She smiled at Alisa. "I want to step outside. Maybe the fresh air will help clear my head and allow me to sleep."

"Yes. That often helps when there are too many thoughts in the head. I will take this to Cora, and then make us some warm milk to drink. By then you will be ready for it."

She didn't want warm milk. She wanted to get as far away as possible. Creed's Crossing was no longer safe, and as long as she was here, everyone around her was in the devil's way. Putting her coat on, she spotted a can of shoe polish. If she used it on her hair, her hair would not be blonde and no one would recognize her. She dropped the can into her pocket and stepped onto the back porch. A gust of cold air made her sharply inhale.

"Can't sleep?" Joseph Coleman asked.

Her entire body instantly quaked. "I did not know you were here."

"I doubt anyone feels much like sleeping. Too many unknowns. You were lucky they did not find you."

She nodded. "Forgive me. I need some time alone."

"I understand."

She stepped off the porch and walked to where several horses stood in a corral. Tiago's steed came to her and she petted his long face. "Want to go for a ride, boy?"

The sound of a door closing caused her to turn and look at the house. She wasn't certain who joined Joseph, but she thought it might be Frank. Crossing the yard, she slipped into the shadows and quietly pulled the barn door open. A small lantern was lit in the far corner, but she didn't see anyone. Certainly no one would purposely leave a light lit in the barn.

Hefting a saddle into her arms, she tucked it to one hip, went to the lantern hanging on a wooden peg, turned the wheel on the wick, and watched as the last flicker of light died. With the saddle tightly clutched in her arms, she stepped back and found herself against a strong chest. A yelp rose from her throat.

"What are you doing out here?" Tiago asked. "And where do you think you're going?" He lifted the saddle from her hold. "You've got to stop running from your problem and face it. Otherwise it will always be there, ready to tap on your shoulder. Furthermore, you are not the only one with a problem. Your problems have become my problems, and they have cost me more than I want to consider."

"What do you want me to say? I'm sorry?"

"Not if you don't mean it."

She heaved a sigh. "I am sorry. But do you not see that the problems keep mounting because I am here?"

"You need to put a stop to them by telling someone what you know. Let those who have the authority go after the men who are doing illegal things. And where do you think you can go without money?"

"I will serve whiskey and beer if I must."

"You silly girl. To make money, they serve more than drinks." He grabbed her chin between his thumb and forefinger. "Why do I love you so much?"

His lips touched hers. Instantly her body warmed from his kiss. Then his lips drifted over her cheek to her ear and words whispered in Spanish filled her ear with warm breath. She clung to his jacket and prayed her knees would support her.

She knew what he was saying, knew he was professing his love, and she didn't want to stop the delicious feeling he sent through her.

He had her pressed to the wooden wall that separated this room from the others in the large barn. His kisses had become more insistent and she no longer understood his breathy words. She pushed against his chest, except she didn't have the strength to move the solid mass of a man. Her stomach clenched as a pearl of fear rolled through her.

He was crushing her between the wall and his body. His mouth covered hers and she could no longer find a breath. She turned her head and managed to squeak a tiny no.

He laughed, deep and throaty. It was a sound that she loved, but not this time.

"No!" she repeated.

"No to what, my beautiful darling?"

She pushed on his chest and he stepped back.

"Are you trying to kill me by taking my air?"

"Don't hold your breath when I kiss you."

She tried to dodge past him, but he held onto her.

"You are not going to run away again." He grabbed some twine from another peg on the wall. "You are staying with me."

"You can't… You wouldn't."

"I will. You are the most stubborn woman I've

ever known. Spanish women know how to obey. Alas, you are not Spanish. You are sunshine and moonbeams wrapped up in a fierce wind."

Holding onto her wrist, he forced her to lie on a blanket that had been placed on a pile of hay. And proceeded to tie her hands to a wooden post.

She attempted to kick him.

"Do it again, and I will tie your feet, too."

16

Tiago rested next to Ingrid in the straw bed.

She huffed and rolled away from him.

He placed one hand on her back and resisted the urge to do more. There was no doubt in his mind that she loved him, but her stubbornness kept her from giving into her heart. She needed to confide in him, but she still didn't trust him. Her inability to trust was the wedge between them, and it hurt. If she trusted him, she wouldn't still be running. You would wrap your arms around me, and put your head on my chest to sleep. What can I do to show you how much I love you and how much I care?

He got up once, found a folded blanket, and put it on them. It was cold but not too cold. The heavy log building was good at keeping the severe cold out, but it was still cold, too cold for Ingrid to take off alone, and he was determined to protect her from herself. He snuggled against her back and listened to her groan.

"I'm not going to do anything to you. You forget that you are a lady, but I have not forgotten that I am a gentleman." Or at least I am trying to be. This is not going to be easy.

"Then untie me."

"No."

In fitful bursts, he managed to sleep until morning light seeped into the barn. He untied her wrists and watched her for a moment. She was so different from the other women he knew. She had an inner strength about her and would never be a meek wife. Growing up without a mother meant she hadn't been duped into a prissy role. Physically she was tough as any man. And she never complained. She carried on no matter what. It was both aggravating and delightful.

He walked away from her and then outside into the sunshine, but stopped long enough to drop the latch on the door. "José, don't let her out. I'm holding you responsible."

The young man nodded. "Si, señor."

As Tiago sat at the table, Joseph looked up. "Ingrid went into the barn and never came out. You kept her with you?"

"Yes. She was determined to take off by herself last night. I kept her to keep her safe and she is still there."

Alisa raised her eyebrows. "Safe? In the company of a man?"

"I am a gentleman. She was quite safe."

"Such behavior is not tolerated in this house."

Tiago couldn't hold back his chuckle. "We weren't in the house. We were in the barn. But my behavior would have been the same. I know not to touch a woman who is not mine. She was safe with me."

Cora's cheeks grew bright red. "He stayed at her side when she almost froze to death. I know he was a gentleman. And I know what he did for me when he found me yesterday."

Joseph never looked up. "But the temptation can be too great to risk such a thing."

Tiago laughed as he slipped an egg onto his plate. "Ingrid would kill me if I wasn't. And I am certain that she is not happy with me this morning for preventing her from running away. She's afraid that she will cause problems here."

Joseph pushed a piece of bread into the yolk and sopped the runny yellow. "That is why I have men patrolling. We take care of ourselves. Always have."

"I owe you much."

Joseph brushed his hand through the air. "My mother and father stood over this ground with Cheéte and protected it from more than a few threats. It is my job to do the same."

"Who is Cheéte?" Tiago asked.

"The Crow who helped my family - Falcon and Bear's father. If it had not been for him, we probably would not have survived."

Tiago looked at both the Crow men, and then at Falcon's son Chase, but Chase had his eyes on Cora.

Joseph picked up his strip of bacon. "It has not been a hardship, as you have provided men to this ranch. We take turns."

"And I need to take food to Ingrid." He started to stand and take his plate.

"I will take your plate and bring you a warm plate for Ingrid," Issy said, as she took the plate from his hand. "More coffee, anyone?"

A few minutes later, he left with a metal plate that contained more food than Ingrid would probably eat. Ingrid was rattling the barn door screaming for someone to release her. "You have done well, José."

Ingrid rammed him like a train and he laughed. "My you are feisty this morning. Now eat so you have more strength. Maybe then you will knock me off my feet."

She took a swing at him, but he caught it and dragged her back inside.

"How dare you!"

"What? Keep you safe? Now eat."

"And what am I supposed to eat it with - my fingers?"

"You think I will give you a fork to stab me?"

"I am not putting my fingers in my food."

"Then I will feed you from my fingers."

She curled her lip at him.

"Lovers do not snarl when they feed each other." He let go of her and she attempted another swing. "Shall I tie you again?"

"You will not rule me!"

"Then sit and eat."

She sat and stared at the plate on her lap. "I am not eating with my fingers."

He squatted in front of her. "Then open wide, my little bird."

***

Part of her did not believe he intended to feed her, and it was all she could do to keep from biting his fingers. But each morsel tasted delicious, and when he licked a crumb from her lips, she thought she might die on the spot. Why did he have to be so wonderful?

For the next few days, he kept her in the barn with him until she complained of wanting a bath. Then he accompanied her into the house to her room to get her clothes, and then to the bathing room. While he stood guard outside the door, she sank into the warm water. Fighting him was useless. She couldn't imagine a more bullheaded man. Yet his constant nearness made her chest heave. She slipped further into the water and hoped the sensation would pass. *If I put my face under, how long would it take?*

She slipped down further until she had covered her nose and mouth.

"Dios!" He yanked her out of the water and then wrapped her in a towel. "You are loco! I cannot trust you for two seconds."

She sputtered, coughed, and then asked, "How did you know?"

"I have ears. And you have the most beautiful body, but that was not the way I wanted to see it."

She pushed her chin up and out. "So look." She pulled the towel from her body. "Take me if you want. Because that is what all men want."

He leaned against the door with his arms crossed over his chest and stared at her. "You are pink and blonde. A real beauty...fit to be an angel. Now get dressed."

"No. Take me. Or are you not enough of a man?"

"Oh. I am a man and I will have you, after I have married you. I only need to keep you alive long enough to do that."

Once she was dressed, he took her to the kitchen and let her have a cup of coffee. "If you can behave yourself, I'll let you chat with Alisa, Adie, and Cora."

Inside she seethed. Did anyone see what was happening? For them to have hope, meant she had to leave. The women chatted about food and children. Her very presence was enough to destroy all of it.

***

Tiago enjoyed the visit from Mark Hunter and his wife Malene. The man had been prepared to help build Tiago's house, but under the circumstances, there was nothing to be done. But Tiago worried about Malene traveling when she was with child.

Mark was an unusual man. He looked like an Indian with his long hair, coloring, and facial features, yet dressed like a white man. But when he spoke, it was obvious that he was an intelligent man.

Mark laughed. "She's healthy and fine. And I am always nearby." He pointed to the youngest child Malene had with her. "I brought that one into the world and I will do it again. Women are easier than horses. At least, women listen and do as instructed. Try explaining to a mare."

Tiago laughed, but he was slightly shocked. He could not imagine even being present during the birth of his children. That was something between women.

Tiago was also surprised at how well behaved all of Malene's children were. They had their schoolbooks with them and would join the others in Alisa's classroom. But what really surprised him was how much the children, especially the three orphans Malene had acquired, loved Mark and respected him.

In facial features, Tiago could tell Falcon and Bear belonged to the same tribe as Mark, but Indians on the Coleman ranch acted and dressed like the rest of the Coleman family. Mark had hair that hung below his waist. He had a broad chest and strong arms, yet he was gentle with all the women, and played on the floor with Adie's little girls as though they were sweet kittens. And when Virginia wasn't looking, he swept her off her feet and tossed her in the air as if she were a feather.

She squealed and played with him. It was obvious there was a special bond between them, but Tiago did not understand it. Mark would chase her upstairs to get ready for the night, and then she would return with a book to read. The man often struggled with printed words, but Virginia would stay curled in his lap until she was sound asleep. Then he would carry her upstairs to her bed.

Adie and her sister spent hours together and wanted Ingrid to join them.

Tiago threatened Ingrid and let her join the young women.

At the end of the week, Mark and Malene went home, leaving Tiago without his own barn and a woman he couldn't trust out of his sight. As much as he enjoyed Mark's company, the visit left Tiago with a sense of sadness, and the realization that he would not have what he wanted anytime soon. *Why am I being punished when I have done nothing wrong?*

***

A few days became weeks, and being constantly tied to Tiago's side bothered Ingrid. Then Andy Lyles appeared, except this time he didn't look the same. Had it not been for the distinctive blue and yellow flecks of color of his green eyes, she would not have believed it was the same man.

He took his hat off and placed it beside him in the barn. His unkempt, dirty hair fell over his forehead and onto his shoulders. He dressed and smelled of a man who had been working cattle and not the least bit like an investigator for the U.S. Treasury.

Tiago talked at length to him and then produced the letters from her brother to her father. Andy read through each one - twice. "What else do you know?"

Ingrid looked at Tiago, and from the stern look on his face, she knew she had better answer. "I only know that my brother was killed someplace along the Santa Fe run. A week after receiving the news, my father was killed as he returned to our house from seeing a patient. He'd been shot in the back three times. Murdered. Three different types of bullets and three different angles."

"How would you know such a thing?"

She stuck her chin out and prayed her trembling didn't show. "I prepared his body for burial." She glanced at Tiago and then returned her gaze to the strange man. "My father was a doctor. I often assisted him."

Andy flipped through the letters one more time and lifted three. "These are the ones we need. I'm going to suggest you destroy the rest."

She nodded and took the letters from him. "This is all I have left of my brother."

"Burn them. Chances are when he was killed, his pockets were rifled. Partially written letters from him to you or his father would point the men to you." The man tented his fingers and brought them to his lips. "For us, this is not over. There is a huge illegal land grab from the government, but within that conspiracy are men willing to do almost anything for money. Your brother knew too much, but not enough to realize how dangerous things were for him. He merely put two and two together, because he was so close to them." Andy looked at Tiago. "In a few weeks, this will come to an end. Not all of it, but enough for you to be safe again. Joseph Coleman has built a fortress of men around this ranch. Until we have completed our investigation and have arrested everyone, you need to stay where you are."

"How will we know?" Ingrid asked.

"I will personally let you know. Do not believe the newspapers. Sometimes the wrong information is released on purpose."

"You have my last letter from my brother, but you know nothing about a Mr. Carmines or a Mr. Hawkins."

Andy cocked his head. "What do you know?"

"I was listening to conversations. I heard their names along with Douglass while…" She blushed. "While spying on the sheriff and his friends. The names were spoken in very hushed tones."

Andy smiled. "Anything else?"

"Mason, but I do not know if that is a first or last name."

"Any more names?"

She shook her head. "No."

"Miz Svensen, I assure you this will be over in a few weeks. I only wish you had told me when I first came. But I understand your fear. Please be assured that the Colemans, your friend Cora, the residents of Creed's Crossing, and the Colima family, have all been investigated." He looked at Tiago. "I am sorry, sir. It is a precaution that we had to take. We must be absolutely certain before we can make a move."

Tiago nodded. "It is understandable. Ingrid knew someone with money was behind this, and she has had her doubts about everyone, including me."

Andy put his hand out to Ingrid. "I promise. His

family is an old and highly regarded one, known for their honesty. They've never had any dealings with any of the men we've been investigating. They will take a few cents less on their beef than deal with a stockyard known for its unethical practices."

Ingrid nodded and shook Andy's hand. "Thank you for telling me. Will it really be over?"

"I believe it won't take us long. I wish your brother still worked for us, and I wish you had trusted me sooner." He stood and brushed the straw from his pants. "I will return with good news. And if you ever want a job as a spy, write to me. We could use a few good women. You know how to keep your mouth closed, use a gun, and listen to conversations. But the next time you decide to run away, change the color of your hair, your first name, and use something more imaginative than Smith."

Tiago laughed. "When this is over, I'm marrying her. I'll keep her busy with babies."

Andy pushed his hair from his forehead, placed his leather hat on his head, and pulled it low on his forehead, casting a dark shadow over most of his face. He said a few words to Tiago in what sounded like perfect Spanish, making Tiago laugh as he took Andy's hand.

Tiago opened the barn door and stood outside, watching the man ride off.

Ingrid joined Tiago and tucked her hand into his.

He squeezed her hand. "Feeling better?"

She nodded. "But still scared. What did he say to you? I didn't understand enough for it to make sense."

"He warned me to be very good, for the women on this ranch are known marksmen."

"Why would he say that?"

He shrugged. "I heard the men talking. Adie killed a man in a street who tried to kill Mark Hunter."

"Malene's husband?"

He nodded. "And Frank's oldest sister killed the two men who shot her grandmother. I think that is enough to make any man think twice."

She giggled. "Maybe you are lucky they have not shot you for holding me prisoner."

"It has gone through my mind while you sleep next to me." He squeezed her hand again. "I want you, my darling. I want you naked in my bed."

Heat rose to her cheeks. "And I, too, know how to use a gun."

"You don't need one to protect yourself from me, for I will never hurt you or take what is not mine."

"So why tie me up every night?"

He laughed and looked up at the sky. "So you don't rip my clothes off of me while I sleep."

Her fist connected with his side.

"Ugh! Why did you do that?" He rubbed his side.

"When I said you are as strong as any man, I meant it." He lifted her still fisted hand to his mouth and kissed it. "I need to talk to Alisa. The temperature is dropping and those clouds look like snow is on the way. I don't think you'll be sleeping in the barn tonight. I won't take you to the bunkhouse with the other men. Alisa isn't going to be very happy with me."

***

Alisa and Joseph agreed to the sleeping arrangement under the condition that the door remain open. And since Tiago couldn't lock her in the barn, he had no choice other than to hog tie her long enough for him to take a bath. He made her sit with her back to the tub, but the minute he left her, she wiggled until she faced him.

"You are terrible." He chuckled.

"You think I do not know what a man looks like?"

"Then why look?"

She huffed and wiggled so her back was to him.

"Be polite. It's darn difficult being a gentleman."

She didn't answer and he laughed as he slipped into the warm water. Quickly he washed and just as quickly, he stepped out, dried off, and pulled on his union suit.

Again, she wiggled and watched as he brushed

his teeth. "Would you like to inspect each one and make certain I didn't miss anything?"

She wiggled again so her back was to him.

He laughed and untied her. "Let's get you into bed."

That night, Cora, Ingrid, and he sat and chatted in their beds well past bedtime. Cora spoke of Chase and it was obvious that she was smitten with him.

Tiago looked at Ingrid and then at Cora. He cupped his hands over his stomach. "Are you?"

Cora's face turned bright red. "No."

"You are lucky." He grabbed the rope he used to tie Ingrid and, after looking at the solid headboard, he tied her to him. Something told him she wasn't going to run, but he didn't want to chance it.

As Cora blew out the candle in their room, Ingrid rolled onto her side and dragged his arm over her.

Tiago muffled his laugh. "Must you make it so difficult for me?"

"You are the one who tied me," Ingrid whispered.

"Then I shall enjoy our night."

"Don't you dare!"

"What are you daring me to do? I'm very good with dares."

"Shh!" Cora giggled.

Tiago chuckled. "Then tell her to go to sleep. She's keeping me awake."

"Go to sleep, Ingrid, before we all get into trouble

with Alisa."

Ingrid snuggled her back to his chest and stomach.

"It's going to be a very long night," he moaned.

"That's your problem. Not mine."

"It might become yours," he whispered.

"Shh!" Cora admonished.

He tried to keep his mind off the beautiful woman in the bed and attempt to find some sleep. But it didn't come easily.

Morning came too soon and he realized the family was stirring. When Frank passed by the open door, Tiago called in a low voice.

Frank backed up. "Did you call me?"

"Yes. Is anyone in the small room?"

Frank shook his head.

Tiago undid the knot that bound him to Ingrid. "Stand guard. I will only be a minute." He relieved himself and returned to the room. "Thanks."

He pulled his clothes over his union suit and sat on the bed watching Ingrid. How have I managed to be this good?

That thought sent him back to his days growing up. His family was really no different than the Coleman's, except his family was wealthy and his mother only oversaw the servants and the kitchen. Here Alisa did everything.

He thought about his daughter asleep in the room

with Virginia. She had not spoken a single word since the day she purposely tumbled from that horse. Ingrid said that her voice was intact. Alisa promised she was learning and at a quick pace. Everyone agreed she'd talk when she was ready.

The aroma of coffee and food made him realize he was hungry. He heard the sounds of Virginia and Alma as they went into the little room. He stood and waited for Alma to appear. She ran into his arms and he picked her up.

She pointed to Ingrid who was still asleep.

"Yes, she is sleeping."

She squirmed from his arms and jumped onto Ingrid's bed.

Ingrid awakened slightly confused. Then held the child tightly to her. "How's my Alma?"

Alma grinned.

"You are bright eyed this morning."

Alma ran to the window and pointed.

"What?"

She pointed again.

Ingrid looked at him and got out of bed. "It's snowing! What fun! Maybe we can play in the snow today."

There was nothing he wanted more than to see his daughter and Ingrid laughing together. Yes, there is. I want to hear Alma's voice again.

Part Three

17

After breakfast, Tiago watched Ingrid and Alma play in the falling snow. He'd never seen much snow in his lifetime, and from the way Ingrid was acting, he was certain that she hadn't either. Lydia's boys came outside with José and played, as did Clarissa and Issy.

Alisa set several bowls out and threatened everyone to stay away from them. Tiago couldn't imagine why anyone would collect snow in a bowl or why she would want it.

Lydia's boys scooped snow into balls and began to toss them at one another. Soon the girls had joined the fight. Adie milked the cows, and then the goats before she fed the chickens. Then she vanished back inside. All the normal chores were being done except the children were not having their daily lessons.

Alisa called everyone inside and had made warm

sweet milk for the family to go with a batch of cookies. After the unexpected midmorning snack, she sent the children to find books to read. Cora pitched in and did laundry. Ingrid came to him and motioned that she needed to go upstairs.

It didn't take much for him to recognize the signs of her womanhood. He waited for her at the top of the stairs. The last time this had happened, they were in the barn. Being in the house was easier for both of them.

That night, Ingrid went right to sleep. But when he woke, they were untied and Ingrid was sound asleep beside him. He couldn't believe she had managed to undo the knot without him knowing it, but she had. He kissed her cheek and took care of his morning rituals, then returned to the bedroom where he pulled clean clothes over his union suit.

Ingrid woke with a smile.

"Did you fail to tie yourself back to me?"

"Oops."

"And how often have you done that?"

"I didn't want to disturb you. Besides, it was all I could do to untie the knot with one hand. If I tried to retie it you would have awakened and then accused me of trying to run away."

"I'm glad you didn't run."

"I feel like a prisoner."

"You are not. I've only tried to protect you from

killing yourself."

"When will it be over?"

He shook his head. "Andy said he would tell us. I am as trapped as you. Shall we go downstairs?"

As he drank his morning coffee, he noticed the bowls of snow were now covered and sitting on the porch. He was still confused about this careful preservation of snow. But his confusion came to an abrupt end as he drank his coffee and watched Alisa put all the snow into a large pan and then mix cream into the snow along with a jar of canned fruit that she had pressed through a sieve until it was nothing more than a slurry.

"Who wants snow cream?" Alisa called.

Everyone dove for their seats at the dining room table. She ladled it out until there was only a tiny mouthful left and she put that in her bowl. Joseph stood and shared half of his with her. His kindness towards his wife always showed, and Tiago admired Joseph for his thoughtfulness.

The days began to tick by and one week ran into another. Standing guard over Ingrid almost made no sense. She seemed happy and hadn't tried to run, but he still didn't completely trust her. He made her follow him out to the stable while he worked with Joseph. Winter was for repairing things and taking extra care of things like saddles and harnesses. Frank and a few men went into town weekly for mail and other things.

Adie came to the barn. "I think these are for you."

"Thank you." Tiago stood and took the letters and package from Adie.

"Frank said there was mail in the box with your name, but he didn't touch it."

"No. No one is allowed to know we are here. It's not safe. We don't know who is watching."

He peeked in the package and opened the letters, but when he saw the one from his mom he wanted to leap for joy. Tortillas! He asked Joseph, "Do you have lime?"

He gathered a bucket of dried corn and the lime and went into the kitchen. There he tried to explain to Alisa, but she looked at him with a blank face. "Then I will make it."

His mother often joined the women when they made tortillas, but he only had her words to follow. He prayed he could carry out her instructions. He put water in a large pan, added the lime, and stirred.

Alisa's eyes grew wide.

Then he added the dried corn kernels to the water, removed any floating kernels, and watched the water boil for several minutes. He burnt his fingers trying to take the hot pan from the stove. Starting to curse, he swallowed the words even though they were in Spanish. No matter what language, it was not proper to curse in front of women, and he had most of the grown women in the Coleman household watching his every move. He shook his hand and grimaced.

Alisa attempted to grab his hand.

"I will be fine." He looked at his burned left hand and realized it contained several small blisters.

"Use this to lift that pan." Alisa handed him two heavy cloths sewn into squares.

He poured the boiled-with-lime corn into her sieve and rinsed it with cold water.

Alisa peered over his shoulder along with Adie, while Lydia and Ingrid stood beside him. He rinsed until he was certain his fingers would never recover from so much cold water, but the cold water felt good on his burned hand. He finally turned to Ingrid. "Please keep rinsing and rubbing the kernels together to get rid of all the lime water."

Alisa looked over his shoulder. "The corn is now white."

He nodded. "My mother said it would turn white. We need towels. The corn must dry."

Alisa spread towels on her bench that she used for making bread and other things. Handful by handful, the corn was transferred from the sieve to another pan of clear water. That corn was lifted from the water and spread on the towels.

"Tonight, we eat my food!"

Ingrid looked at Alisa. The kitchen was far from hot, but Alisa was red-faced and sweating as through it was the hottest day of the year. The change? Ingrid smiled. "Do you have a mill for grinding? I've only seen it rolled on stones."

Alisa went to her pantry and brought out a mill. "I use it to make cornmeal."

Tiago smiled and let out a breath. He blotted the corn on the towels. "You know how to make tortillas, Ingrid?"

"Not exactly, but I've seen several Mexican women make them," she answered.

"When it is dry, it needs to be ground. The rest should be easy."

Alisa shook her head. "You have enough corn for me to feed a whole town."

"According to my mother this feeds the house once."

That night they had tortillas filled with ground meat and cheese. They weren't quite as thin and uniform as his mother made, but they tasted delicious. Alisa served raw onions with them, and her pickled cactus. Tiago piled everything onto his tortilla.

The children laughed as they ate with their fingers. The tortillas cracked and fell apart, scattering the food onto their plates.

José laughed. "You must learn to hang onto your food, Virginia."

Alisa declared them delicious and so did Adie and

Frank. Joseph wasn't as thrilled with the messy meal, but swore it tasted good and was an interesting change.

"Our meat is spicier, but I do not know what my mother uses."

Alisa smiled. "Then write to her and find out."

"I shall."

A week before Christmas, Joseph found a pine tree, cut it down, and brought it inside. The children decorated it with bits of colored paper. Tiago took a scrap piece of tin from the barn and polished it with ashes from the stove before cutting it into strips, punching a small hole in each one, and twirling them. Alisa loved the shiny objects, and hung them on the tree with bits of ribbon.

It was a poor man's Christmas, but no one seemed to notice. His family had a beautiful tree that went almost to the ceiling and was covered in imported ornaments from Spain and Italy. On Christmas Eve, when family and friends gathered at the house, his mother and father would light the tiny candles that covered it. It was magical even as an adult.

In the Coleman house, the women made cookies and sang songs as they prepared for the holiday. Lydia's boys asked for trains and when he heard that they weren't getting very much, he threatened Ingrid to stay in the house while he retreated to the barn. With only a few woodworking tools, he managed to make trains for the boys cut from some pieces of scrap lumber. They were solid and sturdy. He used a heated rod and decorated the plain wood. They weren't fancy trains, but the wheels turned and he was certain Lydia's boys had enough imagination to enjoy the primitive toys.

Now he felt bad about giving Ingrid her present when no one else was getting anything fancy. He made a last minute decision not to place his package under the tree, but to give it to her when they were alone.

Christmas Eve began with a meal of ham, pickled beets, and mashed potatoes. Then Virginia read from the Bible about the birth of Jesus. Christmas morning, the children dashed into the parlor and opened their presents. With Frank's help, Tiago had managed to buy two dolls, one for Alma and one for Virginia. Frank and Adie's twins had little push toys and Lydia's boys were given kites and a board game.

But it was the trains that the boys loved. He tickled each boy on the back of the neck. "I'll get you each a train that runs on a track."

He motioned to Ingrid and took her outside to the barn. "I wasn't certain about this morning when I noticed the adults didn't have presents."

She took the package and opened it. Her eyes widened as she lifted the fancy turquoise jewelry from the box. "They are beautiful. But how did you manage...?"

"I asked my mother for help. I wrote the letter. Adie sent it to her mom, who sent it to my mom. My mother bought the jewelry, and sent them addressed to Adie's mother, who sent them to Adie." He slipped the bracelet on Ingrid's wrist and fastened it. "I am as trapped as you, and this looks so much better than rope." He undid the top few buttons on her blouse and put the necklace on her. He undid a few more buttons and slid the shirt to the edge of her shoulders. "Our women expose more skin. It entices a man."

"You don't need to be enticed."

"No, I don't."

She leaned up and kissed him. He drew her into his arms. Heat coursed through him and he knew he had to end the kiss. "When this is over, I will marry you." He stood back and admired the jewels around her neck. He whispered, "I love you."

"I feel terrible. I had intended to knit a sweater for you, but my yarn and needles were left at Cora's."

He took her hands into his and kissed her fingers. "I will look forward to it next year. For this year is not what either one of us had planned, but at least you are here with me."

Days and weeks dragged on. Frustration mounted and weighed on him, but he knew it weighed on Ingrid, too.

E. Ayers

Just as he rolled out of bed one morning, he heard a gunshot. Pulling his pants on, he flew down the stairs, but was greeted by Alisa who had a slight smile on her face.

"Go back to bed if you wish. There's no cause for alarm." She dropped the rifle into the rack near the back door.

"What happened?"

"Wolf."

He looked out the door and saw a wolf lying on the ground near the chicken house. Barefooted he ran out and realized it had been shot once between the eyes. He swallowed and returned to the house. "They rarely are alone."

"I know. There were three of them, but the other two ran off. Joseph is going to come with me while I milk the cows."

"Would he like me to come, too?"

She shook her head. "No. Go back to sleep."

He went back upstairs and stepped into the little room for morning rituals, and when he came out, Ingrid was standing by the door.

She covered her bottom lip with her front teeth. "What happened?"

"A wolf."

"Oh, no."

"It's dead, but there are two more out there."

"If it is not man, it is beast."

"It has been that way since Cain killed Abel." He stepped out of the bathing room and waited for her to use it.

He led her back to the bedroom. She slipped between the covers of the bed. He followed her and whispered, "Give me your hand."

"Please do not tie me."

"Maybe you need to tie me this morning." Holding onto her hand, he rolled so his back was to her and then pressed her hand to his heart. "I cannot continue to sleep with you. It is becoming too much. I am a normal man with the natural desire for a woman. And you are a very beautiful woman."

Ingrid giggled. "Thank you. I know how difficult it is for you. I know what must be in your dreams. But you have kept your word."

"I need you to keep yours and not leave from here. We have waited this long - we can wait a little longer." But deep inside he was beginning to doubt that they would find freedom and peace.

***

Ingrid watched as the men went to plow fields. It was the dead of winter, but Joseph was getting ready to plant wheat. It was a different way of life on a ranch, and with everyone in the house, there was plenty to do, but plenty of hands to do it. The women took turns doing certain chores, which kept Alisa free to teach. Ingrid enjoyed teaching and often joined Alisa. Frequently, Ingrid worked with José who was still struggling with English. But the boy was learning.

Alisa said he was much further along in his knowledge of science and mathematics, but it was his English that was still holding him back. She worried about his end of year exams, so she often spent extra time with him.

Alma, as usual, was moving ahead with her studies. Alisa slowed her down by adding other things to her curriculum and stressing penmanship. Alma had already passed Lydia's boys in reading and mathematics, and was nipping on Virginia's heels. Alma was gifted and Ingrid hoped that one day Alma would go to college.

Ingrid had wanted to go for further studies when she read about a special college for women in Pennsylvania, but her father needed her and needed an assistant. She read her father's books on anatomy and medicine. Other young women learned to stitch pillows, and she learned to stitch skin. She hadn't realized how much she missed her father until tears formed in her eyes.

"Would you like to play in the dirt with me this afternoon?"

Ingrid looked up from the tub of soapy water

filled with laundry to see Alisa standing in the doorway. She smiled at the woman and answered, "I have no idea what game we would play with dirt."

Alisa laughed. "You will see."

At home, Ingrid did laundry once a week. Living with Cora meant washing once a week, but in this big household, laundry was done everyday except Sundays. The little stove in the laundry room wasn't much bigger than the one Cora had in her privy, but it kept the room warm. As she finished each piece, she hung it on the drying line that was strung across the room several times. It had taken her most of the morning to wash and she was glad when she had finished hanging the last petticoat. She emptied the water from the tubs, dried her hands and mopped the floor.

At noon, they had a simple meal, as the men had carried food with them so that they did not have to return. After the meal, the children were free to read and study on their own. Adie sat at Alisa's sewing machine and did some mending.

Ingrid stared at Alisa. They were about the same height and had the same color of golden blonde hair. Ingrid wondered if she were looking at herself in another twenty-five years, for Alisa resembled her in so many ways. "May I ask what your maiden name was?"

"Anker. Edgar Anker was my father and Mabel

Dolci Anker was my mother."

"D-o-l-c-i?"

"Yes." She giggled. "I wasn't much different from the mail order brides of today. Our grandmothers knew each other and Joseph and I started writing to each other."

"Do you have family in Delaware?"

She shrugged. "My father came from a big family, and so did my mother."

Ingrid held up her finger, and then ran upstairs to retrieve her Bible. She returned to the kitchen. "Here. Dolci. This was my mother's Bible."

Alisa took the Bible and studied the family tree. "Follow me." In the parlor, she took her Bible and opened it to its family tree. Several of the names matched. Alisa grinned. "I think we are related."

Alisa took the Bibles to her writing desk and carefully copied the extra names into hers. "Would you like to add these names to your Bible?"

Ingrid nodded and then took Alisa's spot and added the other family members.

"From the minute I first saw you, I thought you looked like you could have been my daughter. Now I realize we are distant cousins."

The discovery of family, and in particular this family, made Ingrid's heart want to take flight. She couldn't stop her smile and her feet didn't feel as though they touched the ground as she followed

Alisa out the back door. The sharp inhale of cold air brought Ingrid's mind back to reality.

Alisa grabbed what she called wooden flats and then opened the worm box that sat next to the porch. Taking an old, large wooden spoon, Alisa pushed the top layer of table scraps off to the side and began to fill a flat with what appeared to be moist crumbly dirt. Ingrid watched fascinated. She knew that Alisa would occasionally check the box and then send Lydia's boys to find worms. And when the men went fishing, they would dig through the box for worms.

"Now, fill your flat, but leave the worms." Alisa instructed as she moved her flat from the edge of the big box.

It was warm working over the worm box and it didn't take long for Ingrid to fill her flat and, just when she thought she was finished, a wiggly worm appeared in her flat. She tried to catch the worm on the spoon, but gave up, plucked it out with her fingers, and shuddered as she dropped the legless creature back into the big wooden bin.

They put the flats on the kitchen table and Alisa began to pick through the dirt, lifting little capsules from it, and placed them in a bowl. "Search yours for worm eggs. We will take these back outside to the bin. Also remove any large object."

Alisa smiled as she worked. "I love playing in the dirt. I feel like a child, except as a child, I never did play in the dirt."

"Neither did I. My father did not like me to get dirty. And where did all this dirt come from?"

"It's worm castings."

Ingrid lifted her hands from the soil. "Poop?"

Alisa laughed. "Best kind of dirt."

Ingrid's stomach clenched when she looked at her hands and fingernails.

Alisa gently flattened the soil. Using a farrier nail, she drew lines through the dirt. On wooden slivers, she wrote the names of several vegetables. "Place every seed about three inches apart. It makes it easier to lift the tiny plants into the garden."

Some of the seeds were no bigger than fly spots. As they finished each flat, they stacked it on an open shelf system in front of the windows in the laundry room, grabbed another flat, and repeated the process several more times. As they finished up, Adie came into the kitchen with two little girls who had awakened from their afternoon naps.

Ingrid watched as Alisa went to the garden and added a shovel full of dirt to the ash bucket and dumped it onto the worm bin. Then she called one of Lydia's boys to go find a cow muffin, the boy dashed out of the house, seemingly thrilled to get away from daily lessons. With a short-handled shovel and a bucket, he took off across the field. A minute later, he screamed. Four men raced from the stables in the direction of the child's cries.

"Stay," Alisa instructed as she put on her coat and flew out the back door.

A moment later, she returned. "I'm afraid the boys have picked up the fear that has kept us hunkered down here all winter. I'm also not happy to see our visitors."

"I would go for the men, but I cannot leave my batter - it will be ruined by the time I return," Adie offered.

"I will send Clarissa. The men are on foot." Alisa called to her next to the youngest daughter. "Clarissa take Virginia and go get your father. We have Shoshones."

"What are Shoshones?" Ingrid whispered.

"The tribe to the west of us. The Crow and the Shoshones have always been rivals. They don't like the fact that Crows live here, off the reservation, when they are stuck on theirs," Adie said, as she beat her batter.

"Will they harm us?" Ingrid asked.

Adie shook her head. "They have never harmed this family, but the tales of them years ago were not so good. Apparently Clare Coleman saved the life of a Shoshone, and they have never forgotten it."

"So why are they off the reservation?"

Adie shrugged. "They have probably come looking for food."

Bear walked into the house, lifted the rifle from above the back door, and strode to the room where the children were doing lessons. He called over his shoulder. "I don't like this."

"Calm down," Adie called.

"You know there are more out there," Bear bellowed from the other room.

"And they know we are kind to them. So hold your tongue."

Alisa came through the back door and chased Lydia's youngest to find his mother. The three Shoshone men followed Alisa into the house.

From what Ingrid could see, they were young and probably as scared as the child. Ingrid finished wiping the table and motioned for them to have a seat. She made coffee and found a cup for each man.

As she waited for the coffee, she couldn't help but notice the resemblance of these men to the Aztecs. Have they ventured this far north? "Do you speak English?"

"Yes," the youngest-looking man answered.

She poured coffee for all of them and offered cream and sugar with it.

The one man drank his and pushed his cup to her.

"Would you like more?"

The man nodded and she fixed him another cup. One by one, they all wanted more. Ingrid smiled and gave them all more coffee. Slowly they pulled off their coats. They wore elaborately decorated shirts. She pointed to the one man and mimicked the pattern of the black, green, and white beads. "Very pretty."

Adie giggled as she covered the batter so it could rise. "Now he will try to give you his shirt. They are like that."

"Oh, no. I do not want your shirt. I want to learn how to do that. It is beautiful. Did your wife do it?"

The men talked among themselves, and the youngest answered. "His mother uses needle."

Ingrid stood, walked around the table to the man, and looked closely at the beading. Little knots separated the beads and it was all perfectly spaced with tiny stitches that held it in place. "You have a wonderful mother. You tell her she is very good, and you are lucky to have a mother who loves you so much that she makes you beautiful clothes. You have given me much by telling me she does it with a needle."

From this angle, Ingrid could see into the backyard and could see Alisa pacing on the porch. As far as Ingrid was concerned, the men posed no threat, even though each carried a knife strapped to their waist. They were men - like all men. They had families, and women and children that they loved. She returned to her seat and listened to the men chatting in their language.

The man reached into his pouch and withdrew a set of leather strings attached to a larger piece. He motioned to the cups and then to her.

She looked at him and smiled. "For my hair?"

He nodded.

"You understand but do not speak English?"

Again he nodded.

"Where are they?" Adie whined. "Oh, no!"

Ingrid jumped from where she had been sitting and looked out the back window. Tiago was riding at full speed towards the house with two more Shoshones with him. Behind him in the far distance, she could see the girls and the other men. It seemed as though the whole tribe was with them. She squeezed Adie's arm, and then turned to the men at the table. "Why are you here?"

18

Tiago reined to a halt and jumped off his horse. As far as he was concerned, they weren't getting a thing if one hair on anyone's head was missing. He stormed into the house. "Where are the children?"

Ingrid pointed down the hall. "Bear is with them."

He looked behind and saw the empty rifle rack. "Who has it?"

"Bear," Ingrid answered.

"Anyone else with him?" Tiago asked.

"No. Only the children, and I think Lydia is in there, too."

He walked down the hall. When he returned to the kitchen, he stared at the men at the table.

Ingrid pulled the pins from her hair and allowed it to fall free. She gathered it together and tied a leather piece to it. She smiled at Tiago. "I gave them coffee and they gave me this lovely piece for my hair.

See, it has been tooled with a fancy design."

He narrowed his eyes at her. Don't be a fool, my darling.

"They know English, and he speaks it." Ingrid stood behind the youngest man.

Why do I doubt you? "Thank you for telling me that." He turned to the men. "Who is in charge?"

The men conferred and then the younger one said, "I speak English."

"What do you want?" Tiago demanded.

Ingrid frowned at him then knelt beside the young man. "Why are you here?"

"We need food. We are hungry. Our people are hungry."

"What do you want us to give you?" Ingrid asked in her soft voice.

Tiago turned when he saw Alisa walk into the kitchen. Her eyes were washed in tears.

"I think they are holding the girls as ransom."

"We want meat. Beef." He pointed to the cream. "Beef make more, lamb, goat. Our people are hungry."

"No, not my goats. You cannot take my goats." Alisa wiped tears from her eyes.

Ingrid stood. "There are not enough goats to share." She walked out the back door and swung her coat over her shoulder.

Tiago hollered, "No."

Ingrid held up her hand as if to tell him she didn't want to hear his complaint and walked to the men who had Clarissa and Virginia sandwiched among them.

Tiago felt powerless to do anything more than watch, but his fingers twitched near the gun on his side. *What is she doing?*

A moment later, she brought both girls into the house. "Wash up and go to your classroom." Then she turned to Tiago. "This ranch is under duress with all of us here. Supplies are getting low. The Colemans have helped the Shoshones in the past. I know we don't have much we can share, but with letters, they are allowed off the reservation. You have much to do this spring with barns to build and fences to make. I'm sure we can trade help for meat." She looked at the youngest man. "If we help you, will you help us?"

"You give us letters?" The young man asked.

Ingrid looked at Tiago, and he nodded.

Joseph came into the house. "This is one time we can't afford to lose our profit. The market was not good this last time. Prices keep falling."

Tiago put up his hand. "I will help them."

Joseph shook his head. "The Shoshones have always been good to us. They have been fierce warriors and they, too, are confined. They have put me in a difficult spot."

Ingrid opened the box that contained potatoes. "Do you have more at your house?"

Adie shook her head. "Nein. The men emptied my pantry last week."

"Ah, that is where the food came from. Then I will pay for more in town." Ingrid turned to Joseph. "Did you not say you saw wild turkeys where you grow wheat?"

Ingrid turned and looked through the window as if to see where the sun was in the sky. "They are skilled hunters. Take them hunting, and we will have wild turkey tonight for dinner."

"You are loco!" Tiago clenched his fists.

"No. I'm trying to figure out how to feed so many hungry men. They are desperate or they would not be here. Do you think they have come with letters? They could be arrested and hanged. Our government doesn't care about them."

Adie opened a bin and took out several cups of flour.

The one man started to stand and Tiago put his hand on the man's shoulder, forcing him to sit.

Adie turned at the slight commotion behind her. "Ja. Flour."

Ingrid took a cup to the man and sprinkled some in his hand. He frowned and dumped it. "They don't know what it is. Our government gives it to them and they don't know what to do with it. They don't know it is food. To them, it is white, tasteless powder."

Adie took the man's hand and brought him to where she stood by the worktable. "You will learn to make bread."

She made him wash and dry his hands. Then she measured the flour into his hands, which he dumped into a big bowl along with the sugar, eggs, milk, yeast, and salt. When all the ingredients were combined, she started mixing and beating it with a spoon. She let the Indian try mixing. He grinned and took the spoon. She held his hand under hers and showed him.

Tiago watched the two of them with disbelief. Was Adie that trusting, or did she know them by some other means?

Adie took another bowl filled with batter and stuck her finger into it, and then made the Indian do the same. She smiled, pointed to the indentations, and nodded.

A moment later, she put the batter into the oven. "You will like. We will have bread for dinner. She covered the one bowl of batter they had just made. "Yeast." She added more flour, a pinch of salt, some sugar, and stirred it together. "It is like a child, you must always feed it more."

She stirred the contents in the jar until it was smooth, and then put some into another jar. "This is for you to take. You must have it for bread."

Adie pulled a chair out and sat beside the man. "I am tired. I have stood all day skimming cream and making butter, and then bread. Issy and Clarissa can peel potatoes. I will make potato cakes."

"That is more eggs," Ingrid said. "Will we have enough?"

"We can make pancakes tomorrow for breakfast," Alisa answered. "Egg production goes way down in the winter."

Joseph paced the kitchen. "I will take them hunting. Maybe they will hunt the wolves, too."

"What is turkey?" the one Indian asked.

Adie flapped her arms. "Big bird, lots of good meat."

Ingrid fixed more coffee and refilled the cups. "Will you tell the men that they will go hunting with Mr. Coleman, and that we will fix turkey for dinner? Everyone will eat."

The youngest Indian went to the porch and told the men what was being planned. From the looks on their faces, the men were happy.

Joseph looked at Tiago. "Are you willing to go hunting with these men?"

Tiago walked to the younger Indian. "If anything happens to these women or the children, I will personally kill you. Do you understand?"

The man nodded. "We came for food, not to hurt

you."

Tiago walked over to the other Indian. "You understand English but do not speak?"

The man nodded.

"Come with us." Tiago glared at the other man. He was no better than Ingrid when it came to trust, and he didn't trust Indians at all.

***

Ingrid let out a breath as the men rode off. Then she turned to Alisa. "Please, sit. They will take what we give them."

Adie agreed. "Mark supplies his whole tribe with chickens and occasional beef as he builds his ranch. They could learn from Mark, but they, too, are proud, and Mark is not their brother."

"Pride and greed ruin men," Ingrid said.

"The Shoshones seem to have fared better than the Crows," Alisa added.

Adie nodded. She turned to the girls peeling potatoes. "Grate them when you are done. Virginia, do we still have apples?"

"Not many good ones. The bad ones keep going to the chickens."

"Too many spots?" Ingrid asked.

Virginia nodded.

"Bring me two-dozen even if they have spots. I'll

use what I can." Adie turned to Ingrid. "I hope they find turkeys."

"I don't. I hate plucking them," Ingrid whined.

Adie laughed, as did Issy and Clarissa.

Lydia joined them in the kitchen. "I could hear what you were saying. We can mix the wolf meat with beef by grinding it together and frying it."

"I thought it was going to become sausage," Ingrid said.

Adie shrugged. "What is the difference? It was free food."

Ingrid went in search of Alisa. She found her in the parlor. "What is wrong?"

"Nothing and everything. We are taught to share. But we have had many things happen this year."

"And now we are here with our men."

"Oh, please, do not feel bad. We are blessed in so many ways. We will not starve."

"No, we will not, but they are starving. Why did you not tell me that we needed to buy food from town?"

Alisa ran her hand through the air as if to brush everything off and sniffled.

"I will give you money and Joseph can buy whatever you need." She smiled at Alisa. "Remember you are now family, but mostly you are a wonderful friend."

"And you have quit running?"

Ingrid nodded. "I do not want to run from Tiago. He has his flaws, but I've grown to love him, and not because he is handsome or wealthy. He is a good man. And I love Alma."

"She is so bright. As fast as I can teach her, she learns it."

"I know. I just wish she would talk."

"She will when she feels safe again." Alisa wiped the tears from her eyes. "I am being such a fool. I lost a baby, and now I am coming to the end of my womanhood."

"I am so sorry about the baby. But you will always be a woman. Be thankful the hassles of being a young woman are coming to an end. You and Joseph will be free. It is not a time of sadness, but of celebration."

"But I am hot when no one else is, or I'm freezing."

"That, too, will go away."

"It does?"

"Yes." She sat beside Alisa. "How old were you when you married Joseph?"

"Sixteen. Clare wasn't even fourteen when she married."

"Compared to you, I'm an old maid."

"How old are you?"

Ingrid giggled. "Issy is only a few months younger."

"No!"

"Yes. Like Alma will, I finished school early. Then I began to assist my father and study medicine. With my father's help, I was already working as a midwife and assisting during surgeries. He wanted to send me to become a surgeon. But what he wanted and I wanted were two different things. I wanted to study the arts. Now look at me. I'm in Wyoming with a very handsome man."

Alisa smiled. "And when this is over, you have a lifetime ahead of you."

"I hope." Ingrid returned to the kitchen where Lydia was already grinding meat. Ingrid could feel her stomach churning but she wasn't starving. She chopped up onions and peppers and sent Virginia to retrieve a large squash from the cold cellar.

Adie took the large gourd and was going to smash the big basket gourd to open it, but when she raised it above her head, one of the Indians took it from her. He took it outside and when he returned, the top had been carefully removed.

Ingrid knew how difficult it was to cut these large gourds with a knife, for she had several times tried to save it. "You want the gourd?"

The Indian nodded.

She scooped out the seeds, but before she finished saving them, the one Indian snatched a few seeds. She smiled and handed him a few more and saved a few seeds for the Colemans, and then placed the remaining seeds in the oven to toast. The one Sally Lunn loaf came out of the oven and the second one went in.

Adie worked on the apples, cutting away the brown spots and cutting up the good portions to make a layered apple dessert. The bottom was cake-like, the center layer had bits of apple, and the whole thing was topped with a sweet crumble. When she finished that, she created a batter for the grated potatoes to make potato pancakes.

The basket gourd didn't provide much edible flesh, but when mixed with onions and topped with toasted seeds, it would make a delicious side dish.

Lydia spiced the meat and Ingrid made tortillas to go with it. Joseph walked through the door with a wide grin. He presented the women with three wild turkeys.

While Adie and Ingrid cooked, the girls plucked turkeys. Joseph created a small fire pit in the backyard. The men could roast their own turkeys. Adie took the smallest turkey and put it in the oven.

Tiago and the other men ate the wolf and beef filled tortillas, but Ingrid passed and only put some vegetables in her tortillas. She didn't even care about the turkey. Totally exhausted, she excused herself and went to her room.

She was also the first one awake in the morning.

She tiptoed out of bed and readied for the day. The house was quiet as she began to mix up a batch of pancakes and a big batch of cornbread.

Tiago joined her. "How can you trust them?"

"They are men and they are desperate. Adie has told me much about their reservation. Have you not put your dreams on hold to protect Alma and done things you might not otherwise do?"

"But what does that have to do with them?"

"Their livelihood has been taken from them and their dreams crushed. They only want to live in peace. Don't be mean to them. Treat them as men. Their skin is a different color, and they do not have the same education, but they are still men who want to take care of their families. Remember I told you once before 'If you prick us, do we not bleed? If you tickle us, do we not laugh? If you poison us, do we not die? And if you wrong us, shall we not revenge?'"

"Yes. Shakespeare. I, too, am educated."

"Give them a chance."

After breakfast, Tiago talked to Ingrid. "I can take a few men and cut three heads from my herd. You already know I don't have any milk production, but I have pregnant cows. I don't want to lose one, but I understand not having milk. Yet each head lost puts me behind."

"Frank said more cattle could be bought from him

and Joseph. Plus you have the option of going to the stockyards to buy. Some other bulls for breeding might be good." Ingrid patted his shoulder. "In the end, you get more help."

"That is true."

Ingrid looked at the one Indian who had joined them and forced a smile. "We will help you."

A round of commotion started outside. Tiago and Ingrid flew to the front door. Three men rode up surrounded with men from the Coleman ranch. Ingrid instantly recognized the one man.

Andy Lyles dismounted and grinned. "May we talk?"

Ingrid grabbed her coat and greeted the man. "Please tell me we are free."

"Almost." Andy shook Tiago's hand and then turned his attention to Ingrid. "Thanks to your brother, we were able to crack the ring. We knew about the riverboats, and we knew bits and pieces. His information and the added names you provided were the missing links. Not saying we got everyone, but we did get the men pulling the strings. This was a highly organized group of thieves that has been operating for years."

"Are you certain we are safe to return to town and to my land?" Tiago asked.

"There are a few more arrests to make. The department is on a hunt for those men. We will get them. But they are not anywhere near here. As for being safe?" He rolled his palms up. "This is the west. Wyoming is a state, but the law is often what you carry on you hip. No one will ever be completely safe from evil men."

Ingrid nodded. "This gang is gone?"

"Yes. And there will be reward money issued. I'll see that you get what are your shares."

Ingrid and Tiago chatted with Mr. Lyles for a little longer and then bid him a good day.

Ingrid stood on the porch and watched the three men ride off. As they did, a huge weight peeled off of her, and what was left was her grief. Tears rolled unchecked down her cheeks. She sat on the porch steps and buried her head between her knees. For the first time in months, she was free to cry.

***

Tiago stared at her for a moment. Then he sat beside her and placed his hand on her back. He was a man, and men did not cry, but he understood her emotional release. He pulled the kerchief from his coat pocket that he used to cover his nose and mouth when he rode in the bitter cold and stuffed it between her hands. "Cry, my darling. When you are done with your tears, we will begin again."

He looked over his shoulder at the house. There

was much to do and the pressure was on him to succeed. He owed the Colemans too much. I am a Colima. I will prove I am worthy of my family's name.

19

Tiago walked into the house and saw Alisa in the parlor. "Excuse me. Your goats are for cheese and your sheep are for wool?"

She nodded. "They are like pets."

"Do you have extra cheese or extra wool to spare?"

She nodded and opened a chest. It was filled with neatly rolled balls.

"What does it take to make something?"

She reached in and lifted several balls. "One baby sweater set."

"That's too much. What about cheese?"

"We can make more. It is in the cold cellar. They may have one."

"Thank you."

An hour later, Tiago gave the Shoshone men two bulls and a cow. "Save one bull so you have more for next year."

He gave them a block of cheese, and the letters for the six of them to return, and the bill of sale for the three heads.

Without a thank you, they rode off.

Joseph dismounted from his horse. "The Shoshones are not like the Crows. But we must live with them. They will remember. They always do. Proud people. They must be desperate this year."

Tiago knew that feeling, and all the families thrown together were too much on Joseph and Alisa Coleman. Having the Shoshones asking for food was the breaking point for the Coleman ranch. Tiago hadn't realized the additional burden the Colima cowboys had placed on the ranch, and then he came with Ingrid, Cora, and Alma. Now he was glad he had provided the cattle and taken that obligation off of the Colemans. He knew he'd be able to use the help of the Indians once he started his ranch.

Tiago looked at Joseph. "It is time for us to go to town. Tomorrow I will take Ingrid and Cora back to Cora's house. The man who came says we are safe to return to town. We'll take my cart and go now."

"No one is ever safe. That is why we must wear guns."

***

Ingrid looked out the window and realized it was

Tiago with Joseph and Frank in the cart. Heat pulsed through her and it wasn't the good kind. Why didn't he take me?

She stormed up the stairs to her room and began to pack. I'm not staying any longer than I must. As she flipped through Alma's things, she uncovered two wads of money. She counted the smaller one and knew it was hers. Slipping several bills from her pile, she returned downstairs, found Alisa, and stuffed the money in her pocket. "I know Tiago will settle with Joseph, but I want you to have this."

Alisa reached into her pocket.

"No, don't. I don't want any arguments. You are family and you have kept me safe. That is a debt that can never be repaid."

"Then why give me anything?"

"Because you are special to me, and you've taught me so much about living on a ranch. Take the money and do something just for you with it." She giggled. "Maybe some silk bloomers and a matching chemise or…" she raised her eyebrows. "a nightgown that will remind Joseph why he married you. Something so you feel special and pretty."

Alisa blushed. "Joseph does not need reminding."

"The money is for you alone."

Alisa reached out to Ingrid. "Tiago is a good man. He loves you very much."

"I love him, but we are not a good match."

"How can you say that?"

Ingrid smiled. "He is too stubborn and so am I." She put her fists together. "Like bulls, we constantly knock heads."

"But you would not be happy with a man who wasn't strong. You need a man with plenty of backbone."

Ingrid retreated to her room and finished her packing. She was anxious to return to being Cora's renter. But when someone began clanging the outdoor dinner bell, she scooted down the steps to see the origin of the commotion.

Tiago, Joseph, and Frank had returned and were carrying supplies into the house. Alisa stood with her mouth open as food items such as oranges were brought inside.

They had a heavenly feast that night. After supper, Tiago took Ingrid's hand and walked outside in the waning light.

He stopped and drew her to him.

She looked into his eyes that were dark as coal, and her heart swelled with its love for the handsome man.

He ran a calloused finger over her cheek and then his thumb across her lips, dragging her lower lip down. "You are so beautiful, so wonderful, intelligent, and loving." He placed a gentle kiss on her lips. "You made me see that I was doing to the

Indians what has been done to me because of my coloring. We are all men wanting a better life for our family. And I want you forever as my wife."

Her insides quivered at his words. And he drew her to his chest and rested his cheek on her head. His breath fluttered through her hair.

"I know I should not ask you when I have nothing more than land and a few head of cattle. But my pile of bricks and tile will become a home for us. I need you to believe in me and trust me. No more secrets. I love you."

She tilted her head up and his lips met hers. She slipped her arms around his waist and held onto him, for her knees no longer wanted to support her. His tiny kisses rained on her face until he found her earlobe. The sensation of his breath in her ear gave her gooseflesh.

"I will not sleep with you tonight, for I can no longer be that close to you and control my body. I want you too much."

"Where will you sleep?"

"Do not worry about such things." His breath still filled her ear with warmth. "I want to hear that you will be my wife. I will treat you as if you were the queen of Spain."

She pulled away from him. "I have thought about how much I love you. But you need someone worthy of such treatment, another Evita to fill your bed and be a mother to Alma."

"No. We were young and carefree. Now that I have met you, I know the difference. You are the woman I want."

"I am not the woman for you. I am strong willed and independent. I am not a rancher's woman. I am not like Adie or Alisa, or even like Cora. I cannot butcher an animal or sew a dress."

"Do you think my mother does such things?" He shook his head. "She oversees those who do." He took Ingrid's hand and opened it. "You are tough. You are not afraid of work, and you have worked hard while you have stayed with the Colemans. You will make a fine wife for me. I will hire someone to churn the butter and iron the clothes." He chuckled. "With luck, and God's blessing, we will give Alma some brothers and sisters."

She shook her head. "I do not want so many children that my teeth fall out."

He laughed. "Then we will be very careful. When my mother had me, she said enough. My father was very vigilant and they are very happy."

She was glad the darkness hid the warmth on her cheeks. Touching her finger to his lips, she whispered, "I love you, Tiago Colima. I love you with all my heart."

"I know you do, but will you marry me?"

***

Spring sprang with every possible hue of green. Fields were filled in colorful blossoms that waved in the gentle breezes. Snow still topped the mountains and often blended with the puffs of white clouds blurring the line between mountaintops and sky. Sun warmed the air.

In the early morning mist, Tiago surveyed his sea of cattle. His father had offered to send more, but Tiago turned down the offer. He had bought more locally and was pleased with his purchases. The local ranchers were happy to do business with him, and he obtained several nice bulls for breeding.

Tiago rode his horse across his land. He looked around him at the new sprouts of green grass and prayed for a good year. He had cut the bulls from the cows and bought more cows. His herd had nearly quadrupled between his purchases and the arrival of calves. He had plenty of land to support them even through a dry season, and this spring had been dry. Barbed wire separated his pregnant cows from the cows he had placed with his best bulls. These bovines were his future. He turned and looked back.

Several brick buildings came into view along with two windmills. At the top of the crest was a house, three stories with a large, single-story wing on each side and a porch that surrounded the whole thing. It was better than he had envisioned it.

He and Ingrid had selected each piece of furniture from magazines. Now the house was ready for Ingrid. If only he could have given her a honeymoon. Next spring I will take her to my family.

His father had written him about a Van Duzen engine tractor that ran on gasoline. It seemed exciting, but Tiago knew he had no easy access to gasoline. For now, he used horses to plow. When I am bigger and I have grown...

He finished checking his herd, and then went back to the house. The only things left for him to do were to take a bath and put on his best suit. He thought it was customary to receive guests at his house after the wedding, but Alisa put her foot down and said no. It was better to hold the reception at the church. He said breakfast, and Alisa said sandwiches after the wedding. She was as stubborn as Ingrid. But he and Ingrid had taken great care to write individual invitations to the townspeople along with the neighboring ranchers, and would spend almost two solid weeks receiving guests and feeding them cake.

It had been the longest year in his life and it was about to end. There was nothing he wanted more than to make Ingrid his wife. The elusive dream of his own ranch rested before him, a reality still shrouded in a morning mist that reflected the green of nature, of money, of success, and of a future.

E. Ayers

***

Butterflies flittered through Ingrid's stomach to the point that she only had some tea with a piece of bread with honey. She and Cora had spent part of yesterday decorating the church with flowers and bits of greenery.

Her dress had been ordered from a shop in New Orleans and when it came, it was too big. Adie had to alter it. It was the palest shade of pink and trimmed in white with darker pink flowers appliquéd on it.

"Sit still," Cora admonished. "I have less trouble with Alma"

Ingrid tried not to move as Cora pinned Ingrid's hair into an elaborate bun and then placed the wreath made of cloth flowers and pearls on her head. A long veil attached to the wreath went to the floor.

"Mr. Hagger will be here to pick you up in his carriage. Mrs. Hagger said he's decorated his old horse for this occasion. Swore it was good luck to have a gray horse."

"Why do they call it a gray horse when it is white?"

Cora laughed. "Under that white coat he has gray skin."

"Oh."

Cora insisted that Ingrid wear makeup. The rose that had been added to her cheeks was too much. She took toilet tissues and tried to remove it, but her cheeks still glowed pinker than normal. Although she did like her darker eyelashes and her pinker lips. Ingrid looked at herself in the mirror. With her veil pulled over her face, she waited for the carriage.

Adie had Alma. The child was to wear a pink dress that matched Ingrid's. Ingrid didn't want an elaborate wedding, but Tiago insisted that he would give her the perfect wedding and the Colemans were making certain it was.

Since she didn't have a father to escort her down the aisle, Joseph Coleman was taking the honor, and Alisa was standing for her mom. Frank was serving as groomsman. Everything had been planned down to the tiniest detail.

Waiting was the most difficult. Their possessions had been moved to Tiago's house except for all the last minute things that she needed for this day. Cora would be moving in with them in a few days. A young cowboy from a neighboring ranch and his bride were going to rent the house from Cora.

All of Cora's doubts flew away when she saw her little apartment in the wing of the Colima house. She even had her own entrance, and with running water that produced both hot and cold, she was more than excited about working for the Colimas.

Ingrid's thoughts switched from Cora and the new house to the wedding. Ingrid laughed to herself. Yes, I will be a Colima, the wife of a Spaniard and a rancher.

Mr. Hagger pulled to a halt in front of Cora's house. His open coach was lovely. It looked as though every square inch of it was covered in flowers.

She felt Cora's nudge. "I think the bees will have to find some other meadows this spring."

"You are right. It looks as though there is not one flower left near the Haggers' house."

"Are you ready?" Cora smoothed the fine silk veil.

Ingrid smiled. "Very."

***

Tiago was pleased with the simple ceremony, for if he had married at home, it would have been a full Mass and taken over an hour. The local pastor in Creed's Crossing promised to send the Colima's priest a voucher of the wedding, which was acceptable. They would be married before God and, next spring, he planned to return for a visit to his parents with Ingrid. The priest would bless them at that time.

His mother had written a long letter of welcome

to Ingrid and had enclosed a gift of pearl earrings for Ingrid to wear. He had faithfully read every word to Ingrid, for it had been written in Spanish, but he couldn't help laughing when his mother had warned Ingrid that he was stubborn and spoilt. Fortunately Ingrid, also, laughed.

After the simple ceremony, he stood next to Ingrid and received the good wishes of the people of Creed's Crossing. It had taken him a year to accomplish what he had hoped to do in six months, but he had gained respect from the members of the community and not just because he had money, but because they saw him as an honest hard-working man who wasn't going to let anything stop him.

His men were now welcomed in the tiny town of Creed's Crossing and the signs that had once said no Mexicans had vanished. He knew people's attitudes would never change overnight, but it was a start. The town's people actually smiled and bid him a good day.

Creed's Crossing was his home. He had made friends, as had Ingrid and Alma. He was proud of what he was creating and even prouder of his beautiful wife.

Alma tugged on Ingrid's skirt, looked at her father, and then at Ingrid.

"What is it, my little darling?" Tiago asked. He leaned down, giving his daughter his full attention.

"Tell me what you want."

In a perfectly clear voice, she answered, "Does this make Ingrid my mommy?"

The entire room hushed.

In unison, he and Ingrid said, "You spoke."

He gathered his daughter into his arms as he fought back tears. "Yes, she is now your mommy. And there is not a happier man on earth than I am today." He whispered in her ear, "I love you, too, my little darling."

The End

Did you enjoy reading *A Rancher's Dream*
by E. Ayers?

Please leave a short review on your favorite platform and tell your friends! Independent authors count on your reviews to help them succeed. You can write to the author directly at the following website: http://www.ayersbooks.com

About the Author

Born and raised with wealth, E. Ayers turned away from all of it and married a few days after turning eighteen, to the shock and dismay of family and   friends.

A firm believer in love conquering everything, there was never cause to look back. The newlyweds' life-long love became the springboard for   many   future   novels.

Fascinated with the way people deal with everyday problems, E. Ayers has always been an observer and a listener. A simple problem for one person is a mountain for another. Utilizing those common predicaments, the subsequent novels have touched   many   lives.

Today finds E. Ayers writing while living in a pre-Civil War home with a dog and a cat. Rattling around in an old money pit provides one's muse with plenty of freedom. A perfect day is spent at the keyboard, coffee in hand, and everything in the house actually working as it should.

As the official matchmaker for all the characters who wander through a mind full of imagination and the need to share, E. Ayers enjoys finding just the right ones to create a story.

More Great Books From E. Ayers!

Wanting (A River City Novel)
A New Beginning (A River City Novel)
A Challenge (A River City Novel)
Forever (A River City Novel)
A Son (A River City Novel)
A Child's Heart (A River City Novel)
Coming Out of Hiding (a novel)
A Fine Line (a novella) *
Mariners Cove (a novella)
Ask Me Again (a novella)
A Skeleton at Her Door (a novella)
A Snowy Christmas in Wyoming (a novella) *
A Cowboy's Kiss in Wyoming (a novella) *
A Love Song in Wyoming (a novella) *
A Calling in Wyoming (a novella) *
Sweetwater Springs Christmas (anthology) *

Sweet Reads

YOU CAN VISIT CREED'S CROSSING AGAIN... AND AGAIN!

Please enjoy this peek into
A Snowy Christmas in Wyoming*,*
a novella from E. Ayers.

Caroline Coleman hadn't seen the place look this good since she was a teen. The flowerbeds were mulched and tidy. There was a new coat of green paint on the shutters and front door. Garlands of fresh pine wrapped the porch rails that encircled the log house, and a pretty, matching, pine wreath hung on the front door.

She knocked once and opened the door. "Grandmamma. It's me! I'm home."

"Thank goodness, you're here," a voice from a distant room called back. "I was worried about you coming in with this snowstorm on its way."

The stress of her journey slipped from her shoulders as she breathed in the familiar scent of home. Caroline let go of her rolling suitcase and looked around. Inside, everything looked the same, even though it was decorated for the holiday. A beautiful Douglas fir tree, covered with ornaments, stood in front of the window. Its tiny lights twinkled as if they were welcoming her.

The house was neater, cleaner, and there was a

basket of toys next to the sofa. But everything else was exactly the way it had been all of her life. That familiarity wrapped her in a warm blanket.

"Darling, I'm so glad you're here. You're needed. This storm is going to be bad," Barbara Coleman said.

Caroline turned to her grandmother. The woman was holding a toddler whose eyes were filled with tears.

"What are you doing? Babysitting?" She hugged her grandmother and offered to take the child, but the child clung to the older woman.

"I guess you could call it babysitting. I'm trading, and I got the best end of this bargain. This is Sarah Anne Coyote. Isn't she a cutie?" Barbara took the child to a highchair in the kitchen. "Coffee?"

"Thanks. I'll get it. How did you wind up with a child?"

"Long story. You remember Margaret Simpson?" The older woman started fixing a snack.

"Double T ranch, of course."

"Her kids are selling everything since she died. Remember when I told you I was buying some of her land?" She put a handful of baby carrots on a plate, and stuck them in the microwave.

"Yes." Caroline poured a cup of coffee, then watched her grandmother fix a cup of milk with a sipping lid, and hand it to the toddler.

The child's enormous chocolate brown eyes were

still washed in unshed tears and her long eyelashes were clumped with moisture. Chubby hands grabbed at the handles on the sippy-cup and tipped the cup of milk to her mouth. She watched Caroline with a reserved curiosity.

"Are you thirsty? Did you just wake up from a nap?" Caroline asked the child.

Little Sarah pursed her lips and banged on the tray in front of her. "Milk."

"How old is she? She's adorable. She's got the prettiest eyes."

"Thirteen months. She's a little handful. She's really coming out of her shell since she's been here." Barbara put several crackers spread with cheese on the child's tray. "Eat, sweet baby. You like creamed cheese." The microwave beeped and Barbara lifted the plate of baby carrots off the unit's carousel and put them on the child's tray after checking each one. "She's such a good thing. Just never thought I'd be playing with a baby at my age."

"Why did you nuke her carrots?"

"It slightly softens them. Makes them easier to eat. She doesn't have all her teeth."

"Grandmamma, you still haven't told me how you've wound up with a child."

"Well, I'm buying the eastern portion of Margaret's land, which includes her house and barn because it backs up to mine."

"Nice house."

"Yes, it is. I'm hoping to rent it. The one barn is in perfect shape, but the other barn has some problems and that's going to take more money."

Caroline rolled her eyes. Sarah giggled.

"Anyway, when Margaret died, her foreman lost his job."

"Oh, no. Sarah is one of those Coyotes?"

The back door opened and Andy Coyote walked into the kitchen. "Miz Barbara..."

Caroline stared at Andy. He wasn't the scrawny kid she'd known most of her life, and if it hadn't been for the scar across his cheek, she wouldn't have recognized him. His shoulders were broad and he'd grown very tall. The long straight nose, strong cheekbones, and his coloring conveyed his Crow Indian heritage, except he was taller than most.

"Excuse me, I didn't know you had company." He took his jacket off and hung it on the peg by the back door.

"Company? I doubt that anyone would call me company," Caroline shot back at him. She couldn't remember the last time she'd seen him, maybe high school.

He looked at her for a brief second, then grabbed a mug, and poured a cup of coffee.

"Caroline, you remember Andy?" Barbara asked.

"How could I not remember Andy?" Memories of

the young man and his family flowed through her brain like a bad news story.

Sarah squealed with delight as Andy took her in his arms. "How's my baby girl?"

The child pointed to Caroline.

"Yes, that's Caroline," Andy said with a big grin. "Have you been playing with her? I thought you just got up from your nap."

"She did just get up from her nap as Caroline came through the door. I brought her in here for her snack. She hasn't had a chance to play."

He pulled his mobile phone from his pocket and looked at it. "We're in trouble."

"What kind of trouble?" Barbara asked as she cleaned up the crumbs off the child's tray and handed the toddler the last tiny carrot. "Are you talking about the storm?"

Andy turned on the TV and watched the weather channel. "I've been watching the storm track on my phone. I'm gonna need help getting that herd down here. I can't do it alone. If I can find help, I'll leave tonight. That is if you don't mind keeping Sarah for me."

Barbara turned to her granddaughter. "Caroline'll go with you."

Andy turned around and stared hard. "You? You think you can ride herd?"

"Darn right, I can ride. Won't be the first herd I've

ever brought in, but I…" She bit her tongue.

"But what?"

She forced a smile. "Let's just say I always ride with a gun, and I know how to use it."

"Good. So do I. We'll leave at six. Make sure you're saddled and ready to go."

Hot anger boiled through Caroline. "I'll be ready."

She stormed out of the kitchen, grabbed her suitcase, and headed for her room.

***

"She'd better be able to ride. This isn't going to be an easy cattle drive," Andy said.

"That little thing knows every square inch of this ranch and this business. My husband used to say, 'Let her go, and when she's done, she'll come back.' I hope he was right."

"Ma'am, I don't need a prissy female. I need a man for this job or I'll never get that herd back here."

"Oh, she can do it. She and her grandfather moved herds all the time. She's knows what she's doing and she knows this land. Listen to her."

Andy kissed his daughter's nose and put her to the floor. "Are you sure you can handle her overnight?"

"I can handle your daughter overnight." Barbara laughed. "Just don't try to handle my granddaughter, or she'll be bringing you back in a sack."

"Miz Barbara, one female in my life is plenty. I don't need anymore."

***

Caroline cinched the saddle and adjusted the stirrups before tying on her pack. Her mind drifted over the stories of Jessie and Clare Coleman and the things that they endured to start this ranch in the 1840's. She had vowed to write their story one day. Clare was barely fifteen when she married Jessie and went west with him. The handwriting in that diary was difficult to decipher, but Caroline managed to read it when she was a teen. Snowstorms were nothing new, and if Jessie and Clare could survive them, there was no reason why she couldn't do it today. Except instead of doing it with her grandfather at her side, she had Andy Coyote. She grimaced as bile rose from her stomach.

"You ready to ride, Caroline?" Andy asked.

"Yes, I'm ready." She pulled her scarf over her head and shoved her old felted Stetson over the hot pink angora.

"Don't wimp out on me. I need another man for this job, not a fancy Washington, D.C. TV news anchor."

"Well, I have a job to do, and the idea of having you along for the ride has no appeal. As far as I'm concerned, you're strictly brawn, and you'd better do as I say."

"This is gonna be hell," he mumbled as he yanked on his horse's reins.

"That's right, and don't forget it." Caroline put her foot into the stirrup.

Caroline pulled her scarf tighter around her face. An occasional snowflake floated down as they rode. She wasn't going to let on that she was dead tired, but she was certain that if she'd blink her eyes, they wouldn't open again. She had worked yesterday doing the six and eleven o'clock nightly news broadcasts, and then caught an early morning flight out of D.C. Three hours of sleep was not enough.

"Caroline!"

She gasped and righted herself.

"You're falling asleep."

She looked over at Andy and frowned.

"If you talked to me, you might stay awake," he suggested.

"What would you like to discuss?" she snarled.

He chuckled. "You want my opinion on the Senate's newest budget?"

"Oh, save your breath."

"I didn't think so. Why don't you tell me what it's like living in the big city and having a hotshot job?"

"Nothing to tell. I have a condo overlooking the Potomac River. I have a driver who takes me to and from work. The clothes I wear are chosen by someone else, even my hair is styled according to the network's consultant, and I don't have a say so in any of it."

"I think you look mighty pretty. Miz Barbara and I always watch you while we eat our dinner."

"Why are you living in the house with my grandmother?"

"And not living in the foreman's apartment in the barn?"

"Yes." The idea of a Coyote living under her grandmother's roof bothered her. As far as she was concerned they were all filthy criminals.

The only sounds were theirs, the horses' breaths, the soft slap of leather reins, and the thumping of hooves on the frozen earth. Finally he answered, "She didn't want me out there in that small apartment with the baby. She thought it was easier on Sarah if I stayed in the house."

"Where's Sarah's mom?"

"Don't know and don't care." He nudged his horse to pick up the pace.

"Nice attitude."

"Yours sucks, too."

"I don't have a child," she retaliated.

"I have two. I'm not allowed near my son."

She shook her head. "What did you do to prevent visitation?"

"Fathered the boy."

"How old is he?"

"He'll be fifteen in February."

Her mind spun back in time to Andy and Katelyn as teens. They were inseparable. The fun loving, petite female with wide set eyes had always been a fierce competitor in 4H and was an amazing trick rider. Then Katelyn vanished. "So the rumors were true?"

"Half true. I never raped her. We were kids and thought we were in love. When she found out she was pregnant...her dad came looking for me with a rifle in his hand. Three years later, the judge threw it all out. I was forced to sign an order to stay away from Katelyn and my son."

Somehow she understood the wealthy family's rage. She could also imagine Katelyn's tears at being torn from the boy she loved. But Andy was a Coyote, and those boys were hellions. "She still here?"

"If you mean still in the county, no. According to a few friends, she's living outside of Boulder, raising horses, and happily married to some hotshot lawyer."

"And your son?"

"He's with her. She'll tell him the truth someday."

"What about Sarah?"

"Another big mistake. Sarah's not, but her mom was. I'll be honest. My life was a mess. I was living in

Casper when I meet Jessica. We went out a few times and then we started living together. She was hot. Then one day she tells me that she's pregnant. Two weeks later, the warehouse where I'd been working closed. I started searching for any job I could find."

Andy's momentary silence hung in the cold air.

Caroline straightened her back and rolled her shoulders. Fatigue was robbing her body, but she wanted him to keep talking. He was right. Conversation kept her awake.

"It was a bad situation. I needed money and there were no jobs. Eventually, I found a job working back here for Double T. They needed a hand. But Jessica didn't want to come. She wanted to live in the city. Had a big fight. I tried a half dozen times to patch things up. Then the phone quit working and my envelopes were returned with no forwarding address. When Margaret Simpson died, her kids kicked everyone out and started selling everything off. I got lucky and got a part-time job working at Kalab's Store."

"Doing what?"

"Anything. Didn't matter to me. It was a job. Had to cover the payment on my truck and put food in my belly. That's where I found your grandmother. She was complaining to BillieJo Kalab about not being able to do everything. That evening I came out to her house. I begged for a job and a place to sleep."

"My grandmother does not complain about anything."

"Well, call it whatever you want, but those two women were commiserating about how hard life was."

"Oh, big word."

"Knock it off, Caroline. Just 'cause I didn't run off to some big university in Virginia doesn't make me an idiot."

She nudged her horse. "You never were an A student."

"No, I wasn't. But you don't have to get uppity with me."

She looked over at him. "You calling me a snob?"

"I really don't care what you are, as long as you can get this herd back to where I can take care of them. Your grandmother doesn't need to lose her livestock because they've frozen to death."

She hid her snarl. "So how did you wind up with Sarah?"

"I'd been here about three weeks when Miz Barbara got a phone call. Seems Social Services tracked me down. Sarah had been abandoned. She was in bad shape. If it weren't for your grandmother...I don't know what I'd do."

"She's adorable."

"She is. I'll do anything to make sure nothing ever happens to her again."

Ask for A Rancher's Woman, Creed's Crossing
Historical at your favorite local bookseller today!